MURDER
IN OCEAN PINES

MURDER
IN OCEAN PINES

DANA PHIPPS

CEDAR
FORGE

Cedar Forge Press
7300 W. Joy Road
Dexter, Michigan 48130

Published 2018 by Cedar Forge Press
Designed by Thomson-Shore, Inc.
Printed in the United States of America

20 19 18   1 2 3 4

ISBN: 978-1-943290-56-7
Library of Congress Control Number: 2018936831

Here's to the hearts that ache,
Here's to the mess we make.

—Audition lyrics from La La Land (2016)
@Warner/Chappell Music, Inc.

To Tom for giving so much of your time

CHAPTER 1

Greg King was determined to plan the perfect murder. He wanted to be rid of his wife. Divorce was not an option. He wanted all of their assets and investments for himself.

Greg opened the medicine cabinet in the bathroom, and his wife's jar of cold cream popped out, breaking on the tiled floor. Cursing, he picked up the glass pieces and discarded them into the wastebasket. He wiped up the greasy mess on the floor. Smoothing thick shaving cream on his cheeks and grabbing his razor, he began tackling his stubble. "I'll be late for this morning's presentation because of her."

"Damn," he said, nicking himself. He covered the small, bloody spot above his lip with a bit of torn toilet tissue, hoping it would stop the bleeding. "That's just great. I look like crap. Now she's ruined my face."

Fully dressed, Greg entered the kitchen.

"Accident shaving?" Cici asked, as she buttered a toasted waffle.

Greg ignored her and sat down at the kitchen table, sipping his coffee. "I couldn't find my white Oxford shirt I wanted to wear today. Didn't you pick up my shirts from the cleaners yesterday?"

"Oh, I forgot. Sorry."

He raised his voice. "What? You forgot?" He threw his hot coffee towards her, staining her silk robe.

"What the hell's wrong with you?" Cici said. "You could've really burned me!"

Greg ran his fingers through his hair. "How in the world could you forget to pick up my shirts?"

"I said I was sorry. I had other things on my mind," Cici said. "But throwing hot coffee at me? Are you crazy? You ruined my robe." Looking down at her front, she said, "What a mess."

"You're irresponsible. All you did yesterday was go to lunch at Fish Tails," Greg said. Cici's mouth opened, but nothing came out. Greg grabbed his briefcase, stormed into the garage, and backed out his SUV. *What a real pain in the ass she is.*

In the afternoon, after his presentation, Greg drove to Harborside, one of his favorite bars. The restaurant faced the inlet, had a huge outside deck, and was known for its Orange Crushes. Boats pulled into the many slips, and fishing trawlers glided by with their catch of the day.

Greg signaled his number-one bartender. "Hey, how's it going?" Greg said to him.

He answered with a thumbs-up.

Greg slid onto a stool next to an attractive woman and ordered a scotch.

"That looks refreshing," he said to her. "What is it?"

"A mojito."

"I'm Greg King," he said, putting out his hand for her to shake.

"Lisa Wolfe," she said.

"I don't think I've seen you before. Believe me, I'd remember," Greg said.

"I don't come here that often. This is my day off from the

salon," she said. "No haircuts today. I usually take my days off to catch up on things. My dog is at the groomers now."

"So you don't trim your own dog's hair?" Greg asked.

She laughed and said, "No."

"You have great hair. Do you cut it yourself?"

"No, someone at the salon does my hair, and I do hers," she said.

"You've almost finished your drink. How about I order you another?" Greg asked.

She looked at her watch. "Well, I guess. Okay. Thanks," she said.

"You already know you've got great hair, but you're also very pretty," Greg said. "Who did you get your good looks from?"

"Thank you. My mom," she said as she sipped her drink. "You know, you have nice, thick hair. Why don't you drop by my salon sometime, and I'll give you a haircut?"

"Yeah, that sounds great. Hey, before I get that haircut, would you like to go out to dinner sometime?" Greg asked.

She smiled and said, "Sure." She looked at her watch again. "Sorry, I've got to go. My dog is waiting," she said, and she handed him her card and left.

"She's really hot," said the bartender as Greg paid the tab.

"Yes, she's easy on the eyes," Greg said. "And she gave me her phone number." Greg tucked Lisa's business card into his shirt pocket. *Don't want to lose this card. We'll set the dinner date tomorrow. What a nice, tight ass she has.*

Greg drove his black Escalade out of Harborside's graveled parking lot and smiled at himself in the rearview mirror. He'd had a great day. First, he received kudos on a successful presentation in Ocean City. Second, he'd ended his day by meeting Lisa at the bar. The only damper that day was his morning spat with Cici. Why couldn't she be like the other women he met? Yesterday, the jeans Cici wore stretched at the seams. She'd need to buy a size larger soon. He hated that Cici did nothing to improve her appearance. Laziness seemed to be her only talent.

When she didn't have her nose in a book, she cooked, washed the clothes, did shopping, and tidied up the house. If he wasn't married to her, he could hire someone to do that.

He'd found Cici attractive when he'd first met her. Cici was a cute, petite brunette with deep, green eyes and long, silky hair. Her bikini showed off her flat tummy and shapely legs. They made a great-looking couple back then. But why did she neglect herself and gain a few extra pounds every year? Those legs of hers were now thick and dimpled with cellulite. And it was so embarrassing to sit next to her at the beach. No more of that. He avoided sex with her, and his repulsion turned to hate.

He swerved sharply to the right after someone beeped a horn at him. An older man gave him the finger. *Got to keep my mind focused on the road.* Greg adjusted the rearview mirror again. He spread his lips, looking at his white, bleached teeth against his dark tan. He ran his tongue over his front teeth. At 41, his wavy, black hair showed no trace of gray. Beautiful women were drawn to him. He was proud that he was one of the top salesmen of his food-distribution company, and he liked the travel component of his job. Traveling all over the Delmarva area, and staying overnight often, kept him away from Cici. His well-paying job afforded him the opportunity to renovate his house into his dream home, and now it was time to enjoy the good life—without Cici.

He often daydreamed about what it would be like without her. The thought of spending the rest of his life with her was loathsome. Since divorce was out of the question, should he hire someone to kill his wife, or should he do it himself? Growing up in Whaleyville on his father's farm, about 18 miles northwest of Ocean City, he'd learned how to kill animals. He'd had no problem at an early age chopping off a chicken's head or shooting squirrels with an air gun. He wouldn't want to chop off Cici's head, and shooting her with an air gun certainly wouldn't work. But he strongly believed after the last few years of boredom with her, he was up to the task.

⚔

Cici had looked forward to Saturday. She and Greg were invited to his boss's daughter's wedding and reception. Cici had bought a striking black dress for the occasion.

"How do I look?" she asked Greg as she spun around.

"Fine," he said. "But you'd look better in it if you took off some weight. You ought to go on *The Biggest Loser*."

She frowned. "Thanks a lot. I'm trying to lose weight. You really know how to ruin my mood. I really love this dress."

"The dress is nice," said Greg.

"You look great in your suit," she said.

They drove to the church, and after the wedding, they headed to the Dunes Manor Hotel in Ocean City, where the reception was being held. Cici found their table for eight people, and she and Greg were the last ones to take their seats.

"This is my wife, Cici," Greg said. People introduced themselves to her.

"Great job on getting the Top Salesman Award, Greg," said Gus, one of the sales reps.

Greg knew most everyone—colleagues and clients from work and their wives. But he didn't know the gorgeous brunette who was seated opposite him and Cici.

"Gus, who is your lovely date?" asked Greg.

"This is Susan," he said.

"How lucky you are, Gus, to have such an attractive lady."

Cici asked Susan, "How do you stay so slim? Losing weight is a real battle for me."

"I work out some and watch what I eat. Believe it or not, it's hard for me too," Susan said.

Plates of food were brought to the tables, glasses were filled with wine, and the room was lively with chatter. Over a hundred people filled the room. The band started playing, and Cici was looking forward to dancing. "Greg, I love this song. Let's dance."

"Maybe later, not now," he said. Cici took a bite of her buttered roll and watched as couples filled the dance floor.

"Gus, do you mind if I have the next dance with Susan?" Greg asked.

"Sure, if it's okay with her."

Susan and Greg walked out to the middle of the floor and danced to the music. "You are the best-looking lady here. Even prettier than the bride," Greg said.

Cici grabbed her purse from the table and stormed into the restroom. She threw her purse onto the sink's counter. *What a husband. Making a fool of me in front of all his colleagues. Insulting me this morning.*

She left the restroom and saw Greg and Susan doing a line dance together. "You've got to be kidding," she said. Cici sat down at the table, alone. The music stopped, and the band played a slow dance. She saw Greg grab Susan and hold her close as they moved on the dance floor. The next thing she knew, they were nowhere to be seen. And where the hell was Gus? Cici wanted to cry. And scream. Instead, she drank two full glasses of merlot.

Cici spotted Greg going into the restroom. She waited for him outside of the men's room in the hallway. She quickly approached him when he came out. "How could you embarrass me like that? You spent too much time on the dance floor with that woman," Cici said.

"I didn't spend a lot of time with her. Only danced with her three times. I was having a good time. I thought you were too," he said.

"Are you serious? Why couldn't you dance with me? I felt like a fool in front of your friends. You know I like to dance. I hate you! That was a rotten thing to do. I was so hurt."

"I didn't mean to hurt you. You're making too much of it," said Greg. "We can dance the next one."

"I could just kill you," she said.

"Ha," he laughed.

"What's so funny?" Cici asked.

"Nothing," he said.

Greg had changed so much. Cici couldn't remember the last time they'd had sex. Was it six months ago? Longer than that? He smoked a pack a day, smelled of booze, left the house unexpectedly, and came home late at night. He shot insults at her more frequently. She'd kept some of these changes in his behavior from Amie, her most trusted friend. She couldn't kid herself any longer. She would talk to Amie. She needed some advice. Should she and Greg get counseling? No, she'd skip the counseling and just ask him for a divorce.

Monday morning, Cici laid out her walking outfit on the bed. She looked into the mirror, placing her hand on her tummy. "I'm too fat. No wonder Greg didn't want to dance with me. He's ashamed of me." Cici stepped onto the bathroom scale nude. Disappointed at seeing a pound gain, she sighed. *The diet just isn't working at all.* She glanced out her bedroom window across the street at Amie's house to see if she was coming. She stepped into the bathroom to brush her teeth and, seeing the time, said, "Oh no!" Amie would be waiting outside for her if she didn't get dressed quickly.

Amie walked across the street in her yellow microfiber fleece outfit. Outside the slider's screen door in the kitchen, Cici heard Amie's loud voice. "Cici, where are you? It's chilly out here," Amie said as she wrapped her arms around herself.

"Coming. Putting on my jacket. Be right out!" she yelled,

and then bolted out the slider, slipping her right arm into the sleeve.

Cici emerged from her house wearing her light jacket, navy blue shorts, a long-sleeved top, and white sneakers. While waiting outside, Amie tapped her foot and put her hands on her hips. Amie asked, "Did you oversleep?"

"No, I couldn't find my tennis shoes," Cici said, feigning a smile. "Sorry."

"Not a problem," Amie said. They met with a hug.

Cici pulled away first. "I need this walk."

"We can jog a little when we get to Pintail Way," said Amie.

"My diet isn't working," Cici said to Amie. "Ate too much crab dip at a wedding reception."

Cici was always on a diet on Mondays. Watching her weight hadn't been a priority. The weight gain snuck up on her, and she felt it was too late to do anything about it—and so hard to give up her Ben and Jerry's ice cream. It angered her when her mother told her to take more pride in her figure and also told her Greg might lose interest in her if she didn't lose some weight.

In the beginning of their marriage, she'd felt secure because they always had money in the bank and gave the appearance of being a successful pair. They were happy back then. Cici enjoyed pleasing Greg by fixing him all kinds of gourmet meals. Eating seconds was not a problem for her.

She never exercised as much as Amie. Walking and jogging a little was enough. She used to jog two miles, three times a week several years ago. Not anymore. Her idea of a good work-out now was to curl up with a novel off the best-seller's list.

She loved her beautiful home that Greg updated. She enjoyed reading in their great room located in the back of the house and gazing out at expansive views of the St. Martin's

River. She was proud of the large, glassed-in sunroom that had a panoramic view of the river, and she could see condo row in Ocean City's skyline in the distance. The lights from the high-rises were beautiful at night. Two of her four bedrooms faced the street. The other two faced the river. Big windows let in plenty of light, and vaulted ceilings made the space feel twice as large. Greg had enhanced the great room with a well-stocked wet bar, installed a large maintenance-free deck, and remodeled the kitchen and baths.

Their walk took them around Cici's house onto Teal Circle toward Ocean Parkway. They increased their pace. "My shorts feel tighter this morning," Cici said.

"You should sign up for the Zumba class I teach at night, now. I think it would do you some good," Amie said.

"I know. I'm going to do it," Cici said. "Figure I'd better take dieting more seriously. I need to be slim and trim like you," Cici said.

She began perspiring as they walked toward Lookout Point near the river. Both of them observed the waterfront homes as usual. No two homes were alike, and some were neglected. "Look at that house over there on the point. I really like that huge blue crab over their garage door," Amie said. "And look at that one," Amie said as she pointed. "They hung up blue sheets for curtains, and the contour folded side is showing. Must have just moved in."

Cici made no comment. Instead, she just stared downward at the pebbles in the road. The silence hung heavy. Amie squinted in the sunlight and stopped. "Cici, is something wrong? You're awfully quiet." Amie brushed a lock of her long, blonde hair back from her face.

Cici's eyes welled up, but she didn't cry. She was beyond that. She felt a lump in her throat. "I've been meaning to talk to you about Greg and me. Greg came home after one o'clock in the morning last Thursday night smelling of liquor. It happens a lot."

"What's going on?"

Words tumbled off Cici's tongue. "Greg has been behaving like a jerk for awhile now. Maybe it's the pressure from his job. I don't know." She explained his obsessive behavior and lack of sex in their marriage. "I never know when his mood will change or when something will tick him off. He threw coffee at me."

"What?" asked Amie.

"He's hit me. Pushed me once on the cement steps going down into the garage. I fell and scraped my knee." Cici told her what happened at Greg's boss's wedding reception. "From the way he's treating me, I bet he's interested in someone else. I think I should hire a private detective," said Cici. "I'm thinking about divorcing him."

"Geez, this is breaking news. I've witnessed Greg insulting you, but I can't believe he's hit you. I've always felt you deserved better. I really want to hear more, Cici, especially about the coffee thing, but I've got to get to work. And Cici, I know of a P. I. you can hire. We'll talk later during lunch at my office. I'm really sorry to hear about this." Amie gave her a quick hug and rushed home.

Three hours later, Cici adjusted her bifocals and read the Ocean Pines brochure she found in Amie's office.

"What a great place to buy a home. Ocean Pines has nine miles of waterfront property and has over 3,000 shaded acres nestled on Maryland's Eastern Shore. Built as both a residential and resort community, the developer intended it to be built as a vacation-getaway, a second home adjacent to Ocean City, Maryland. It began to be developed 45 years ago and now there are approximately 15,000 full-time residents and 23,000 summertime dwellers. Assawoman Bay, Manklin Creek, and the St. Martin's River surround 7,400 homes and 8,500 platted lots. The people in Ocean Pines love the 18-hole golf course, yacht club, four pools, community center, marinas, playgrounds, and tennis complexes. There are walking trails and parks, and they have their own police force and fire comp . . . "

"What are you reading?" Amie asked, as she walked into her office.

"All about where we live. If you're done with your conference call, let's eat. I'm starving," said Cici. "I almost picked up a crab cake from the Southside Deli for Greg's dinner, then thought, he doesn't deserve one, the way he's been acting."

"Thanks for picking up the crab cakes," Amie said. "They smell delicious."

They moved into the empty conference room and sat down to eat. Amie bit into her crab cake, licking her lips. "Yummy." With her mouth full, she said, "I can't think of anyone who doesn't like a jumbo, lump crab cake. Can you?"

"No, but then I'm someone who loves to eat everything," said Cici.

"You crack me up," said Amie.

"How's the real estate business going?"

"I'm selling about 35 percent foreclosures, but they say the housing market may pick up in the spring of 2014. We'll see," said Amie.

Cici changed the subject, saying, "Since my marriage is falling apart, I was thinking about your first marriage. Have you seen Carl at all since your divorce?"

"No, but I heard he was still living in Salisbury."

"Can't believe after two years, he told you he was gay," said Cici.

"A year and a half. I don't even like to talk about it." Amie quickly changed the subject. "Cici, I know a private detective," Amie said.

"Who?"

"Patrick McCombe. Like me, he went to Salisbury University. He used to be a cop, but now he has his own business in Bishopville. I helped him find an office space to rent there."

"No kidding, Bishopville. That's not far at all from my house," Cici said. "Greg makes me feel so inadequate. He filled my tires with air and left for Wilmington this morning. He said I neglect taking care of my car and should be more astute about things."

"Well, it still was nice of him to do that," Amie said.

Cici rolled her eyes. "Greg underestimates me and makes me feel like my grandmother made me feel when I was little," Cici said. "I rarely could please her. I was so afraid of her."

"You were a tough kid to have put up with such a wackadoodle grandmother," Amie said.

"Tough? Not really. I thought if I told my mom how mean she was, my grandmother would beat me, and who knows what else. I could write a book about her and call it *The Big Bad Nanna*."

She then told Amie about the coffee incident. "Have you told your mom about Greg and you?" asked Amie.

"No, not yet," said Cici. "It would upset her, then she would upset me. Don't want to hear her incessant scolding. I can just hear her say, 'I told you so.' I don't want to be made to feel like a little, stupid kid. I want her to think my marriage is okay right now."

"Is your mom still liking living in San Diego?" asked Amie.

"She and Sam love it out there. They just moved closer to the beach. She's having terrible problems with both of her knees now. She said she needs full replacements."

The skies were darkening, and several raindrops hit the

windows. Thunder boomed in the distance. "Whoa, hear that? Time to go home," said Cici.

"Call Patrick McCombe," said Amie.

"I will." Fully sated from lunch, Cici drove back to Teal Circle in the downpour.

⚓

"Let's toast," he said to Lisa. She raised her glass. "May we spend good times together," Greg said. She clinked his wine glass. The Sunset Grille was his favorite. He loved showing her off in the main dining area, which looked out onto the numerous docked yachts. Her shiny, raven hair draped across her lovely shoulders. He wanted to kiss the nape of her neck. She volunteered she was 29. Greg told her he was 37. He hoped to end their evening at her place.

Greg pulled into her condo's parking lot off Route 50. The three-story building faced the Assawoman Bay. They entered her place through the rear entrance. Walking down Lisa's long corridor, Greg glanced at each of the three small bedrooms off the hallway. The hallway opened up to an L-shaped living room and dining area. A galley kitchen was behind the dining room. The living room looked out onto the bay. Beachy knick-knacks cluttered every table and countertop. "You must love sea shells," said Greg. *Would hate to dust this place.*

"And light houses," said Lisa.

"Whoa!" Lisa's dog jumped up onto Greg's legs. "Your dog is huge," Greg said as it sniffed his leg. "What is he, a lab?"

"Meet my beautiful black lab, Toby," she said.

"Hi, there." Greg scratched Toby between his ears.

"Be right with you. Have to feed him. Help yourself to a drink. I have some white wine in the fridge."

"Do you have any scotch?" asked Greg. She pointed to the

corner cabinet. Lisa fed her dog and then walked back down the hallway while Greg sipped his scotch. He heard the toilet flush.

A minute later he heard her say, "Come on back here." Greg walked back down the hall with Toby following. He saw her naked in the bedroom, lying on top of a down comforter covering a queen-sized bed. He took off his clothes and lay on the bed beside her. He put his arms around her and kissed her passionately, not missing the nape of her neck. He felt her wetness, and as she ran her fingers over his thighs, she said, "You know, you're really exciting me."

Greg was breathing heavily and felt he couldn't hold off. He was inside her, and she moved her body with his.

"You're the best," she said, sighing deeply.

Lying on top of her, after they finished, he felt the heat from her body.

"Don't get up," she said.

"I wasn't planning to," he said as he caressed her smooth skin and kissed her. Toby jumped up, putting his two paws on the bed, and licked Greg's foot. "We have company," he said. Greg rolled off her body and lying next to her, placed his hand on her breast.

Lisa fell asleep on top of her comforter as Greg lay there. He glanced at the pictures hanging on her wall. One caught his eye that he didn't like—a painting of a farm and silo. It reminded him of his father's 30-acre farm. He missed Gal, his pet pygmy goat. That was the only thing about living on the farm he enjoyed. But his father ruined that for him. His father wanted to sell Gal to a neighbor, who wanted Gal's milk to make goat cheese. Greg begged his father to let him keep her, but his father told him to find another pet. He never forgave his father for taking away his cute, little goat who was so friendly to everyone.

Greg hated the chores that went along with living on the farm. He didn't miss it or the chickens. And most of all, he didn't miss his family.

He looked over at Lisa, peacefully sleeping next to him. How sweet she looked. But Cici? She never looked sweet like that. Lisa stirred and woke up. Playing with his hair, Lisa said, "You could use a haircut. It's getting a little long in the back. Come in next week." They made love again, and then it was time for Greg to go home.

"You can stay here," she said.

"I wish I could. But I have to work on the computer to prepare for a meeting tomorrow, and all my stuff is there," said Greg. "I'll be in next week for that haircut, though." And Greg kissed Lisa goodbye.

In the late afternoon the next day, Greg started the 90-horsepower motor of his pontoon and got it up to 20 knots. Cruising along the river was one of his favorite things. He respected the water and avoided the crab pots. He filled his lungs with the smell of brine and enjoyed the company of the geese and gulls. No one was on the river. He sipped a cold beer and took in the view. He slowed down and drifted along in the middle of the river. His mind went to work. He knew how he was going to kill his wife.

Greg was very familiar with Cici's routine. She walked with Amie every morning except on weekends and rainy days. Cici normally took a shower after she returned from her morning walk, and Amie usually went to work afterwards. His plan would work if it didn't rain. He needed to buy a bike, Lycra shorts, a tight-fitting jersey, and a helmet.

The weekend arrived, and Greg decided to scout the garage sales in his neighborhood, held every Saturday. Driving to Terns Landing, he spotted a men's bike in a neighbor's driveway.

He looked it over. He was not real familiar with bikes, so he needed to talk to the seller of the bike. Greg found him in the rear of the garage.

"Nice-looking bike you have here," Greg said to the athletic-looking, broad-shouldered man. "Can you tell me a little about it, how much you're asking for it, and why you're selling it?"

The seller said, "Well, it's a hybrid. It's an upright bike with brakes and gears. I've had it for a little over two years. I've been riding quite awhile, but I need something more challenging. I want a road bike, which is an upgrade. They have different handlebars, and I want to be able to ride up hills with it. I need a bike that goes faster."

"I just want a sturdy bike for riding around the neighborhood, but I don't need a slow bike," Greg said.

"This bike is in great shape, and it's fast enough for riding in the neighborhood. I can sell it to you for 30 dollars," said the seller. "Test-ride it."

Greg got on the bike and pedaled it down the court. He was pleased with its speed in third gear.

He purchased the bike and thanked the man. Satisfied with the good deal he'd just made, he lowered the back car seats and found ample space for the bike in his SUV. Greg covered it up with a blanket. Unfortunately, he couldn't find a helmet at any garage sale and had to purchase that and a cycling outfit at the outlets off Route 50. He paid cash and threw away the receipts. He hid the helmet and clothes under the blanket also.

Sunday morning he decided he'd winterize the boat and oil the boatlift. It was hard for him to see the summer season coming to an end. But on a good note, he was meeting Lisa for lunch at Crab Alley and then spending some time with her at her condo.

On Monday morning, Greg woke up to a beautiful, Indian summer day. There wasn't a cloud in sight. He thought it would've been perfect to take the pontoon out for a run. He couldn't do that now. He'd already drained the gas. Smartly dressed in his long-sleeved shirt, gray slacks, black loafers, beeper on his belt, and iPhone in his hand, he checked himself in the full-length mirror. He confirmed the week's weather forecast on his iPhone.

He stepped into the kitchen. Cici's back was to him. "I'll be in Wilmington until Wednesday. Have to leave soon. My tank is low, and I have to fill it up," he said to Cici.

"Have a good trip," she said, but he was already in the garage and didn't hear her.

He got into his Escalade and drove onto Route 113 north towards Wilmington. If the plan he'd concocted worked, Cici would be history the next day. He'd worked hard for what he had. *Let's see, the river house is worth $850,000; the pontoon, $15,000; there's almost $400,000 in the 401k; the inheritance from the farm is around $675,000; not to mention stocks, bonds, life insurance, cars, savings and checking accounts, and more—I deserve it all.*

CHAPTER 2

Amie called Patrick McCombe.

"Hey, long time no talk," Pat said.

"How are things?" Amie asked.

"Business is great. Husbands and wives are cheating. People are committing insurance fraud. It's all good," Pat said.

Amie laughed.

"What can I do for you? You still with Paul? Not another husband fooling around, I hope."

"No. I'm not married. Paul and I broke up six months ago," said Amie.

"Oh, sorry."

"I'm not. We weren't really compatible," Amie said. "I'm calling to give you a heads-up. A friend of mine by the name of Cici King is going to call you about her situation. I'd like you to handle her case," Amie said. "You were a big help to me."

"Of course," Pat said. "And I would love to see you. It's been awhile."

"Me too," she said.

"Is she having problems with her husband?" asked Pat.

"Most definitely," Amie said. "She's too good for the likes of him. I hope she calls you soon."

"Okay, I'll do my best, and thanks for sending business my way."

Amie didn't care for Greg. He made her feel uncomfortable, and sometimes Amie caught him staring at her. He made her flesh creep. He was disrespectful to Cici, like telling her Macy's doesn't carry her size now, or her backside couldn't fit into a seat on a plane. She easily tired of his boasting that he was a scratch golfer and a top salesman, and that he had the nicest house in the neighborhood. Even though Amie thought his house was perfect, Greg never seemed to be happy with what he had, which in her opinion made him a miserable husband. She was glad Cici was hiring a private detective and contemplating getting a divorce.

She knew getting a divorce was traumatic. Hers especially had been. She had asked her friend, Pat McCombe, to spy on her husband, Carl. She couldn't understand why Carl skipped love-making as much as he did. And she couldn't understand why he didn't seem in the mood when she occasionally wore bikini panties and pranced into the bedroom topless. Amie was sure he was seeing someone else. He was, but not the way she thought. Pat followed him to a gay bar one night in Rehobeth Beach. He saw him getting pretty chummy with another guy. When Amie got the news, she confronted Carl. He admitted he was gay, but still loved her. He didn't want their marriage to end. Amie couldn't believe he wouldn't give her a divorce because he was afraid of the backlash he might receive from living in the tight-knit town of Salisbury. Asking her to stay married to him and keeping up a false front that all was well was out of the question. It was a contentious divorce. She hoped Cici's divorce would be easier than hers.

She knew if Cici divorced Greg, she might not be living across the street from her. They might sell the house and split the proceeds. Amie wasn't crazy about Greg, but she loved the house Greg renovated for Cici. She hoped to have a house on the water with a great view someday, similar to Cici's. As a realtor, it was easy for her to keep tabs on any new, reasonably priced, waterfront property. Amie enjoyed her job as a realtor and was one of Cathell Realty's best agents.

Although they were opposites, she and Cici remained best friends. Divorced and 32, Amie was two years younger and taller, standing a little over five feet, six inches. She taught Zumba classes two nights a week in the church's social hall on Racetrack Road. She played pickleball as well as mahjong at the community center.

Amie saw a new waterfront listing in her price range come on the market. She wanted to show the listing to Cici. Pointing to the picture of the house, Amie said, "It's on Pintail Point and has a great view up the canal."

Greg walked into the kitchen as they were viewing the listing. "Let me take a look," he said. "Not bad. Looks like the right size for you. Maybe a little small for two people."

Cici and Amie looked up at Greg from the table. "What are you talking about? It's over two thousand square feet and has a two-car garage," said Amie.

"Too small for us," he said. "Especially if Cici continues to gain weight," he said.

"Why don't you take a walk?" Cici said. "And leave us alone."

"You're the one who needs a walk." He smirked as he left the kitchen.

Amie raised her voice, calling after him. "You're a pain in the ass, you know. I don't know how Cici can put up with you! Sorry, Cici, he makes me so mad."

"Don't be sorry. You can butt in anytime you want," said Cici.

Looking at the listing, Amie said, "The house is at the end of a canal anyway." Amie snatched her cell phone out of the purse. "Call Pat, would you?"

⊰⊱

In Wilmington, Delaware, Monday evening, Greg set the snooze alarm on his iPhone for 4:45 a.m. and turned on the TV with the remote while in bed. He started to watch *The Late Show* but fell asleep, leaving half of his scotch untouched on the nightstand.

His dream that night rang true. Greg was 10 years old again, back in his sordid house in Whaleyville. He was sitting at the dinner table with his family in their cramped kitchen—his mother, father, and grandmother. Outside he could hear the chickens squawking, and if he stretched his neck, he could see the tops of the corn stalks swaying outside the kitchen window. What a revolting-looking family he had sitting around the kitchen table—his obese mother in her soiled apron, his toothless grandmother with her rolled-down knee-high stockings around her ankles, and his short, overweight father, burping loudly after swallowing his cold beer. Greg watched them shove food into their mouths.

Greg looked up as his grandfather walked into the kitchen, carrying a dead gray squirrel and cottontail rabbit in his two hands. Smiling, he said, "Shot 'em with my .25-caliber pistol. We'll have stewed squirrel for dinner tomorrow." Greg watched him sit down and set the dead animals on the kitchen table. His grandfather picked up his fork to eat the roadkill on his plate. "This is delicious venison. Didn't cost me a cent either." With his mouth full of food, his grandfather said, "Sonny, as long as the meat is fresh, it doesn't matter how the animal died."

Suddenly, his grandmother screamed and grabbed her stomach in pain. Greg watched in horror as she broke out in puss-filled lesions all over her body.

"Rabies!" his father yelled.

His dream moved to inside the barn, where Greg saw his father standing over a live chicken and holding an axe in his right hand. "Be a man, Greg, and kill this chicken. Don't want roadkill for dinner again."

While his father firmly held the chicken down on the worktable, Greg stood over it and lifted the axe over his right shoulder. He brought the axe down hard and chopped off the chicken's head, blood splattering on them. His father grabbed the severed chicken, plucked its feathers, and submerged it into a pot of boiling water.

Greg shot up in bed with beads of perspiration on his forehead and his heart pounding away. He stumbled into the hotel's bathroom, turned on the light, looked into the mirror at his sweaty brow, and splashed cold water on his face. He walked back into the bedroom, turned the light on, and sat up in bed, resting his head against the pillow. The clock registered 3:00 a.m. Greg's heart rate finally slowed down, but he couldn't stop thinking about the family he hated and abandoned. He turned off the light. The dream was mostly true, except for the puss-filled lesions. He was reliving his life on the farm in his dream.

Tuesday morning, the alarm startled Greg out of a deep sleep. He left the hotel in the early hours of the morning, slipping out the side door, dressed in his biking outfit. Greg headed back to Ocean Pines in his Escalade with his helmet and duffel bag beside him. He parked in the Food Lion's parking lot, put on his helmet, opened the trunk, took his bike out, and hopped on it.

Greg veered onto the parkway. It was still too early for him to see any signs of Cici and Amie. He turned left and headed towards his house. The bike's handlebars were sweaty. He wiped his hands on his pants. Don't give up now. You can do this. Greg hid his bike and helmet behind a sea oats bush in the back of his elderly neighbor's yard next door. He knew his neighbors, Mr. and Mrs. Cole, wouldn't be there, since their permanent home was in Red Lion, Pennsylvania. The retired couple had already turned their water off and left for St. Augustine, Florida for six months. Greg and Cici kept their front door key to keep an eye on things until they returned in April. They had done that for the past nine years. The rest of their family lived in Chicago, so Greg was elected to watch their house.

Most of the neighbors on his street, except for Amie and another elderly retired couple, Mr. and Mrs. Adams, were not permanent residents. All the houses were unoccupied except for the summer months.

Nice and quiet. Empty houses. He moved closer to his house. But, not taking any chances, Greg hid behind his neighbor's crape myrtle bush, waiting for Cici to return from her walk. Beads of sweat covered his forehead. His heart rate was rapid. He wiped his face with his sleeve.

Then at 8:45 a.m., Greg heard Cici's voice.

Cici sprinted towards her house and, looking back at Amie, called out, "See you later!"

"Okay. I'm leaving to do some food shopping. I'll pick you up some Lean Cuisines," she yelled back.

Greg watched Cici go around to the back of their house. Cici bounded up the steps of their deck. She should be showering soon.

Five minutes later, he entered the door facing the river, and listened to the sounds in the house. He grabbed a knife from a kitchen drawer. He could kill a chicken. He could kill her. No backing out now. As he crept towards the bedroom, he couldn't wait to sweep the shower curtain aside. As he edged closer to the bedroom, Greg didn't hear the shower's water running. Instead, he heard Cici singing to music on the radio. As he stepped softly on the hallway's ceramic, tiled floor, he saw the bedroom door ajar. He poked his head around the opened door. He quickly pulled his head back, even though she wasn't facing the door.

Damn. Why isn't she in the shower? He looked at his watch. *Plenty of time, though. On schedule. Get in the shower, Cici. Don't have all day. Should have brought a newspaper to read. But patience is a virtue.*

Standing on top of her bedspread, dusting the ceiling fan, Cici sneezed. Something like a cob web and "dust woolies" dangled from the blade of the bedroom's ceiling fan. She wiped the blades one by one with a rag while she hummed the Beatles song "Let it Be," playing on 97.1 FM, *THE WAVE.*

Why can't Greg be like he used to be? He was so protective of me. What a great catch he was. He wasn't that wonderful man anymore. No more cruising together on the river in the pontoon boat once a week. Now he goes by himself. Amie was right: I do deserve better. Glad to have called Pat. Wonder if he will find out anything. Bet he will. For so long she had been in denial. Afraid of the truth. Not wanting to confront Greg. If Greg couldn't stand her anymore, why didn't he ask for a divorce?

So, she'll be the one to ask for a divorce. *Wonder how he'll react. The property will have to be divided. He won't like that. Then there's alimony to be paid. He won't like that either. Will he keep the house? A lawyer can figure all this out. Sure do love this house. That's going to be a problem.*

If they split everything, she would have to find another place to live. Amie could help with that.

She definitely would need a job. Should she work at night and attend classes in the daytime? Cici used to study radiology. She could do that again, but that costs money for classes and books. So she would need to live off some of the assets she and Greg now shared. Money for a condo, money for the bills, and money if she went back to school. She was young enough to start over. She just needed a good lawyer. She'd have to pay him too.

Okay, that does it for the dusting. Woolies are gone.

Greg continued peeking on and off. *Damn it, woman, get in the shower.* What a sight she was. If he had seen her chubby butt like this 10 years ago, he never would have married her. *Come on, get moving.* He looked at his watch again, then peeked. He saw Cici ease off the bed and walk into the bathroom. Finally.

Greg heard her slide the curtain over, still humming "Let it Be." He put the knife on top of the dresser. The shower was running in the tub. He hoped to take her by surprise. The door was slightly ajar. Greg crept into the bathroom. He yanked the curtain aside. With her back to him, the sudden action jarred her and made her gasp, but she didn't have time to turn around. Greg slammed her forehead into the tiles above the faucet. He forcefully grabbed the back of her head with both of his hands and banged her head a second time into the ceramic tiles. She buckled, and her knees bent as she dropped to the bottom of the tub. The shower water trickled down over her body. She landed on her side with her eyes closed and her mouth slightly opened. Greg closed the curtain.

He slipped on rubber gloves from under the bathroom sink and went back into the bedroom. Greg opened the bureau drawers. He quickly threw underwear, socks, and shirts onto the bedroom floor. He took various pieces of jewelry worth over $2,000 from Cici's vanity box. Might as well add his eighteen-karat gold wedding band too. He quickly gathered his commemorative, rare coins, two autographed baseballs of Brooks Robinson and Rabbit Maranville, and about $300 from Cici's wallet. He put the cash and items into a plastic bag. He took a leak in the bathroom. After seeing her at the bottom of the tub in her death-pose, he turned to get the knife to finish her off. Greg was sweating profusely. Now, it was easier for him to stab her. No screaming and fighting back. Don't want any defense wounds.

He heard a knock at the door. *Holy shit! Who the hell is that?*

The knocking continued. Greg wiped his brow. *Go away.* He wouldn't dare take a look who was on the back deck for fear of being seen through the sliders. *Is that Amie back already?* Greg glanced at his watch. *Give me strength.* The clock was ticking. Greg heard a man's voice say, "Cici?" Knock knock. Knock. Knock.

Get out of here. Shit, the slider screen door was unlocked. *Hope whoever it is, doesn't come inside.* Sweat dripped down his cheeks. The rapping on the slider door stopped. It was finally quiet. He heard crunching on his front driveway. He carefully peered out the bedroom window and saw his other elderly neighbor, Mr. Adams, in his front yard. *Is he with his wife?* Mr. Adams retreated down the street towards his own house, a few houses down from Amie's. *Good.* From the bedroom window, Greg saw him walk back alone, but would he return? Mr. Adams was hurriedly walking on his own sidewalk toward the front door of his house. *Why had he come here? Was it important?*

Greg needed to get out of the house fast. It was way past the time he'd planned to leave. He panicked and grabbed his knife. He looked out the window again. No sign of anyone. Was it so important that Mr. Adams could return to the house again? And what if Amie came back from the store?

Greg looked at his Rolex. *Crap.* He wiped his brow with a handkerchief. It was imperative to get moving to make his appointment in Wilmington. He threw the knife back into the kitchen drawer and scrambled out of the house as fast as he could with the items he pretended were stolen. Greg opened the back door of Mr. Cole's house next door and laid the plastic bag of stolen items inside on the floor beside the door. *Thank goodness my neighbors are in Florida.* He hurried to his bike and helmet hidden behind the sea oats bush. He rolled up the rubber gloves and stuffed them into his pocket. He put on his helmet and sunglasses and mounted his bike. He rode out onto his street and pedaled as fast as his legs could move.

Greg glanced towards Amie's house. Her Saab was gone. She was probably still at the store. Then he saw Mr. Adams and his wife walk outside to the curb, where a car was idling in front of their house. The elderly couple stepped inside the car where a waiting driver sat behind the wheel. Would they recognize him riding by on his bike? Greg lowered his head and quickly rode past them and onto Ocean Parkway.

He was just another biker on the main drag. He turned onto Route 589 and left his bike leaning against the outside wall on the north side of Rite Aid. Eventually someone might be tempted to take it. *No worries.* He walked back towards the Food Lion and got into his SUV. He took off his helmet and placed it on the car seat next to him. Looking into the rearview mirror, he backed his SUV out of the parking space, took a deep breath, and prepared to head back to Wilmington.

It was a good disguise. He congratulated himself on thinking of it. As he left the Food Lion parking lot, he glanced towards the side of Rite Aid and saw that his bike was still there. Certainly, someone would take it. He headed north and drove quite awhile before he spotted the place he planned to use on Route 113 to change his clothes.

The police would probably question him when they found Cici. Always the spouse was suspected first. He had to contact his clients to establish his alibi and make the police think he had been working in Wilmington. After pulling into the parking lot of a convenience store near Wilmington, he checked his phone for emails and answered what was necessary. He laid his head back on the car seat. He wondered if Cici was still lying at the bottom of the tub. Was she just unconscious? *Have to accept whatever happens, though. Should have hired someone to do this. Maybe she's brain-damaged. How do you deal with that? Was this the best way to have done this?* Would the cops pin this on him? His hand shook as he picked up his calendar and appointment schedule. Greg then confirmed his late-afternoon appointment and made a few calls to a couple of restaurant managers to see if there were any problems with food deliveries.

Greg walked into the store and went into the men's restroom stall with his duffel bag. He put on his shirt and slacks for work. He placed his helmet and cycling outfit into the bag. He needed to get rid of them. Damn, the Dumpster behind the store was full.

Maybe people would forget about the cyclist man walking into their store. At least his outfit disguised him. But the camera, if working, might tell something different. That could be a worry. It would show a cyclist walking into the bathroom, but not out. Maybe their camera would be turned off, or maybe the restroom was out of the range from the camera. *Should have planned better.*

In his car, Greg called his home phone and left a voicemail. "Cici, I'll be home Wednesday around dinner time. I'm sorry I threw coffee at you the other day. I'll buy you another robe. See you soon." He swallowed and found the next line difficult to say: "Love ya." He drove off.

Greg made a sharp turn off Route 113, and at a nearby playground park, Greg grabbed his duffel bag off the car seat, walked over to a large trash receptacle, and dumped it.

CHAPTER 3

Amie unpacked her groceries and glanced out of her window towards Cici's house. Cici's Buick was in the driveway, so she should be home. She had picked up some frozen diet meals that were on sale at the Food Lion and wanted to drop them off at Cici's house before returning to Cathell Realty.

When she had been in Food Lion's parking lot, Amie had stopped in her tracks. *Was that Greg in a cyclist outfit, getting into his Escalade?* But she had never known him to go bike riding. He couldn't have come back from Wilmington this early. Cici had never mentioned he was a biking enthusiast.

After pulling into her driveway, she walked across the street to Cici's house, carrying a grocery bag. She knocked on the screen door, but there was no answer. She opened the unlocked screen door, placed the frozen foods in the freezer, and then heard the radio playing in the background.

"Cici, where are you?"

Silence.

"Cici! Must be deaf."

Was she in the shower? As she walked towards the bedroom door, Amie yelled her name again. Amie entered the bedroom, heard the water running in the bathroom, and was surprised to see the bedroom in disarray. She walked towards the master bathroom and called out her name again. "Cici, I'm here!" No answer came from behind the shower curtain. Amie felt uneasy. She reluctantly slowly pulled the shower curtain aside. Lying on the bottom of the porcelain tub floor was Cici, her face covered in blood. Amie screamed. She turned off the shower and quickly dialed 911 on Cici's bedroom phone. Trembling, she yelled into the receiver, "My neighbor's in the tub. She's passed out. There's stuff scattered all over the bedroom."

The 911 operator asked, "Where are you?"

Aime gave her the address. "Please hurry."

"Does she have a pulse?"

"Wait, let me check."

Amie tried to feel for Cici's pulse, but she was so distraught and nervous, she couldn't keep herself from shaking. Amie rushed back to the phone.

"I don't know if she has a pulse. I couldn't feel it!" She frantically screeched, "She's soaking wet!"

The 911 operator got her name and said, "An ambulance is on its way."

With quivering hands, Amie tried again and again to find Cici's pulse. She heard the gravel crunch outside the bedroom window. The fire rescue squad's ambulance had arrived. With her knees tucked under her, Amie stared at Cici's bloody forehead and her swollen face. Her eyes welled up.

Amie heard voices and heavy shoes tramping loudly on the floor. "Back here!" she yelled.

The paramedic crew rushed into the bedroom with an Automatic External Defibrillator and jump bag, a respiratory airway kit. Quickly, they put on rubber gloves and assessed the scene. A paramedic attendant was in charge. Amie got up and out of the way so the paramedic could work on Cici.

He knelt down and, looking at Cici even though her lids were closed, said, "Hi." He then asked, "What is your name? . . . Ma'am?" He got no response from Cici and immediately located the space at the top of her sternum. The paramedic rubbed hard there, trying to rouse her and get a pain response.

"Is she alive?" asked Amie.

"Yes, but unconscious," said the paramedic.

"Thank God," said Amie.

Worcester County Deputies arrived on the scene. They were members of the Worcester County Quick Response Team. Amie turned around to see a robust man, well over 300 pounds, and his deputy enter the room.

Amie looked up at the man. "I'm Hank Phillips, Chief of Police from the Ocean Pines Station. They call me Hulk." He asked Amie, "Did you make the call to 911?"

She stood up and introduced herself before answering, "Yes."

Inhaling and exhaling laboriously, the chief asked, "Why are you here?"

Someone yelled across the room to him. "Hey, Hulk, there was no forced entry."

"Be with you in a sec," said Hulk. He looked back at Amie and repeated, "Why are you here?"

Amie shook her head. "I found her like this about 15 minutes ago. I'm her neighbor." Amie explained why she came to Cici's house.

The chief's eyes scanned the bedroom. "Is Cici married?" he asked Amie.

Amie told Hulk that Cici's husband was in Wilmington on business. "I'll call him and let him know what's happened," Amie said.

"No one disturb the crime scene!"

Amie jumped at Hulk's booming voice. She took a closer look at the things strewn around the bedroom.

The chief dialed a number on his cell phone. "Joe, need you to come out here." Amie couldn't quite make out what he was saying to this guy Joe. Hulk looked at his deputy and said, "I want a fingerprinting kit as soon as possible."

Ten minutes later, more gravel crunched outside in the driveway. Amie looked at the detective who entered the bedroom. *Handsome guy in his black suit and dark T-shirt.* He greeted Hulk, walked past one of the deputies, edged up behind Amie, and looked over her shoulder at the paramedic with Cici. Amie glanced at him. "I'm Detective Joe Crabbe. I'll be in charge of this case."

"I was the first one here to find Cici, I mean, Mrs. King," said Amie.

"Ooooh, oh," moaned Cici.

"She's awake!" said Amie.

♔

The paramedics checked her airway and pulse. Cici was breathing. Her respiration, circulation, and skin color were noted. "Take her blood pressure," the EMT said. He hooked up the Automatic External Defibrillator to determine the oxygen level in her blood. The rapid trauma assessment checked her from head to toe. The EMT felt for bumps and swelling and looked at Cici's neck and spine.

The attendant rolled her on her back, and said, "Looking for neck or back traumas. Don't see any. Check for broken bones and blood loss." They finally covered her naked body with a blanket.

While this was happening, another police officer arrived on the scene. He and the deputy were spreading magnetic dust on many surfaces in the house. Hulk said, "We'd better get a palm or footprint." The snapping of pictures was heard.

After the EMT's assessment was completed, the lead paramedic attendant said, "Lead to go."

Cici was gently lifted and placed on a stretcher. The paramedics rolled the gurney through the bedroom door, into the great room, and then outside onto the deck, handling it gently. As they carried her down the outside deck's steps, everyone followed.

Amie said, "Wait. I'm going with her to the hospital." Hulk stopped her.

"Miss Weiss, if you don't mind, please follow the ambulance. Detective Crabbe is going to ride inside with her. He may get a statement from Mrs. King. Sorry."

"I was expecting to go," she said. Amie walked towards her Saab.

The stretcher's wheels were raised, and Cici was loaded into the ambulance. Amie peeked into its opened doors and then got into her Saab.

Cici didn't see her, but she noticed a paramedic start her IV. Her eyes were darting back and forth. She spotted a tall man outside the ambulance doors. She saw him staring up at the sky. He was watching a small airplane pulling a sign advertising Hooters on Route 50. It swung around and flew over Cici's house. Cici wondered who he was, and then she saw him step up into the ambulance. She closed her eyes because the light bothered her.

The ambulance accelerated, flashing its red and blue roof lights.

Cici opened her eyes and moaned. "The lights are too bright," she said.

The paramedic bent over her. "Hello." The paramedic gently said, "You're in an ambulance. What's your name?"

Shaken, she said, "Cici King. What? Why am I in an ambulance?"

"We're heading to the hospital. You were unconscious for a while."

The ambulance arrived at Atlantic General Hospital. The paramedics rolled Cici into the ER. An admitting clerk got the necessary information she needed. A nurse assigned a bed to Cici in the emergency room area.

"What happened to me? What are you doing?" She held an ice pack to her head. A Physician's Assistant came in and began stitching up her forehead. "Ouch!" Her left eye was swollen shut, and blood stained her forehead and nose. She touched her swollen nose. "Things are blurry. I feel sick to my stomach. What hospital is this?" she asked the nurse.

The paramedic told her the name of the hospital. "You were found unconscious on your bathtub floor. Do you remember how you got injured?"

"What? I don't remember anything. And I really feel nauseous," she said. Cici grabbed the nurse's arm. "I'm pretty scared."

"Don't worry. The doctor will take a look at you soon," said the nurse.

The nurse applied a new ice pack to her head. Little good it did because, just then, Cici vomited on the floor in the ER room. Someone quickly came in, closed the curtain, and cleaned up the mess.

A few minutes later, her privacy curtain opened, and a middle-aged man in a white jacket appeared. He sat down on a stool next to her and introduced himself. "Mrs. King, I'm Dr. Chu." He picked up her chart. "You've had a nasty blow to the head, which required stitches. How do you feel?"

"Horrible," Cici said.

"Can you tell me what happened to you?" he asked.

"No, I can't remember. Wait a minute." She paused. "I do remember dusting the ceiling fan, and then I took a shower. I don't remember anything after that."

"Can you tell me what medications you're taking?"

"Something for high blood pressure. Starts with an *L*. Can't remember," she said. "Maybe my husband knows."

"You're doing fine. Do you remember if you're taking a blood thinner?"

"No."

"Are you allergic to any medications?"

"Not sure," said Cici.

"Have you had any prior head injuries?"

"Not that I recall."

"What is your blood type?"

"O positive."

The doctor shined a small light into her eyes.

"The light is too bright," Cici said.

"I'm just checking out your neurological functioning and am going to test your mental status." He examined the neck area. "I'm inspecting your ears for any signs of bleeding. Nope, looks good," he said. Both eyes were black, and one was swollen much more than the other one.

"It looks to me like you have a concussion."

"A concussion?" she asked.

"Like I said, you've had a nasty blow to the head. A concussion can jar the brain. I'm ordering a CAT scan to evaluate the extent of your head injury."

"Oh, that's just great," she said.

"Just routine."

"What are you looking for?" asked Cici.

"The CAT scan would show if there was evidence of bleeding under the skull or within the brain tissue. Don't worry. We'll take good care of you," he said.

"How in the world did this happen?" Cici asked again.

"Hopefully we'll find out soon," the doctor said.

⚔

A little east of Wilmington, when Greg was just about to call on a huge account, his cell phone rang. This could be the call about Cici. Amie's name popped up on his iPhone.

"Greg, glad you picked up. I'm heading towards Atlantic General Hospital. Cici's being taken there by ambulance," said Amie.

Gotta act like the concerned husband. "The hospital? Is she . . . What happened?"

"I had to drop off some things for her and walked into the house." She explained to Greg what had happened to Cici. "The bedroom was trashed," said Amie.

Greg said, "What? I can't believe this. No way. I'm coming right home. It'll be about two hours. I'm still in Wilmington. Stay in touch, especially if you learn anything new."

He disconnected and notified the hotel that he could not return due to an unexpected family emergency. He asked the manager, "Please forward my bill, clothes, and notions to my home address." The hotel staff knew Greg, since he often stayed there as a guest.

Greg stopped at a red light on Route 113. "Fuck." He banged the steering wheel with his palm. He was a freakin' idiot for not finishing the job. But he hadn't counted on Mr. Adams coming, and what if he'd turned around and had come back to Greg's house? Then Greg would be stuck there, unable to get back in time to make his appointments in Wilmington to establish his alibi.

He knew he totally blew it and was back to square one. *Wait a minute. Maybe not.* Amie didn't tell him how bad Cici's injuries were. She didn't say Cici was okay at all. She could be in grave condition.

⚱

Detective Crabbe couldn't get a statement in the ambulance from Cici. He needed to talk more to Amie, and of course, question Mr. King.

Amie parked her car and rushed into the hospital. She ran over to the admitting clerk and said, "My friend just arrived in an ambulance. Her name is Cici King. Do you know how she is?" Before she could answer Amie, a familiar-looking man approached her at the desk, overhearing her conversation. It was Detective Crabbe. He kind of reminded her of a slim and younger version of Vincent D'Onofrio on *Law and Order.*

"Any news?" Amie asked.

"No, not yet," Crabbe said. "Sit down. Let's talk awhile." *Maybe she did this to Mrs. King.*

"I hope they find out who hurt Cici," she said.

"Hopefully we'll find out soon," said Crabbe.

"This is scary. I'm going to have to get a security system installed after this," Amie said.

"That's a good idea." Crabbe suggested one for her to use. "There's been a recent rash of house burglaries in Ocean Pines, including three in the span of eight days and another last weekend," Crabbe said. "Three in a month is the norm, and they're usually along the lines of a boyfriend trying to break into a girlfriend's house."

"I'm getting an alarm system for sure, right now."

"Why, do you have an untrustworthy boyfriend?" asked Crabbe.

"No," Amie tried to stifle her laugh. "And Mrs. King doesn't have a boyfriend either. I wish she did. Not one that would break into her house, though."

"Why do you wish she had a boyfriend?" asked Crabbe.

"Because her husband's a jerk," said Amie. "I called him, and he's on his way here from Wilmington."

"They don't live together?" asked Crabbe.

"Yes, they do," she said. Amie called the security company recommended by Crabbe.

"I'd like to hear more about her husband," said Crabbe.

Amie held her index finger up and said, "Wait. I have the security company on the line now."

Crabbe would have to wait to hear more about Cici's husband. He got up to get a cup of coffee from a small station set up with paper cups, a coffee-maker, creamer, and napkins opposite from where they were seated.

Joe Crabbe was a seasoned detective, putting in almost 30 years. Crabbe had started as a cadet in Ocean Pines at the age of 18 and moved his way up. He was an honest and hard-working officer. He was good at what he did and had solved many cases in all the years he was on the force. Crabbe was also an excellent sharpshooter and practiced at the range often. He had been married for 17 years when his wife was diagnosed with ovarian cancer. After four years, she lost her battle. He was grief-stricken for a long time. After she was gone, Joe wasn't interested in getting married again. He sold his house after his wife died and moved to an oceanfront, two-bedroom condo in Ocean City.

He loved his St. Bernard, Old Bay, who adapted well to the smaller living quarters. Old Bay was obedient and loyal to his master. Sometimes Crabbe would have a beer at the Purple Moose Saloon on the Boardwalk in Ocean City. The trusting dog relaxed on the sandy beach, 20 feet away from the saloon's front door. When Crabbe finished his beer and came outside, Old Bay would run up to him and wag his tail. Of course, that probably was because Crabbe always rewarded him with a gourmet doggie cookie after leaving the bar.

Sitting next to Amie, Crabbe lifted his head after taking a sip from his second cup of coffee. He watched a man rush through the hospital's emergency room doors. Seconds later, that same man, a little out of breath, approached Amie and asked, "How bad is it? What's her condition? What in the hell happened?"

"Haven't heard from the doctor yet," Amie said to Greg.

He sat down opposite Amie. "Well, where is he?" asked Greg.

Detective Crabbe didn't take his eyes off him. Amie explained the scene in the bedroom after she'd called 911. Greg lowered his head and stared at the floor, wringing his hands and shaking his leg. He said nothing.

Detective Crabbe got up and sat next to him.

"I assume you're Mrs. King's husband."

He raised his head. "Yes, and who are you?" Greg asked.

"I'm Detective Joe Crabbe, lead investigator on this case," he said to Greg.

"Greg King," he said to Crabbe and firmly shook his hand.

Crabbe gave him his business card as his cell phone hummed. "I'd like to ask you a few questions, but I have to answer this phone call first." He raised his cell phone for Greg to see. "Don't leave the hospital."

"Of course not," said Greg. Greg got up and walked down the hall towards the gift shop. He looked at the flower arrangements and bouquets. He bought a beautiful bunch of colorful mums, daisies, and carnations and walked back to the emergency ward.

He sat back down near Amie, bouquet in hand, and asked, "Where did that detective go?"

"Not sure," said Amie.

"I don't know who he thinks he is, telling me not to leave the hospital, ordering me around like that," said Greg.

"He's just doing his job," said Amie.

Greg rose from his seat, laid the floral bouquet down, and started pacing back and forth in front of Amie. He walked over to the admissions desk. "Can you please tell me about my wife's progress?" he asked the clerk. Greg returned to his seat. He said to Amie, "She's getting a CAT scan."

Crabbe walked back to the emergency area. After an agonizing wait, the doctor located Greg, introduced himself, and said, "Your wife has a concussion, a hematoma at the site of the head injury. She's now resting after her CAT scan. We're treating her with an ice application every half hour for the next two to four hours. Rest is important to let the brain heal. I want her to stay overnight to keep an eye on her."

"Did she say anything about how she got the concussion?" asked Greg. Crabbe listened to him carefully, watching his demeanor.

Doctor Chu said, "I wish I knew how she got it. She only remembers doing some household chores then taking a shower."

Greg asked, "When can I see her?"

"You can go in now, but only stay a few minutes. Who is your family physician?" asked Dr. Chu. Greg gave him the doctor's name and told Dr. Chu the name of her blood pressure medication. "I'm going to prescribe Ambien to help her sleep after she's discharged," the doctor said.

"Thank you, Doc." Greg abruptly got up, grabbed the flowers, and headed in the direction of Cici's ER room. He slid the curtain aside, poked his head into her cramped cubicle, and saw her lying there on the gurney.

Crabbe had to postpone questioning Greg. He had a funny feeling about this guy. He got up and walked back inside the area that housed the private patient emergency rooms. Crabbe showed his badge to the nurse behind the desk. He waited there, crossing his arms.

Five minutes later, Greg came out of Cici's cubicle, and Detective Crabbe approached him.

"Mr. King?"

"I'd like to ask you some questions now," said Crabbe. "How is your wife doing?" Greg updated him on her condition. Crabbe said, "Let's sit down where you were before." Amie passed them as they walked out the doors from where Cici and the other patients were being seen.

"You can't stay too long," Greg said to Amie.

"I know," said Amie, and she continued walking down the hall.

Crabbe said, "I've already examined the crime scene with the sheriff. We dusted for prints. There was no forced entry into your house. Your bedroom was ransacked, and you need to tell me if anything is missing."

Greg could feel perspiration on the back of his neck and on his palms. "You think someone wanted to kill her? This has all been too much. It's crazy. Have there been burglaries on our street? I haven't heard of any."

"No, there haven't been any burglaries on your street, but some on other streets. You probably know that Ocean Pines is the largest residential community in Worcester County. There are more calls for domestic violence in Ocean Pines than robberies. But we have our share of armed robberies and burglaries in the area also. After we talk, if you forget anything or think of something that could pertain to the case, don't hesitate to call me. I'll also be talking to your neighbors, and I'll be canvassing the neighborhood."

"Good, good," Greg said while nodding.

"Do you normally leave the doors unlocked?" asked Crabbe.

Greg said, "Pretty much during the day. It always seemed like a safe neighborhood, but we lock up late at night. And we have Neighborhood Watch."

"That's ironic, because you don't have many permanent neighbors on your street." Crabbe paused for a moment. "Well, it certainly looks like someone did try to kill her," said Crabbe. "Where were you this morning and up until now?" the detective asked.

Oh boy, now the questions begin. "Surely, you don't suspect me?"

"I want to catch the guy who did this. I want to rule you out, not freak you out. This is a routine thing. Following protocol, you know. I question everyone."

"Sure, okay. I was in Wilmington, checking on my customers. I got a call from my neighbor that my wife was in the hospital. I drove to the hospital as soon as I heard."

"Was that Amie Weiss?"

"Yes."

"How long were you in Wilmington?"

Greg cupped his hand under his chin and said, "I left yesterday morning."

"Where did you stay in Wilmington?"

"The Radisson."

"Did you stop along the way when you returned home today?"

"No."

"Did you send any text messages or make any phone calls?" The detective noticed perspiration on Greg's brow.

Greg cleared his throat. "I made some business calls Monday. Had to cancel my afternoon appointment today. Called the hotel and some clients today. I also phoned Cici and left her a message that I was coming home tomorrow." Crabbe noticed Greg's crossed right leg shaking up and down.

"What time was that?"

"Around lunch time, I think."

"What did you do Monday night?"

"Not much. Had a drink at a bar. Watched TV. Went to bed early."

"What bar?"

"The one in my hotel."

Crabbe finished scribbling and put his pen and notepad in a pocket inside his jacket. "When you get home, take inventory of any missing items. I need to know what they are, if any, and I can look in pawn shops in the area to see if they ended up there. I'll be talking to you again. And, like I said before, don't forget to call me if something important to the case comes up."

Crabbe couldn't put his finger on it, but he knew something didn't feel right. *Smug fellow when he first arrived in the emergency ward.* He'd talk to Greg again to establish a detailed time line of his movements, pinpoint when he left the hotel, and check his alibi at the time of the assault. Did he have the opportunity to do this? First, he'd check to see if he was at the Radisson that morning, and then he'd run a background check on him and zero in on his cell phone records.

⚓

Amie popped her head in to see Cici after Greg's turn. "Cici, you look awful."

"Yes, I know. Like the walking dead," she said.

"The doctor said you don't remember what happened. Maybe you'll remember tomorrow."

"You know something, Amie?"

"What?"

"Greg left in a flash and brought me flowers, but you'd think after what I've been through, he could muster up a hug at least. You'd think he'd show more compassion," she said as tears rolled down her cheeks. Sobbing, she barely could get the words out. "He's so . . . detached. He, he . . . cringed when he saw my face. How bad is it, Amie?"

"Your face is swollen, and you have a number of stitches in your forehead," Amie said.

"I thanked him for the bouquet. He wanted to know what happened, and that was it. I can't explain it, but he seemed like he wanted to leave quickly because he had something to do—and not stay with me."

"Don't get yourself upset over him. Your emotions are very fragile right now. He left Wilmington as soon as I called. He seemed worried when he was sitting in the emergency area, and he was pacing back and forth," she said. "You'd better get some rest. The nurse said I could only stay a minute." As she said that, the nurse walked into the room, placed her hand on her right hip, squinted her eyes, and gave Amie a hard stare.

Turning her back to her and pointing her thumb over her left shoulder towards the nurse, Amie whispered to Cici, "That's Nurse Ratched's twin sister. Get some sleep if you can."

"Don't make me laugh. Oh, this rotten headache."

"Bye, Cici. Whoever did this to you is a monster."

Amie walked toward the hospital exit and shook her head.

The next morning, Cici woke up with a pounding headache. She didn't get much sleep. The staff kept coming into her room during the night to check on her.

Dr. Chu entered Cici's hospital room that she had been moved to overnight. The walls were painted a pale green, and there was an unoccupied bed next to her. Her bed was next to a window that looked out onto the parking lot. Body lotion,

Kleenex, a water cup, and a sanitizer bottle cluttered the table next to her bed. Her morning breakfast egg looked untouched on her tray beside her.

"Not hungry?" Doctor Chu asked.

"No, but I drank my orange juice," Cici said.

She liked Dr. Chu. He was maybe in his early 50s, medium height, with short, jet black hair. He was a cute, Asian guy with a pleasing smile. He slipped his pen inside the pocket of his white lab coat and walked over to her bedside. "How are you feeling this morning? Your memory any better?" he asked.

"I still have a dreadful headache, and I still don't remember a thing."

"Do you know how you got here?" he asked.

Cici ignored his question. "I can't stand this headache."

He walked over closer to her. He lifted her eyelid and looked into her eye with his retinoscope. "It's not uncommon to have persistent headaches for a week and up to a month or more after a concussion. Do you remember me telling you that you were found unconscious in your bathtub?"

"Yes."

"Do you remember I told you your house was robbed and ransacked?" asked Dr. Chu.

"Wait. We were robbed?" Cici was still confused and couldn't put the puzzle pieces together. Yesterday's events were still foggy.

"Will I regain my memory about what happened?" asked Cici. The doctor explained that her memory may come back.

Dr. Chu proceeded to examine her and asked questions to test her ability to pay attention and remember things. "These questions are challenging," Cici said.

"You're doing fine, and you're solving problems quickly. I'm not too concerned you can't remember what happened to you in your bathroom, because you can answer other questions not pertaining to the accident quite well."

Cici smiled.

Dr. Chu finally said, "Well, I'm going to discharge you today, but I want you to follow these instructions when you get home." He handed her a paper. "When you get home apply ice to your head to ease the pain."

He prescribed a pain killer for her and said, "Get plenty of rest, drink lots of fluids, and avoid housework and exercises for awhile. Also, please don't do any activities that would put you at risk in the future. Keep away from bright lights, and no watching TV for a week. I want to see you next week, and by then, I'll let you know when you can slowly return to your regular activities."

Cici was happy to hear she was leaving the hospital.

"Oh, by the way, a detective was here and wanted to talk to you. I didn't want him questioning you here at the hospital while you were recovering. He'll probably get in touch with you at home."

As the doctor left her room, he glanced back, pointed his index finger at her, winked, and said, "Take it easy."

She nodded back and smiled. Cici then dialed her home number. It was busy.

Cici finally reached Greg on his cell phone and said, "The doctor is discharging me today. Can you come and pick me up?"

Greg answered, "I wish I could, but I'm up to my eyeballs with work. That's good you're being discharged. Could you please call Amie and see if she's free to drive you home?"

"Do I have a choice? What if she can't?"

"Call me back if she can't," said Greg.

"I can't believe we were robbed. Did you talk to the police?" Cici asked.

"Yeah. Do you remember anything now about the assault?"

"No," said Cici.

"Okay. Gotta go. Talk to you later." He hung up, looking at a photo of Cici on the bookshelf next to his desk. He picked up the picture frame and spoke to her, "You're indestructible. I try to kill you bitch, and you can't die. You've got a skull tough as iron."

Cici couldn't believe Greg wouldn't pick her up. *He's not going to change.* To add to her frustration, she couldn't scare him enough to stop him from smoking. Asking him to give up alcohol was futile.

As Cici held her ice pack to her head, she called Amie. After the third ring, she picked up. "Amie, guess what? The doctor is discharging me from the hospital today."

"That's great!"

"Yes it is, but I have a problem. My wonderful, sweet, adoring husband can't pick me up. Is there any way you could drive me home?" she asked.

"Of course I can. What time are you being discharged?"

"Anytime before 1:00 p.m.," Cici said.

CHAPTER 4

Greg chipped his ball out of the bunker onto the green at Lighthouse Sound's number-one handicap hole. He putted it into the hole from there.

"Wow," his friend Merv said. "Great par."

His foursome liked the course but complained about the high cost to play there. "Too bad South Pines Golf Course closed. That was an enjoyable course to play and worth the price to go there," one of the foursome said.

Merv said, "Yeah, and now it's completely abandoned, overgrown with trees and shrubs. The clubhouse is a wreck. Thought they were going to build houses there."

"No, it's a dinosaur now," said one golfer. "They scratched that idea."

Greg and the guys went to Harborside after their game, talked mostly about golf, and had a few drinks. "How's the wife doing, Greg?"

"She's going to be fine, thank you."

"Yeah, heard the sheriff talk about your home invasion on WBOC this morning. He mentioned they were looking for a suspect," one golfer said.

"Yeah, they'll find him. Got a good detective on the case," said Greg. When the guys tired of talking about their golf games, they finished their beers and left. Merv remained behind with Greg.

"You look sharp, Merv, in your matching golf shirt and cap." Greg was used to seeing him in his crusty, old handyman digs.

"Do you think Cici would mind if I stopped by and saw her? I hope they catch whoever did it pretty soon," said Merv. "Even my wife is nervous about the robbery."

"I'm sure Cici would like it if you stopped by. You're pretty charismatic. You've already won Cici's affection. That would be nice if you visited her," said Greg.

"I'll call her, and see if she's up to visitors yet," Merv said.

Greg hovered over his scotch. "Merv, can I pick your brain?" asked Greg.

"Sure."

"Of course this is all very hypothetical," said Greg. "So," he sipped his scotch, "if you wanted to plan the perfect murder, how would you do it?"

"Don't tell me you're planning to kill someone?" Merv laughed.

"No, of course not. Just play along with me, Merv. How would you do it?"

Greg's cell phone rang. "Excuse me, Merv." He pointed to his cell phone and whispered to Merv, "My boss." Merv nodded.

"Yes, she's going to be okay. She's had it pretty rough." He paused. "I'm not able to check on any clients right now. Please have customer service call my accounts, and when things improve on this end, I'll call on them." Greg told Merv that his boss, Mr. Case, was very understanding.

"So, how would you do it?" he asked Merv. "How would you plan the perfect murder?"

"I wouldn't." Merv took off his Nike golf cap and wiped his forehead with the back of his hand. His tattooed arm was sunburned from the hot sun on the course. His curly, brown hair fell messily on his forehead.

"Oh, come on, Merv. This is make-believe. You're a smart guy, except you drink too much."

"Yeah, well, you drink a lot yourself," said Merv.

"I never got a DUI," said Greg. "Awhile back, you spent some time in jail after your second DUI. Did you ever meet a murderer when you were there?"

He scratched his sweaty scalp. "As a matter of fact, this one con killed someone. I didn't hang out with him or anything like that. He was pretty weird. Anyway, he put antifreeze into some poor guy's drink, and he died."

"But he didn't get away with it, did he? So it wasn't the perfect murder," said Greg.

Merv said, "On *CSI*, one guy poisoned his wife with arsenic. He added it to her food little by little over a period of time, and she finally died."

"Did he get caught?" Greg asked.

"It's *CSI*. Sure, he got caught. What would you do?" asked Merv.

"I haven't the faintest idea. Off the top of my head, I can't think how to do it," Greg said. "I watched a documentary on *48 Hours* about a doctor who left his hospital between surgeries, drove home, and murdered his wife in their bathroom, stabbing her with a knife. The doctor drove back to the hospital to perform his next operation. He was late for his second surgery and left evidence back in their bathroom at his home. Homicide detectives found him guilty." He snorted. "Even a doctor can't plan the perfect murder."

Greg finished his scotch and looked past Merv. He glanced towards the bar at the hot chick bartender squeezing an orange. Taking his eyes off her, he said, "Think about it, Merv. Gotta go. Have to get a haircut. See you around."

Merv's input wasn't very helpful. The golfers had mentioned the old, abandoned South Pines clubhouse. *Maybe putting Cici's body there could be the answer. But how to kill her and get her there was the question.*

Greg parked in front of "Hair Today, Gone Tomorrow," a small salon in a strip mall.

He didn't have to wait long at all. Lisa took him right away. She pumped up his hydraulic, adjustable barber chair and began clipping the back of his hair. "Don't take off too much," he said.

"Don't worry. I'll take care of you. You'll like it. Just wait," said Lisa.

"What time do you get off?" he asked.

"I can't see you tonight, but can after that. And I'm free Friday night," she said.

"Want to go to the casino?" Greg asked.

"Sounds like fun. And your place afterwards?" Lisa asked.

"I like your place, and besides, I miss Toby," said Greg.

Lisa laughed and said, "Okay, but my place is a mess. You'll have to put up with it."

♔

Amie helped Cici gather her things together in her hospital room. "Boy, am I glad you're leaving this place," said Amie, shaking her head.

"Yeah, but the doctor said I have to rest all week. No morning walks for awhile," said Cici.

"Just get better. Walks can come later. Cici, something has been nagging at me."

"What?" Cici asked.

"After our walk yesterday, I went shopping at the Food Lion. In the parking lot there, I thought I saw Greg wearing a bike helmet and getting into his Escalade. I can't be one hundred percent sure, but it did seem odd."

"He was in Wilmington."

"Yes," said Amie. "Well, that's what I thought."

"Wait a minute. Are you suggesting Greg could have done this to me?" asked Cici.

"Cici, who knows, but look how he's treated you in the last several months. I want to tell Detective Crabbe I thought I saw him."

"Amie, I can't believe Greg would do such a thing. He doesn't even own a bike."

"Well, I said I wasn't completely sure. When I called him to tell him you had been taken to Atlantic General, he did say he was in Wilmington, and it would take him two hours to get to the hospital."

"It couldn't have been him," said Cici.

Amie shrugged her shoulders. "Did you call Pat?" asked Amie.

"Yes, and I'm waiting for him to call me back," said Cici. "I want to tell Greg how he's hurting our marriage. I want to put my feelings down in a letter to him. I want to know how he really feels."

"Seriously, Cici? Why don't you just ask him?"

Amie dropped Cici off in her driveway. The house was quiet. Cici checked all the doors when she got inside and locked the sliders. Cici didn't care about the mess in the bedroom. Powder from fingerprinting was everywhere. One good thing, it didn't look ransacked. Greg must have straightened up. She had more important issues to solve.

After resting a bit, Cici began her letter to Greg. She selected a pale, blue note.

> Greg:
>
> I feel that I'm not good enough for you any longer. I can't remember the last time we made love. What can I do to make you happy? You leave unexpectedly and don't tell me where you're going. You smoke and drink more than ever now. Please tell me what's wrong. I want our marriage to work; we can't go on like this. If you want a divorce, tell me. I know I've gained weight. Is that it? Are you upset that we don't have children? We hardly talk anymore. You seem so unhappy. I feel like it's my fault. Am I wrong? If things don't improve, we need to end the marriage. We need to talk.

She put the note in an envelope, wrote his name on the outside, and placed it on his nightstand. But she had second thoughts. Amie's right. She was going to confront him when he got home. She took the letter off his nightstand and put it into her drawer on her side of the bed. She waited for him. It wasn't long before Cici nodded off.

The noise from the garage door shutting awakened her. *He's home.* She glanced at the clock—11:45 p.m. Greg walked into the bedroom and threw his jacket onto the chair.

"You're up. I thought you'd be asleep by now," said Greg.

"We need to talk," said Cici.

"What about?" asked Greg.

"About us."

"What about us?"

"Your actions this past year have been horrible. You act like you hate me. You stay out late almost every night. We don't make love anymore. We . . . "

"Wait a minute, I don't want to do this now. I'm tired and want to go to bed. I have a big day tomorrow," said Greg.

"Then why did you come home so late? Where were you? You didn't even want to be here after what happened to me."

"I told you to call me back if you couldn't get a ride home. Look, Cici, sometimes a man has to chill after a hard day at work. I didn't want to bother you. The doctor said you needed to rest. Do you realize how tough my job is? I bring home a huge salary, if you've noticed. Look at this house. It's beautiful. You don't even have to work. Why are you complaining?"

"Why do you insult me all the time?" asked Cici.

"I don't insult you all the time."

"You've been drinking. I smell it on you every time you come home late at night," said Cici.

"You know I like my scotch," said Greg.

"I'm not happy. You call this a marriage?" asked Cici.

"What do you want, Cici? A divorce?"

Cici opened her nightstand drawer. "Here, read this."

Greg grabbed her letter and ripped the envelope open. He finished reading it and said, "I don't want a divorce."

"Then tell me what's wrong with you. Why do you do the things you do?"

"Damn it, Cici, I told you I was tired and didn't want to talk about this right now. You're driving me nuts." He stormed out of the room, went into the guest bedroom, and slammed the door.

Cici flinched. Her headache worsened. She was too upset. She couldn't fall asleep right away. Her marriage was a joke.

*

Early the next morning, Cici arose with an achy head. The house was noisy. Greg's car was gone, and he'd left the TV blaring. She noticed that the note was still on top of her night-stand. *Well, talking to him last night didn't accomplish anything.*

She went into the bathroom and filled a cup with water. She emptied some ibuprofen out of the bottle and swallowed two pills. Cici got her robe out of the walk-in closet. She glanced at her wardrobe. She still kept her clothes from when she was a lot slimmer. She really needed to shop for more outfits in her current size. She looked over at Greg's wardrobe. Nice-looking suits and ties. On a whim, she searched through the pockets of his sport jackets. *What's this?* She pulled out a business card from a beauty salon and saw the name Lisa on it. *Maybe I should make a visit to this salon. Maybe get a wash and blow-dry and see this Lisa girl.* She put the card back into his jacket's pocket and walked back into her bedroom. She noticed the light was blinking on the landline phone. Cici hit the *Play* button to retrieve messages and listened. The first message was from Greg. It had been recorded on Tuesday. He said he would be home on Wednesday and was sorry for throwing coffee at her. The second message was from Pat. It was brief. "Mrs. King, this is Patrick McCombe. Just returning your call. Call me back when you can." Cici erased his message.

The TV blaring in the great room was getting on her nerves. She heard a loud knock at the back door. Cici unlocked the door and let Amie inside. Amie wore aviator sunglasses, tan shorts, and a red halter top and light jacket. Her hair was pulled back tightly in a ponytail.

"Greg's car is gone, and I thought you could use some company," Amie said. "I brought some goodies. Glad to see the door was locked."

Cici said, "Be right back. Have to turn off the TV." Cici heard the end of the broadcast on WBOC, a local TV station in Salisbury: " ... and the Worcester County Bureau of Investigation responded to Teal Circle in Ocean Pines, where there was a home invasion and a reported assault and burglary. Anyone with information regarding this home invasion, please call the Ocean Pines Police Department at 410-524-1112."

It then hit Cici how serious this was. Would the robbers be stupid enough to return? Maybe she'd keep a sharp knife in her night table drawer. Cici reentered the kitchen. "Dr. Chu said I'm not supposed to watch TV for a week. He said my brain needs some down time. The brain has to work to keep track of what's happening on the TV screen. What a hindrance."

Amie said, "Don't worry, I'll get you caught up on *The Good Wife*." Cici laughed.

"Look what I've brought," said Amie.

She held a box of donuts and pastries from the bagel shop in her hands. Amie put the donuts down on the granite-top island and said, "Screw the diet for now." And she began brewing some decaf coffee. Cici shuffled in her fluffy slippers towards the kitchen table and dimmed the recess lighting because the sun brightened the kitchen enough. Cici gave Amie a big hug. They sat on blue-and-white checkered slipcovers on the Parsons chairs surrounding a glass-top kitchen table in front of the sliders.

"How's your headache?" Amie asked.

"Not gone yet."

"Look at these cheese Danishes from the bagel shop. They'll make you feel better. Let's dive into them," Amie said.

The coffee's aroma filled the huge kitchen. "By the way,"

Cici said, "last night Greg and I argued. I took your advice and confronted him. Didn't do any good. I showed him my letter too. He left the room and spent the night in the guest bedroom," Cici said.

"Sorry, Cici. Guess both of our ideas didn't help the situation." Cici told Amie in detail about their argument while she munched on a pastry.

Amie fetched the coffee mugs, and when she turned to get cream from the fridge, she noticed a note written by Greg for Cici stuck under a magnet on the stainless steel door. Amie began reading it to herself.

Cici:

I read your note again. I've been under a lot of stress lately from work. I don't want to talk about it, but I'll see you in two more days. I have a conference in Dover. I'm staying at the Dover Inn. Take care of yourself.

Amie gave his scrawled note to Cici. "This was on the refrigerator."

Cici put her glasses on to read it. She looked up at Amie and then reread the note again. She said to Amie, "So abrupt and businesslike. Seems so cold. But at least he wrote me a note. He must have felt somewhat guilty. I listened to my phone messages this morning. Greg did say he loved me in a message he left me while he was in Wilmington."

Amie said, "Come on, Cici. Do you really believe he's the same guy you married?"

"You're right. He's not."

Exasperated, Amie asked, "Call Pat. He may have tried to call you."

"He did. He left me a voicemail. We're playing phone tag."

"We can meet here while you're recuperating, and then you can make up your mind if you want to hire him or not," said Amie.

"I'm on it," said Cici. "Were you two college roommates?"

"No, but we did live in a coed dorm after transferring from Wor-Wic Community College."

Cici said, "I remember the good old days at Wor-Wic. We had fun working in the evenings at the Marlin Moon after classes all day. When classes were finally over, I met Greg. That was right after my mom moved to San Diego with Sam. You know, I never thought I'd get married," Cici said.

"Why was that?" asked Amie.

"Long story. I'll try to make it short. When I decided to go on the pill and saw a gynecologist, he diagnosed me with endometriosis. I had to undergo a laparoscopy to remove scar tissue and growths to alleviate the pain."

"Didn't you know something was wrong before that?" asked Amie.

"All the girls I knew in high school complained of painful menstrual cramps, bloating, and headaches, so I thought what I experienced was normal. Anyway, the doctor told me my fallopian tubes were badly scarred and probably would block a man's sperm from reaching my eggs. I worried over the fact that no man would want to marry me if I couldn't have kids."

"Here all this time, I thought Greg didn't want children," Amie said.

"No, he knew about the situation before we got married, but the subject of kids never came up."

"Well, maybe it wasn't important to him."

"I don't know. I had been pretty upset when the doctor told me the news, and I became depressed. I was prescribed an anti-depressant. It helped, and I felt much better after several weeks."

"Cici, I learn something new every day about you. And I don't ever remember you being depressed," Amie said.

"Hey, that's way in past. If Greg and I were to divorce, it's a good thing we don't have kids."

Cici looked up at the kitchen clock. "Merv is supposed to come by in about 10 minutes. He asked if I'd mind his coming over," said Cici. "I don't care if he sees me in this robe. I'm comfortable around him and can be myself."

"You want me to leave, Cici?" asked Amie.

"Actually, I'd like you to stay if you have the time," said Cici.

"I'll have to change into some work clothes soon, because I'm showing a house at noon, but I can stay just a little bit longer," said Amie.

Merv's arrival was prompt. He walked into the kitchen carrying a wrapped package and sat down at the kitchen table, joining the girls for coffee and pastries. He wore a sport shirt, a golf cap, a pair of jeans, and running shoes. He was the same age as Greg, a bit thinner, and had a slightly receding hairline.

"Whoa, you have some mean-looking black eyes," said Merv.

"Yep, I look like a raccoon," said Cici. "Thanks for stopping by, Merv. Are you working today?"

"No, don't have a job until Saturday," Merv said. "Cici, I was so shocked to hear what happened to you. You look like you're really hurting."

"I am," she said. "Inside and out."

"I told Greg I hope they catch whoever did this to you. Here, I've brought you a little something," he said.

Cici unwrapped the box and smiled when she saw Merv gave her dark chocolates from Candy Kitchen. "Oh, I love these, Merv. Thank you."

"It's the least I could do. My wife feels for you too. She says hi."

"Did you see her recently?" asked Cici.

"No, I can't because of the restraining order. You know, she doesn't want me around because of the drinking. She gets scared with me behind the wheel of our car, given my past history. We chat on the phone, though. She said if I give up alcohol, she'll take me back. It's so hard for me to turn down a cold brew though," Merv said.

"You should enlist in getting some real help, Merv," said Cici.

"Greg tells me the same thing. Did you lose much in the robbery?" Merv asked.

"I haven't taken a complete inventory yet, but I looked inside my jewelry box. A lot is missing. I'm giving the detective a list tomorrow."

"I can't imagine anyone coming in your house and robbing you. It seems so strange that your house was chosen. I know it's the largest home on the block, but there are many beautiful mansions in Ocean Pines. Look at Terns Landing. Some of those homes aren't even occupied until the summer. Can't understand it. You and Greg are here permanently. You'd think the robber would have cased the area and hit one that was vacant. Why yours, I wonder? Maybe he thought no one was home, and when he found out you were here, he panicked. Did you hear someone in your bedroom?"

"No, can't remember what occurred," Cici said.

"Oh, that's too bad. Maybe you got a glimpse of him, and he tried to kill you, afraid you'd recognize him."

"That's what Greg thinks happened," Cici said. They all talked some more about Merv's theory.

He finished his coffee and cheese bun and said he'd best be going. "Hope you get your memory back and feel better, Cici."

After Merv walked down the deck's steps, Cici said, "He's always been so thoughtful. I wish Greg had some of Merv's attributes."

"Those two sure do stick together, though," said Amie.

"I know. It's either crabbing, fishing, golfing, gambling, or drinking."

"Lots of drinking. He needs an intervention," said Amie. "Look what Merv's losing in life."

⊰⊱

Crabbe parked his vehicle on Cici's bumpy driveway. He caught a glimpse of Merv Grady as he left Cici's house. Inside Cici's kitchen, the girls heard a car door slam. Amie looked out the front window and saw Crabbe lock his car and head towards the side of the house, boots crunching on the gravel. He knocked on the back door.

Amie let Crabbe in. Cici remained seated and said, "You caught me at a bad time. Look at me in my dirty robe. I'm going to stay in my seat." She put her hands on her pinkish cheeks. "I think I'm blushing with embarrassment."

Crabbe waved his hand. "No need to feel embarrassed. Do you want me to leave? Sorry I popped in on you. I can come back another time."

"No, I'm not going to look much better than I do now even if you come back in a couple of days," said Cici.

He offered his hand for her to shake. "How are you feeling?" he asked.

"Well, I'm not ready to vacuum the floors yet," Cici said. Crabbe turned down her offer of a cup of coffee and donut, but sat down and looked at the food on the kitchen table.

"Chocolates for breakfast?" he said. Cici laughed. "Mrs. King, I'm trying to solve this case as soon as possible. When you feel up to it, please let me know if any personal items were stolen from you."

"I plan to do that," Cici replied.

"Were any of your neighbors home at the time this happened to you?" asked Crabbe.

"Don't know. My neighbors aren't here permanently, except for Amie and an elderly retired couple, Mr. and Mrs. Adams. They live three doors down from Amie. You could question them. But that's it," said Cici. "My other neighbors return in the summer."

"As a matter of fact, I did speak to Mr. Adams. On the day of your attack, he came to your house in the morning and knocked on your door. No one answered. He said his car wouldn't start and he had to take his wife to the hospital for her chemo treatment. He was hoping you were home to give him a ride. I asked him if he saw anything unusual or an unfamiliar person walking in the neighborhood. He said all was quiet except for a cyclist riding by."

"I'll have to call her and see how she's doing," Cici said.

Amie said to Crabbe, "Hey, I forgot to tell you. I thought I saw Greg that same morning wearing a cyclist outfit."

"That's interesting. Where was this and what time?" Crabbe scribbled on his pad as Amie spoke. "Mrs. King, do you have a recent picture of your husband? I want to show it to employees in gas stations and convenience stores along the route up to Wilmington," he said.

"Is he a suspect?" Cici asked.

"No, Mrs. King, but I want to cover all the bases. I have to question everyone. I did speak with the Radisson Hotel manager. He did say he thought your husband was there that morning. There was nothing unusual about his cell phone records. But I have to find out if he had enough time to come down here and attack you and then return to Wilmington."

"Seriously?" said Cici.

"Have to check it out, Mrs. King. Let's just say your husband is a person of interest right now. Be cautious."

"You're scaring me," Cici said.

"Just be on guard." Cici asked Amie to fetch a photo album from the bookcase in the great room. When she came back with the album, Cici selected a recent photo of Greg and Merv on his boat and gave it to Detective Crabbe. Holding the picture and lowering his eyes, he said, "I recognize the guy next to your husband. In fact, he just left your house. Merv Grady."

"That's my husband's friend," said Cici.

"I know him as *10'55*," said Crabbe.

"What?" said Cici.

"That's just the criminal term given to someone arrested for drunkenness and disorderly conduct."

"Oh my. I know he's an alcoholic, but he's a really nice guy," said Cici.

"I have a few more questions to ask you. Does your family live here?" asked Crabbe.

"No, my mom and my stepfather moved to San Diego. My dad died when I was three."

Crabbe asked, "Does your mother know Mr. King well? If so, may I have her phone number?"

"Why?" asked Cici.

"I'd like to hear her opinion of your husband."

"Oh," said Cici.

"How's your marriage, Mrs. King?"

Cici stared at him for a minute and then looked at Amie. Amie nodded her head.

"Not real good at the moment."

"How so?" the detective asked.

Cici told him about Greg's behavior, and then all the words just spilled out. Her tears flowed. Amie put her arm around her, and Detective Crabbe said, "I'm sorry my questioning has upset you."

She wiped her eyes and quickly composed herself,

embarrassed for crying. "You don't really think he had any-thing to do with this? And why would he rob our house?"

He gently said, "I don't know the answers to your questions, Mrs. King, but I intend to find out. When you were in the shower, did you hear rummaging in your bedroom? Did you call out?"

"Don't remember."

"Were you startled?"

"Don't remember."

"What does your husband do for a living?" he asked.

"He's an account manager for a food service distributor. He has major accounts all over the Delmarva area."

"Is he currently traveling?"

"Yes, he'll be back tomorrow," Cici said. "Last night, he wrote me a note after I wrote him one." She got the notes for Crabbe and handed them to him.

"Can you think of anyone who might want to harm you?" Crabbe asked.

"No."

Amie hit Cici's arm. "What?" asked Cici, staring at Amie.

"Tell him about Greg's hitting you," said Amie. Cici then told him about the physical abuse.

"Have you seen anyone suspicious-looking in the neighborhood?"

"No."

"I haven't either," said Amie.

Crabbe read the notes. "May I keep the originals?" Cici thought for a moment and nodded yes.

"I will return them to you."

"I'll make copies now on my printer in the den," said Cici. "That way you can keep the real ones."

When she came back from the den, Amie whispered

something to Cici. Cici turned to Crabbe and told him that she was going to hire a P.I. and why. Crabbe knew Patrick McCombe. "He's a good private detective. Well, I think that's enough for now. I have to question your husband when he returns. Thanks for your time."

"Oh yes, I forgot. Just a minute." She gave Crabbe her mother's phone number.

As soon as Crabbe's car pulled out of Cici's driveway, Cici looked at Amie and said, "He's a handsome guy . . . Oh no. Oh shit."

"What's wrong, Cici?" asked Amie. "Did you forget to tell him something?"

"Forget about my being embarrassed in my soiled robe in front of Detective Crabbe. He saw me butt naked in the tub, didn't he?"

Amie nodded, wrinkling her forehead. "Yep."

"I want to crawl in a hole," Cici said, shaking her head.

"I'm sure he's seen his share of naked bodies, Cici," said Amie.

Outside in his patrol car, Crabbe called Cici's mother, Mrs. Johnson, and identified himself.

"Is my daughter okay? Do you know who did this?" she asked.

"Not yet, but I'm working on it. That's the purpose of my calling you. What's your opinion of Mrs. King's husband?"

"He seems nice. He's somewhat opinionated, but he's talented. He's worked hard improving their home. I know it cost him a lot, but he has a good job. He's had his job a long time. Cici is lucky to have him. Why? Is he a suspect?"

"Person of interest. When's the last time you saw him?"

"We flew out there three years ago. Cici came out here two years ago without him. She said his job was demanding at the time."

"Do you recall any incidents or problems Mrs. King may have mentioned about her marriage?"

She paused too long. "Hello? Are you still there?" said Crabbe.

"Sorry. Not really. Greg wouldn't harm a hair on her head. He's not the man you're looking for. I just know it. How is Cici doing?" Cici's mother asked.

"She is healing. Has some stitches that will need to come out. Mrs. King will need to take it easy for awhile. Her memory of that day is sketchy."

"You shouldn't be wasting your time talking to me. You need to get out there and search for the culprit."

"Believe me, I am. Thank you for your time, Mrs. Johnson." *Culprit, my tail. You mean beast.*

CHAPTER 5

After dinner the next day, Greg let Crabbe inside his house. Greg wore white Bermuda shorts, a Green Turtle T-shirt, and flip-flops.

"Let's talk in the kitchen," Greg said. He searched for his lighter in his shirt pocket and pulled a cigarette out from its pack. Crabbe asked him if he could sit down.

"Yeah, take a seat," Greg said. Greg grabbed his lighter and lit his cigarette. Crabbe noticed his hand shake. He inhaled deeply and exhaled, blowing his smoke towards Crabbe.

"How's your wife?" asked Crabbe.

"She seems a little better. Here's the list of stolen items and my wife's list too." He said Cici's wallet was empty, but he wasn't sure how much money Cici had in it.

Crabbe said, "Glad Mrs. King is home from the hospital. You must be relieved." He watched Greg's facial expression. Greg remained straight-faced. Crabbe asked, "How's your marriage?"

Greg frowned, and he took a deep breath. When he didn't answer, Crabbe asked, "Have you been unfaithful?"

"What's that got to do with the robbery? Am I a suspect? Do I need a lawyer?" asked Greg.

Crabbe's eyes narrowed, and he said, "No, you don't need a lawyer, but you didn't answer my questions."

"I've never had an affair."

"Is your marriage a happy one?"

"My marriage is fine."

"Tell me about your wife," Crabbe asked Greg.

Greg took a moment before he answered. "She's great. A good cook. Loves to read and play mahjong with her friends."

"Do you love your wife?" Greg's fingers tapped on the table.

"Of course! You really need to get this personal?" asked Greg. "Next, are you going to ask me about my sex life?" Greg looked at his watch.

"Well . . . ," said Crabbe. "How is it?"

"This is ridiculous. My sex life is fine." *I hate this guy.*

"So, no problems?" Crabbe scribbled on his pad. "Does Mrs. King have any enemies that you're aware of?" asked Crabbe.

"Everyone likes her." Greg told him who her friends were and that she kept in touch with the people she used to work with at the Marlin Moon Restaurant. The back of his neck felt moist.

What really threw Greg was Crabbe's next question. "Do you own a bike?" asked Crabbe. More finger tapping.

"Why is that important?" His left knee started bouncing.

Ignoring Greg's question, Crabbe asked, "What about a helmet?"

The armpits of Greg's shirt were becoming wet with sweat. "No, I don't own a bike or helmet."

"Do you mind if we go outside and I take a look inside your pontoon?" asked Crabbe.

"Are you serious? Why? You think I'm hiding something in there?"

"May I look?"

"You won't find anything of interest in there," said Greg.

"Is that a no?" asked Crabbe.

Greg was silent a moment. "I have a warrant to search your boat," Crabbe said. He grabbed the warrant from his inside coat pocket and showed it to Greg.

Greg said, "Fine, but it's a waste of time for you and me."

They walked out to the pier. Greg lowered the boat on the lift and unsnapped the canvas over the seats and compartments. The 25-foot pontoon could seat 18 people, so Crabbe had a lot of areas under the seating to search. Crabbe looked inside the compartment in front of the helm and lifted the cushions to search underneath each seat.

"See, I told you it was a waste of time," said Greg. "You thought I hid the stolen items in there, didn't you?" Greg asked.

They went back inside, into the kitchen, and Crabbe sat down at the table. Greg's hand shook as he stared at Crabbe and lit another cigarette. He sat down and put his hand in his lap. Crabbe's next battery of questions were, "Is Mrs. King close to her mother?" Is she thoughtful?" "Does Mrs. King nag?" and, "Is she bossy?"

Greg wanted to tell him she was a pudgy wimp. Greg's knees were both bouncing. "Okay, I've had enough of this. You said I didn't need a lawyer, and I think I do. Why don't you just ask me if I attacked my wife?" He noticed Crabbe had kept his eyes on him a little too long.

"Did you?" asked Crabbe.

Greg inhaled from his cigarette. "No. I did not," Greg said, as his words mixed with the rest of the smoke that came out of his mouth.

Crabbe finally put his pen away. "You're not helping my investigation by not answering my questions, Mr. King."

"I'm hiring a lawyer."

"We're not finished here, you know." Crabbe got up and left.

Greg watched him get into his patrol car. Crabbe was a thorn in his flesh. He was like a plague and he rankled him. Greg hadn't counted on a determined detective that just wouldn't go away.

He fixed himself a scotch and carried it into the den. He sat down at his desk, folded his fists against his cheekbones, stared out the window, and tried to think what he would do next. But Crabbe domineered his thoughts.

Under his breath, Greg said, "Thinks he's a hotshot. Badgering me. Asking personal questions. Getting angry at me. What a prick."

⚎

"Pat's coming this afternoon around three. Thanks for recommending him. "I have an appointment at the hair salon this morning. Have to drive to Ocean City to get my hair trimmed," said Cici.

"You can drive so soon after your concussion?" Amie asked.

"Oh, probably not. You're right."

"I can drop you off and wait if you just need a trim."

"Have to do a little detective work," said Cici.

"Huh?" said Amie.

"Tell you in the car," Cici said.

Cici, wearing dark sunglasses, walked into the salon and sat down, waiting her turn. The place was very nice, surprisingly posh. The receptionist asked her if she wanted something to drink and told her homemade sugar cookies were on the side table.

Lisa walked over to her minutes later. "Mrs. King?" Cici nodded. "Follow me and sit in that black leather chair over there by the vase with pink flowers." Lisa was dressed in a long-sleeve black blouse; a tight, short, black cotton skirt; and matching tights. She wore thick makeup, and her hair was held by a clip at the back of her head, above her ears. Strands of hair dangled along the sides of her cheeks.

Cici sat in the comfortable leather chair. Lisa said, "This is so weird. I'm supposed to go out on a date this week with a guy whose last name is the same as yours," said Lisa. "Are you related to a Greg King?" Lisa asked.

"That's my husband's name," said Cici.

Lisa dropped her brush. She bent down to pick it up. "Are you joking? Tall guy with dark hair? A food sales guy?" asked Lisa. Cici nodded. "No way. Is that why you're here? Did he tell you about me?" The hairdresser next to Lisa stared at them.

"No, I had no idea my husband asked you out," said Cici.

"Yeah, right," she said.

"I came in here to get a haircut. How old are you anyway?" asked Cici.

"Twenty-nine. Why?"

"Greg's in his 40s. You can do better than that, can't you?"

"I didn't know he was married. I don't go out with married men. I guess you don't want your hair done, do you?" she said.

Cici said, "No, thank you," and got up and walked out of the salon. Amie heard all about it as she drove Cici back home. "I'm looking forward to talking to Patrick McCombe. I want to find out more about Greg's philandering," said Cici.

That afternoon, Patrick McCombe was right on time. Cici and he met in the great room of her house. He was wearing a beige shirt with his tapered white slacks. Cici smiled when she shook his hand.

"Please get comfortable. Would you like something to drink?" asked Cici. "Amie should be coming by any minute."

"No, thank you, Mrs. King. I'm sorry to hear you were assaulted and robbed."

"Please call me Cici."

"Sounds like you had a tough time," he said. "And call me Pat. I heard about it on the news, and Amie filled me in."

"Right. The police don't have a suspect yet, but Detective Crabbe said my husband is a person of interest."

"Really? Joe Crabbe is a friend of mine," he said.

"Oh, I didn't realize that," she said.

Cici explained why she wanted to hire him. "Can you help me?"

"Yes, if you want to accept my terms," said Pat. "What, in your opinion, makes you think he's cheating?"

"Well, for one thing, I found out something this morning. He made a date with this young hairdresser." She explained what had happened in the salon. "Didn't realize it would be that easy to discover he's not a faithful husband. But to answer your question further, we haven't had sex in eons. He's so anal about his body. He works out at the gym to keep in great shape. Maybe he's keeping fit for the ladies or one particular salon lady."

Cici told Pat more about Greg's behavior. Amie walked in on their conversation. She plopped down on the sofa after saying hi.

He turned from Amie to Cici. "Has he ever been physically abusive?"

"Yes, a few times," said Cici.

Amie interjected, "He belittles her in front of me. He flirts with women in front of her. Big time."

"Tell me about your husband's background," Pat said.

Cici told Pat about his job and talents. "He was an only child. His parents are dead now. I don't think he ever visited them on their farm since we got married. He told me he was ashamed of his family and couldn't stand his mother. Greg thought they were uncouth rednecks. Greg didn't like the life on the farm, and he didn't want to raise chickens all his life, which disappointed his father, who was almost 70. He communicated very little with them. Greg moved out after he graduated from high school and was offered a football scholarship at Salisbury University. Greg got a student loan and worked on the weekends at a grocery store to cover extra expenses. Other than the salesmen at his company, he has one close friend by the name of Merv Grady. When his parents passed away, he inherited their farm and sold it."

"Hope he got a good price for it."

"A bundle," Cici said. Cici told Pat what activities he and Merv Grady did together and where they went bar-hopping.

Pat jotted down notes on a pad. He looked up at Cici and said, "I'm sorry to hear your marriage isn't going so well and he's mistreating you. You said he's hurt you in the past. Aren't you worried that he may have attacked you?"

"You sound like Detective Crabbe," said Cici.

"Well, remember, I used to be a cop. I have the same kind of instincts he has," Pat said.

"Well, yes, I thought about it, but I just can't accept it."

"Just the same, Cici, be careful," said Pat.

"I will, believe me," said Cici.

"Let me tell you something about my agency so you know about the services we provide. First you'll have to sign an agreement if you wish to retain my services. I require a retainer of $750, and that would be used at the rate of $65 an hour. You'll be responsible for any expenses incurred during the course of the investigation, such as out-of-pocket expenses, mileage, travel and photographic costs, and so on. Any portion of the retainer not used would be refunded to you. You must agree to provide me with all possible facts available relating to the investigation. I'll provide you with field reports and a free DVD copy of all findings upon final settlement of the account.

I'll conduct the investigation in a discreet and unbiased manner, and all that information related to the investigation would be handled in the strictest of confidence between you and me. I can't make any guarantees as to the results or outcome of the investigation."

Cici nodded her head, sighed, and asked Pat, "May I have a moment with Amie?" Pat left the great room and walked out onto the deck. Cici looked toward the deck and back at Amie. She lowered her voice, "Greg might know that $750 is missing from our savings account. Where am I going to get $750 to pay a retainer without Greg finding out?"

"Cici, I can loan you the money, and you can pay me back later," Amie offered.

Staring at the floor, looking deep in thought, Cici shook her head and finally said, "No, I can't accept your money, but that's very kind of you. I guess I could sell a portion of my sterling silver place settings my aunt gave me. I never use the set, and I have 8 place settings. I wouldn't have to worry about Greg wondering where $750 went."

"Sounds good to me. I know a place on Route 50 where you can sell your silver, or ask if Elizabeth's Treasures in south Ocean Pines would be interested," said Amie.

Amie told Pat to come back into the room. "Do you still want me to investigate, now that you know he has an eye for the ladies?" asked Pat before he took a seat.

"Absolutely," said Cici and she signed and dated the agreement.

Pat said to Cici, "Okay, for starters, give me your husband's full name and the type of car he drives. And the name of the hotels he usually frequents in the Delmarva area." Before he left, Cici gave Pat all the information he needed to start his investigation.

"Thanks for driving me to the beauty salon today," Cici said.

"Good detective work, Cici," said Amie. Cici laughed.

"Greg's a slimeball," Amie said.

"I can't stand him," Cici said.

Amie said to Cici, "Pat's a great-looking guy. Did you see his arms? He's really buff. I kept staring at his opened shirt at the collar revealing his hairy chest." Cici laughed. Amie paused and stared ahead for a moment. "He's got a seductive smile. Even though he was unshaven, he looked sexy as hell, like that eccentric doctor who stars on *House*. It's been several months since I've seen Pat. Wonder if he's dating someone."

"Uh oh, look out, Pat," Cici said. "I believe you're smitten with him. You never noticed his good looks before this?"

Amie said, "Yes, but we were just friends then. We never dated. Either he was going steady with someone, or I was seeing Carl."

She wants to talk? Can't tell her I want a divorce. Sounds like she's thinking of a divorce from that stupid note. Can't tell her the truth. You see, Cici, I want to kill you. I can't stand you. I don't want to divide the property with you. What the hell do I say to her?

Greg walked over to the wet bar in the great room and poured himself a stiff drink. All was quiet in the house except for the sound of the refrigerator humming in the kitchen. He picked up his drink and gulped it down. *Need to see Merv.*

Ten minutes later he was knocking on Merv's trailer door, just off Racetrack Road.

"Well, it's about time you visited me in my lovely castle. It's a piece of shit, right?" Merv said.

"That's what you get for getting too drunk and turning up on your wife's front door step, violating your wife's restraining order. You're lucky you're not in jail, and she told the police she didn't want to press charges. Fat chance if she takes you back."

"I really miss being with her and being in my real home. How about a cold brew?"

"Sounds good," said Greg. He looked around the trailer. Empty cans of beer filled the kitchen sink and the top of the counter. The place was untidy. A gray layer of dust covered every surface. Ashtrays were full of cigarette butts. "You need AA and a maid, Merv," Greg said.

"If I knew you were stopping by, I would have called Merry Maids to clean up this dump," Merv said. "How come you're honoring me with this visit?"

"Since we were robbed and Cici was att—" Greg said.

"Is she doing better?" Merv interrupted.

"I think so. Anyway, because of what happened, we're both a little nervous these days. I thought we could use some protection. Do you need your gun? If not, could I borrow it?" Greg asked.

"Why, planning the perfect murder? What about your rifle?" asked Merv.

"It's locked in a chest in the garage, but I wanted something I could keep in my nightstand. We would feel much safer that way."

"Well, I don't plan to use it, that's for sure. I doubt if anyone would want to rob me of my empty beer cans. That's why I'm not worried about keeping my front door key under the flowerpot outside. Sure, you can borrow the gun."

"Thanks, bro." He took a swig from his can of beer. "I'll return it after they catch this guy."

Reaching for his gun at the top of the kitchen cabinet, and with his back to Greg, Merv said, "I can't help but ask you this, but the other day when you asked me if I had any ideas about how to commit the perfect murder... seriously, did you have anything to do with Cici's concussion?"

"Man, are you nuts? No, of course not! You should talk. Look at the way you treated your wife."

Turning and making eye contact, Merv said, "Well, I never

gave her a concussion. I was drunk and completely out of it. I had to see her. I missed her."

"You practically punched the front door in," said Greg.

"I just wanted to talk to her. I wanted her to take me back. I left when I saw it was no use," said Merv.

"I realize that," said Greg. "You really scared her."

Merv said, "Yeah, yeah, but she knows how much I love her. But back to your wife . . . I know Cici gets on your nerves a lot. Personally, I think she's terrific. But your interest in trying to figure out how to commit a perfect murder, well, it just made me wonder why you even brought up the subject."

Greg snorted and said, "You watch too much *CSI*. Yes, Cici drives me crazy at times, but I wouldn't kill her, Merv," said Greg. "I've been questioned thoroughly by the detective on the case. You know they suspect the spouse first. But I have an alibi. They have no clue who did this."

Greg put the gun in the trunk of his Escalade and headed to Dover to make his 2:00 p.m. appointment. He was unusually jumpy, especially after talking to Detective Crabbe and now Merv. He must have checked and double-checked his rearview mirror more than a dozen times. Despite the cool air outside, he was perspiring and wiping his forehead with his sleeve.

He had lost his cool with Crabbe. The guy got under his skin, and he had let him know it. He didn't want to slip up. Had he? *Can't offend the great, lead detective.*

Another mile and he would officially be in the city limits of Dover. His shoulders jerked as his cell phone buzzed. Merv was on the other end. "Hey, Greg, I'm really sorry, bro. I didn't mean it when I asked if you really gave Cici a concussion. I know you couldn't have done that to her."

"No problem, Merv. Hey, listen, how about if we play 18 holes at Rum Point, a week from this Saturday? My treat."

"Wow. That's a gift. I have a driveway to pave that Friday.

I'll get it done in one day so I don't have to finish it up on Saturday. So, I'm free. Thanks, my rich, good friend."

Greg took a deep breath and smiled. Merv could have been at the top of his game, if he hadn't been such a screw-up. He could have had his own construction company. Now he was just the neighborhood handyman, living in a rundown trailer. *He just can't control his drinking. Don't want to stop him again from assaulting another guy with a beer bottle. Never forget the day he crashed his vehicle through an iron fence, hitting a house on Coastal Highway.*

Greg checked into the Dover Inn and then called on two of his customers. He took orders for their needed supplies and produce selections. He stopped at another hotel in the area to discuss the pricing of a new line of meats with the chef-in-charge. Luckily, he landed a new account that made his day. Driving past the Dover Air Force base a little before sunset, Greg accelerated back to his hotel, hoping to avoid any speed traps along the way. Turning into the inn's parking lot, he licked his lips to moisten his dry mouth. A scotch would soothe his soul in the downstairs bar. And that's when he met Della.

She sat at the bar across from him. Greg couldn't keep his eyes off of her. The bartender set a scotch down on the counter in front of Greg, telling him that the pretty lady on the other side of the bar was paying for it. Greg smiled, nodded towards her, and said, "Thanks for the drink." *My stars, she's gorgeous.* Her beauty dazzled him. She walked over and took a seat next to his barstool and introduced herself. He liked outgoing women. And he couldn't help but notice this one had a dynamite body too.

"Have I seen you here before?" she asked, squinting her eyes.

"Probably. I stay here often on business." He put out his hand. "Greg King. And who are you?"

"Della Summer," she said and shook his hand.

"Pretty name," said Greg.

"Thank you. What business are you in?" she asked.

"I'm in food sales. How about you?"

"I'm a representative for a top-of-the-line national eyewear company. I sell frames to optometrists, opticians, and oph-thalmologists in the entire state of Delaware. So we both have something in common."

"Do you like what you do?" asked Greg.

"Yes, I have a lot of freedom with this job. It's a solid company."

"Good for you," said Greg. "Are you staying here in the hotel?"

"Yes. You too?"

"Yep," Greg said.

"So I'm also guessing you don't have a wife who misses you? I don't see a ring on your finger."

Boy, she's burning with curiosity. He snickered, "No, I'm divorced."

"Well, that's another thing we have in common. Do you have any kids?"

"No, my ex-wife couldn't have children," Greg said.

"Oh, sorry."

"I really didn't want any kids," said Greg.

"I have an 18-year-old son who works for the Red Cross. He's stationed in Germany, temporarily. I hope he won't be transferred to any war zone or some hot spot."

"That would be horrible. You're an awfully young mother for having an 18-year-old," said Greg.

"Yeah," she laughed. "I was pregnant at my high school prom in my senior year." She giggled. "Where do you live?"

"Near Ocean City. I have a house on the river."

"That's nice. I'm a city girl. I live in a high-rise in Wilmington."

Shoptalk came easily since they were both in sales. Greg talked about himself and was pleased that she seemed to show some genuine interest in him. He bragged about his numerous assets.

"Do you play golf by any chance?" asked Greg.

"Yes, I do. Why?"

"I golf a lot. Maybe we could play sometime," Greg said. "I'm a member at Rum Point. It's right on the water and always has a breeze. Well-maintained fairways but tons of traps. It's very challenging. And the homes along the river are beautiful. The greens are fast, and it's environmentally friendly. I'd say it's tough but fair. Nice clubhouse too."

Della said, "We should play there sometime. My uncle is a golf pro. He gave me lessons when I was in my early 20s," Della said.

"Well, we definitely have to play there now," said Greg.

"I'm in an especially good mood today," she said. "I sold a total of 19 pairs of eyeglasses, and the doctor wants me to come back in three weeks."

"Nineteen! What an eyeopener." She laughed as she punched his shoulder. "Your sales pitch had to be spot on, and I bet your bedroom eyes were a perfect model for the glasses. I hope the doc was an old fart."

Della laughed and said, "I'm not the slightest bit interested. He's married. No chance."

Greg couldn't help glancing at her breasts in her tight red bodice. He felt like ripping off her blouse.

"How many weeks do you get for your vacation?" Della asked.

"I usually take three weeks," Greg said.

"It would be fun to go to the Florida Keys," Della said.

"That would be fun." Greg said.

"I've always wanted to go to the Florida Keys. Have you been there before?" she asked Greg.

"No, but I'd like to go there with you." They chatted some more and ordered refills. She put her hand on his thigh. *I like this woman's forwardness.* He could feel himself getting an erection. "Let's go upstairs. Your room or mine?" he asked.

As he hoped, the both of them ended their evening in her hotel room. Once in her room, she slowly stripped off her clothes. She said, "Now take off your shir—" He silenced her by brushing his lips against hers, then pressing them hard against her. He kissed her breasts. She looked at him and unbuttoned his shirt. He unzipped his slacks. She ran her tongue over his lips and neck. She gently touched him. He groaned. They fell onto the bed. Her hips moved against him and he wrapped his arms around her, as she rubbed against him again. Greg entered her as she arched her back. They finished quickly in pure ecstasy. *Good-bye, hairdresser-mojito girl.*

Much later, the heavy drinks he consumed plunged him into a sound sleep.

The next morning Della and he set a date for a rendezvous at the Dover Inn again.

⚜

Detective Crabbe did not have much success canvassing the neighborhood. No one had seen anyone in the vicinity of Cici's house the day of the robbery, except for a cyclist. Crabbe had stopped at several gas stations and convenience stores on Route 113 on the way up and back from Wilmington. He showed the cashiers Greg's photo, but none remembered him being there.

Crabbe asked the hotel registrar if Greg was there that morning. "Yes, I think he was," he said. The hotel's security systems didn't indicate he left real early in the morning. However, one camera showed someone leaving by a side door, wearing a helmet. The cameras in the convenience stores miles from Wilmington didn't show anyone resembling him in their stores. The cell phone tower information revealed he made a call to Cici that Tuesday around 12:45 p.m. in the Wilmington area. Crabbe timed the drive to Ocean Pines from Wilmington and believed Greg had ample time to kill his wife, if he left early enough in the morning. But Crabbe had nothing to connect him to the crime.

No items showed up at any of the pawn shops. And another door closed in the investigation. A few released former suspects, who had committed petty robberies in the Ocean Pines area, did not pan out. The petty thieves proved to Crabbe that they had solid alibis the day of the robbery.

Crabbe had a hunch about Greg, and his hunches were usually right. He did have Amie and Greg's neighbor saying they saw a cyclist wearing a helmet that morning. And the security camera at the Dover Inn showed someone leaving the hotel with a helmet on very early in the morning. It was a long shot. In court, under oath, they couldn't be one hundred percent sure it was Greg. But Crabbe felt it was indeed Greg riding that bike that particular morning. He just couldn't prove he was the mysterious cyclist. The best he could do was to continue to keep an eye on him.

He didn't know why, but Crabbe had this deep urge to protect Cici. His fixation on Greg, not surprisingly, came from a genuine feeling that Greg was a looming threat to her. He planned to give Pat a call. He knew if he was cheating on Cici, it didn't mean he was a murderer. Crabbe needed something more. He needed something crucial to the investigation. He hated not having a solid lead. And of course, Greg's background check had come back clean.

C HAPTER 6

Pat had followed Greg to Dover, Delaware. He pulled into the parking lot at the Dover Inn. From a short distance, he had watched him unload his bag and clothes on hangers from the trunk of his car. He waited until Greg entered the hotel lobby before getting out of his car. He walked into the lobby while Greg was checking in. Pat ran his video camera. He watched Greg take the elevator up to the second floor. Pat climbed up the stairs and got off at the same floor.

Monday, October 28, Pat, Cici, and Amie met in the realtor's conference room to hear Pat's findings. Cici was chewing on her fingernail. Amie sat across from her and reached over to pat her shoulder. Pat sat on the other side of Cici and got right to the point.

"I never look forward to meeting with my clients when my findings are like this. Cici, your husband was with another woman in his hotel room until the next morning."

Cici looked at Amie and said, "Don't feel sorry for me, Amie. I'm not going to have a meltdown. I had my suspicions."

Looking at Pat, she said, "I had a feeling you had something like this to tell me. Especially after my visit to the hairdresser's the other day."

Amie looked at her and said, "Cici, you had him pegged."

"I'd like you to read this, Cici." Pat handed her the surveillance report. Cici polished her lens with a Kleenex, put on her glasses and began reading. She looked up at Amie. "Have you seen this?"

"No, I haven't, but Pat told me just what he told you."

"I prepared myself for this." She let her eyes run down the report from left to right.

DISCOVERY INVESTIGATIONS, INC.

4531 St. Martin's Neck Road
Bishopville, MD 21813
Phone: 410-352-1133
Fax: 410-352-6674

SURVEILLANCE REPORT

Date: Wednesday, October 23, 2013

Case: Cici King	**Time:** 8:30 a.m.–11:50 p.m.
LPI: Patrick McCombe	**Weather:** Clear and Cool
Subject: Greg King	**Visibility:** Excellent

WEDNESDAY OCTOBER 23, 2013

8:30 a.m. Licensed Private Investigator, Patrick McCombe, departed from the DII office and proceeded to Teal Circle. This LPI observed the Subject leaving his garage and heading towards Ocean Parkway.

3:40 p.m. LPI McCombe continued following the Subject in his car. The Subject's black Escalade bearing MD tag BMN743 arrived in the vicinity of 6400 Dupont Highway, Dover, Delaware 19901—the Dover Inn after stopping for lunch and calling on accounts. The Escalade is registered to a Mr. Gregory King. A position of surveillance was established by this LPI. The Subject got out of his car. He is described as a W/M in his early 40s, approximately 175 pounds, 6' 1", has black hair, and he is wearing a white Oxford dress shirt, gray long slacks, a black blazer, and black loafers. The Subject is observed unloading the trunk of his vehicle and carrying his clothes and bag into the hotel.

(Video obtained)

3:55 p.m. LPI McCombe left his car and walked into the lobby of the hotel. LPI observed the Subject checking in at the hotel's reception desk, walking to the elevator, and pressing the second floor button. LPI McCombe took the stairs to the second floor and observed the Subject entering his room. This LPI noted the Subject's room number, 2207. LPI walked back down the stairs to the lobby.

(Video obtained)

4:15 p.m. LPI McCombe sat down in the lobby and began reading the paper.

4:45 p.m. LPI McCombe observed the Subject walking out of the elevator and into the bar of the hotel. The Subject was observed ordering a drink and conversing with the bartender.

(Video obtained)

5:15 p.m. A W/F, approximately 35–38 years old, 5' 5" tall, with short reddish-brown hair, and weighing approximately 120 pounds enters the bar. LPI McCombe observes her carrying a brown case and placing it on the floor near the Subject. This LPI observes her kissing the Subject on the cheek and sitting down on the barstool next to him. The W/F now will be referred to as the suspected paramour. Both were observed talking to one another and drinking.

(Video obtained)

6:30 p.m. LPI McCombe observed the Subject and woman leave the bar together and get on the elevator to the second floor. This investigator waited for the elevator to return to the lobby level.

(Video obtained)

6:50 p.m. LPI McCombe entered the elevator and proceeded to the second floor and went to the door of Room 2207. This investigator put his ear to the door and heard a female and male voice inside the room.

7:00 p.m. LPI McCombe took the elevator to the lobby floor, exited the hotel entrance door, and got into his car. This investigator moved his car to an unoccupied space in the parking lot directly underneath the patio of the Subject's room. A position of surveillance was established by this LPI.

8:22 p.m. This LPI observed the Subject outside on the patio of his room, #2207. The Subject closed the sliding glass door to his room from the patio. He was observed smoking a cigarette and speaking on his cellular telephone. LPI McCombe observed the Subject continuing to smoke a cigarette and talking on his phone.

Cici slammed the report down on her lap. "That was probably when Greg called me to tell me he was getting an alarm system installed," said Cici. "He said we could talk when he got back home and apologized for being such a brute. Son of a bitch. He's a snake in the grass. Greg's a no-good, deceiving cheat and liar. This is ridiculous. I'm getting a divorce as soon as possible. Pat, I want the name of a good lawyer." She read on.

8:35 p.m. The Subject is observed opening the sliders to his room, entering his room via the sliding glass door, and closing the sliding glass door to the patio. LPI McCombe observed the interior of the Subject's room was bright, the blinds were open, and the television was illuminated inside the room. The same woman, a W/F in her mid-30's, with short reddish-brown hair, parted on the side, 5'4" to 5'6", wearing only red bikini panties, was walking in the room. The Subject was observed finishing his cigarette and shutting the blinds.

(Video obtained)

10:15 p.m.–10:30 p.m. The Subject is observed by this LPI entering the outside patio through his room and lighting a cigarette. The Subject's room is now further illuminated, and the blinds are now open. The suspected paramour walks out onto the patio and is observed with the Subject, holding a glass in her hand. She is wearing an oversized white robe. This investigator observed no other people in the Subject's room. The Subject is observed throwing his cigarette butt over the patio rail. The suspected paramour is observed handing a glass to the Subject. The Subject drank from the glass. Throughout this time frame, LPI McCombe observed the Subject and the suspected paramour embracing and passionately kissing each other several times. The Subject was also observed caressing the suspected paramour's breasts.

The Subject and the woman are observed entering the room from the patio and closing the sliders and the blinds.

(Video obtained)

Again, Cici slammed the papers down on the conference table, eyes blazing. "What a hypocrite. I'm such an idiot," Cici said. "Wonder how many times he's cheated on me, the ass." She read on.

11:30 p.m. LPI McCombe observed the lights went out in the Subject's room and terminated surveillance. This LPI entered the hotel lobby and checked in and got a room for the night.

DAY TWO SURVEILLANCE

Date: Thursday, October 24, 2013
Time: 7:00 a.m.–8:03 a.m.   **Visibility**: Good
Weather: Windy and cold

7:00 a.m. LPI McCombe took the elevator to the lobby of the Dover Inn Hotel to begin surveillance. This investigator was informed by the desk clerk that the Subject had not checked out of his room.

7:25 a.m. Subject was observed checking out at the reception desk and exiting the lobby. He was observed loading his bag inside the trunk of his car. LPI McCombe observed the Subject reentering the hotel and sitting in its lobby.

7:35 a.m. LPI McCombe observed the previously described suspected paramour getting out of the elevator and walking over to the Subject. They are observed kissing and leaving through the lobby door. The LPI observed the suspected paramour is carrying a brown case.

(Video obtained)

7:50 a.m. LPI McCombe observed the Subject and suspected paramour walking towards a red Kia, bearing license number

EYES4U. She was observed opening the trunk, putting her brown case inside, and closing the trunk. This investigator observed the suspected paramour putting her arms around the Subject, caressing his face, and kissing him. This investigator observed the suspected paramour entering her vehicle. The Subject was observed entering his vehicle. The Subject and the suspected paramour were observed departing the area in their separate vehicles.

NOTE: An MVA database was run on the suspected paramour's vehicle. The following results were produced:

2008 Kia DE tag EYES4U

Owner: Della Summer W/F 5'5" tall, 115 lbs., DOB 06/23/77

(Video obtained)

8:03 a.m. LPI McCombe discontinued the surveillance, departed the area, and returned to home base.

Cici's face reddened, her mouth clenched, and her hand trembled as she finished reading the report. She threw it onto the table. "That lowlife. I want to see the video. This is like reading the book before seeing the movie."

Greg squeezed in some late-afternoon delight Monday at a hotel in Rehobeth Beach, Delaware with Della. Being with Della again so soon was heavenly. Flaunting her shapely body in front of him in her pink see-through negligee did the trick. In double-quick time, he stripped off his shirt and pants, roughly grabbed her, pulled her straps off her shoulders, and passionately kissed her breasts. She tossed her negligee on the floor, and he took her as she sat on the edge of the bed. Their lovemaking session was hot and heavy, the best ever.

"I love you so much," she said.

"I want you all to myself," he said. Greg placed his hands on her irresistible breasts, gently squeezing them. She giggled.

"I'm so lucky that I saw you that night in the bar," Della said. "When can I see your house? And when are you going to take me out on your boat?" she asked.

Greg answered, "The boat has already been winterized, so we'll have to wait until the spring."

"How about the next time you're in Wilmington, you come see my condo. It's on the 21st floor with a great view of the city."

"Love to," said Greg. "Okay, let me see." He looked at his calendar on his iPhone, and he told her the date he'd be coming back to Wilmington.

"Aw, I have to wait that long?" said Della. She mussed his hair.

"I agree, to wait an hour is too long. Have to go to Norfolk in a couple of days. Be back Saturday. But the days will fly by," said Greg.

"I guess I'll have to suffer and wait," Della said. She pursed her lips in a pout.

"I have big plans for us, Della. But I have to confess something to you. When I first saw you at the bar that night, I couldn't believe my eyes. You were the most beautiful girl I've ever laid my eyes on, and I wanted you so badly. Here's the hard part. I lied to you. I told you I was divorced, because I wanted to spend time with you at the bar. I asked my wife for a divorce months ago, and she didn't want to give me one. I don't love her. She just doesn't get it. I haven't touched her in months. I'm hardly ever home. I've been with her for 10 years, and she's changed so much. She's a bitch. Forgive me for not telling you."

Della said, "That sucks, Greg. It sucks that you lied to me and sucks that she doesn't want a divorce. I want to be with you. I think I'm in love with you, but I don't want to be your mistress."

"No, that's not what I want either. I want you and you alone. I want to get rid of my wife." Greg's description of Cici was full of negative adjectives.

"Well, I guess I have to give you points for telling me the truth. Do you have a picture of her? Can't you hire a good lawyer?" asked Della.

"I am now. I need the best. My wife will probably raise holy hell. I have to admit, I don't want to split any of the assets with her. Financially, she's done nothing to contribute to our marriage. But now that we've met, I don't want to lose you. I don't care if she takes half of everything I own. And I don't carry a photo of her. Why would I, knowing how I feel about her? I bet she'll probably fight hard to take everything she can from me," said Greg.

"She can't do that. I don't know her, but I hate her for making you miserable. It's not fair."

"Don't worry, sweetheart. I'll take care of everything."

"Sounds like you could use some help with the likes of her," Della said.

Greg felt that in order to keep Della, he'd better call a lawyer as soon as possible. Della changed everything. If he could have her, it wouldn't be that hard to let go of some of his wealth.

After seeing Della, he made a quick stop at Merv's. Greg walked up Merv's mobile home steps. Greg picked up the front door key after lifting up the flowerpot. He looked behind his shoulder at the road. No one was in sight, and Merv had told him he'd meet him at Harborside after completing a power-washing job on a house in Ocean Pines.

He walked back into Merv's bedroom carrying a bag, and he pulled out his wedding band from the bag. He placed the plastic bag with the stolen items under Merv's futon. He walked into the kitchenette. Greg placed his wedding band in the corner of the cluttered kitchen window sill. He put Merv's key back in its hiding place, got back into his SUV, and headed to Harborside to wait for his friend.

Greg and he had spent some good and some bad times together. He had met Merv at the Fenwick Boat Repair Marina five years ago. While there, they talked about each other's boat problems and how much money it took to keep their boats afloat and running every summer season. Given the slump in the economy, his handyman business was slower than usual, and he told Greg keeping the boat for pleasure was not affordable any longer. So Merv consigned the boat. He had helped Greg often to remodel his house and their friendship had grown.

When Greg arrived at the restaurant, he saw Merv's truck in the lot. He was already sipping a beer at the bar. "I was just about to call you," said Merv. They sat outside on Harborside's deck and watched a fishing trawler cruise by. Merv wore his Orioles baseball cap, but looked unkempt from powerwashing all day. Greg drank from his glass of scotch.

"I thought about your little game of committing a murder without getting caught," said Merv.

"Yeah, what?" asked Greg.

"Set fire to the house while the person is sleeping."

Greg's eyebrows shot up. "Seriously? Not very creative, Merv. That wouldn't guarantee the person would die from the fire. The noise from a smoke detector could wake him up. You'd have to make it look like it wasn't arson. Is that the best you can come up with?"

"Geez, Greg, you're really taking this whole thing too seriously," said Merv. "Ask the bartender."

"No, not interested."

"Then, I'll ask him."

"No, Merv. Don't do that."

"Well, have you come up with any ideas?" asked Merv.

"Um, well, you could hide the body after you stabbed the person. Hide it somewhere in the wild where no one could find it. The body would decompose and be eaten by critters, and nothing but bones would be left. There would be no sign of stab wounds or a weapon either."

"Where would you stab him, in the woods or somewhere else before you got to the woods? And suppose hunters came along and discovered the body before decomposition?" asked Merv.

"Enough of this, Merv. Game over," said Greg.

After two drinks, he left for home.

Greg smelled the beef paprika cooking in the crockpot when he entered into the back of his house. He saw Cici, stirring the pot and putting some of it into a large Pyrex bowl. "Smells delicious," he said, as he walked over to the wet bar.

She didn't answer him but snorted and whispered under her breath, "Wish it was arsenic Alfredo."

He fixed his usual drink and flopped on the couch, but then decided to get up. He carried his drink outside onto the deck. He sat down on the lounge chair, leaned back, and watched a young teenage boy drift by on his paddleboard on the calm river.

Cici would freak out if she knew about Della. She was exactly what he wanted from the first and felt they were meant to be. Greg closed his eyes and pictured Della nude in his mind, holding her and fondling her breasts. What a dazzling woman.

Cici banged the refrigerator door shut. She snapped the plastic lid on top of the bowl, covering the cooked dinner, and mumbled, "Cheat, liar, drunk, smokehound. Makes me sick being in the same room with him."

Greg snuffed out his cigarette and sipped the last of his drink as he watched a sea gull skim the water. *Aahhh. So relaxing.* He walked back towards the kitchen and opened the slider. Once inside, he turned to lock the door, his back to the kitchen. "Cici, why don't we talk about our marriage like you suggested?" he asked as he slowly turned around.

She wasn't there. Cici had gone out the front door and was walking across the street with her arms full of some beef paprika for Amie.

Greg drank a lot of scotch that night. The heavy drinking and his exhaustion helped him to drift into his dreams on the soft couch.

⅃

The next day, after adding a new client in Pocomoke City, Greg returned home and changed into a dark gray T-shirt, tennis shoes, and casual pants. He drove to Merv's trailer and knocked on his front door. A few minutes later, Merv swung the door open. "Hey, bro. What's up? It's late. Selling a lot of French fries?" asked Merv.

Greg couldn't help but be amused at Merv's appearance. "Can't hide that beer gut, can you?" he said to Merv. Greg looked at his disheveled hair and his soiled, oversized, sleeveless white shirt, pulled down outside his pants. Greg stood taller than Merv except when Merv wore his leather cowboy boots. "Hard day at work?" Greg asked.

"You'd look like this too, if you installed weatherstripping all day," Merv said. "Want a beer? You gotta bring your own scotch. Can't afford that $50 brand you drink."

"A beer's fine," said Greg. He walked over to the sink in the small kitchen. "When are you going to clean up this messy countertop, Merv? How can you live like this?"

"I can't. I'm getting rid of the six packs in the fridge and staying out of the bars. My wife always said she'd take me back if I gave up my drinking."

"Doubt if that'll happen. What's in your glass?" asked Greg.

"Soda. I'm serious, Greg. I'm going to AA. I want my wife back. I'm tired of living in this pig sty. I want to live in my own home."

"Well, good luck to that, Merv."

Greg turned around, rested his hands on the edge of the countertop and looked out the kitchen window above the sink. He then lowered his eyes to the sill. "What's this, Merv? It looks like a wedding band." Greg picked up the ring and looked at it more closely. "It has my initials inside it. This is my wedding band. The one that was stolen from my house."

"Judas Priest! Are you crazy? Let me see it. Just a minute, you think I stole it?" Merv rotated the gold band between his two fingers. "Are you pulling my leg? Okay, very funny, Greg. I get it. You came here to tell me the cops found your loot," said Merv. "Congratulations," slapping Greg on his back.

"No, they didn't . . . I think you stole it."

Merv's mouth dropped open. "Wha—Bull shit! You're nuts!"

"This certainly is my ring," said Greg. "I'm going to search your house for the rest of my things."

Merv looked at him as if he were speaking Chinese. He said, "No you're not, Greg. I can't believe this. Why would you think this of me?" Greg ignored him and began opening all of the kitchen cabinets. He then walked straight into his bedroom with Merv following his lead.

Greg got down on his hands and knees and pulled out the plastic bag from under Merv's futon.

"What's this, Merv? Your latest stash?"

"You son of a bitch!" Merv grabbed the bag and stared wide-eyed at Greg. "You planted that there. You're trying to frame me. Get the hell out of here," Merv said. He was sweating. "You can't pin this on me . . . Just a second." Merv's face was red as he spit out his words. "You're trying to have me take the blame for attacking Cici. I was right. You did try to murder Cici. You bastard."

"That's right, Merv. I did try to kill her. And you had your suspicions, and I couldn't have that."

Merv lunged for Greg. Greg pulled out Merv's Glock 19 9-millimeter semiautomatic handgun from his waistband and shot him point-blank in the front of his head. The bullet traveled through the brain, exiting through the back of the head. He dropped to the floor like a stack of wooden blocks. Merv's lifeless eyes were open. His body lay on the rug next to his futon. Greg looked down at him.

"Sorry, bro. Couldn't trust you if you got drunk and blabbed to someone that I may have given Cici a concussion. And now, this'll get Crabbe off my back. You would've died of cirrhosis of the liver anyway. I know you thought I was treating you to golf on Saturday. Screw that idea."

Greg dialed 911. Soon after, Detective Crabbe arrived at the scene. He bent down and put his two fingers on Merv's neck, feeling for a pulse. Greg was sitting on the edge of the futon, elbows on his knees, resting his head on his closed fists. He stared down at the blood-soaked rug.

"You don't have to do that. He's already dead," said Greg. "I can't believe he did this."

"What happened here?" Crabbe asked.

Greg said, "I came over to see Merv and have a few drinks with him. I saw my ring in the corner of his window sill. I accused him of stealing my things. He said he bought it at a pawn shop. I didn't believe him. Why would he want a wedding band? Besides he doesn't have any money to throw around, except to buy beer. He couldn't afford to buy my gold wedding band. I got suspicious and started looking for the missing items inside the kitchen cabinets. When I entered his bedroom, he acted kind of funny and all. Especially when I got near his futon."

"Funny? What do you mean?" asked Crabbe.

"Like, he was wringing his hands, bouncing back and forth. His eyes darted around where the bed was, and he was sweating. He was yelling at me to get away from his futon and to get out of the room. I really got suspicious then. I bent down and looked under the futon, and there it was. The plastic bag full of the stolen items. I felt like my head was going to explode. He was the one all along. He tried to kill Cici. I wanted to choke him. I got up, and when I turned around, Merv had his gun pointed at me. I freaked out, made a grab for the gun, and we wrestled for it. Both our hands were gripping the gun, and while we were fighting for it, the gun discharged and killed Merv. I can't believe this happened, and I can't believe he's dead," said Greg, shaking his head. "He was my friend," he said. "Or at least, I thought he was my friend."

The ambulance arrived, and Crabbe secured the scene. The bedroom showed signs of a struggle. Papers covered the rug and the desk chair was tilted. A lamp was on the floor. In the kitchen, the cabinets were wide open.

Crabbe said, "So it was self-defense, you're saying?"

Greg said, "Yes. It was self-defense. He was bent on killing me when I discovered he robbed us and injured Cici."

"Why would your good friend hurt your wife and rob you? It doesn't make sense to me," said Crabbe.

"It makes sense to me. His business was sporadic. He wasn't making much money. He wanted his wife to take him back, and if she did, he had to continue to support her and pay the bills. So why not rob us? He knew about an inheritance I received, and we were well off. I often treated him to golf. Cici could have recognized him that morning when he was in our house, and that set him off to try to kill her."

Crabbe said, "You sound like you have it all figured out." Greg just stared at him.

The EMT's lifted Merv's covered body and placed it inside the ambulance. It drove off without the siren blaring. Crabbe looked at Greg. "We need to go down to the station and get your statement of what happened here. I hear your side of the story, but obviously, I can't hear Mr. Grady's side. You see, a prosecutor may say you acted intentionally in causing his death or at least took action that led to his death. I have to hold you there, and you will need to contact a criminal defense lawyer without delay."

"So I can't go to Norfolk and call on clients?" asked Greg.

"No, you can't. For God's sake, a man has been killed. This is extremely serious. There will be some sort of a homicide charge," said Crabbe.

"May I call my wife, please? And a lawyer?" asked Greg. "Can you recommend a criminal lawyer for me?"

"Follow me to the police station," said Crabbe.

Greg called Cici, who was still up, reading *The Beachcomber* in bed. He told her exactly what he'd told Crabbe about Merv's death.

Cici put down the newspaper and said, "What are you saying? He stole from us? And he was the one who attacked me? No, it can't be true. I can't believe Merv did what you said. He was always nice to me. Merv came by when I was recuperating to see how I was doing. He seemed so genuine and caring."

"Well, he did it. I have to find an attorney. Detective Crabbe has arrested me."

"What? But it was self-defense," said Cici.

"There still has to be an investigation," said Greg.

"You're lucky you weren't killed. You must be exhausted."

"I think I'm still in shock," said Greg. "I defended myself when I saw that Merv was going to shoot me. It's justifiable self-defense. I didn't start the altercation. I should be able to have the charges dismissed."

Crabbe let him keep his cell phone in the detention room, but made him give up his wallet and keys. Crabbe's office was just outside Greg's holding room. Inside, Greg had a small cot, sink, and toilet. At least it had a nice-sized window. Might as well call it prison.

The next morning Greg met with a criminal lawyer whom Crabbe suggested. He was being charged with involuntary manslaughter.

CHAPTER 7

Cici dialed her mom's number to get some things off her chest. "Glad I caught you. Have some things to tell you."

Her mom asked, "How are you? Have they caught the robber?"

"Wait. There's so much to talk about. I know Detective Crabbe talked to you about Greg."

"Yes. Do you think the detective is out to get him?" asked her mother. "Greg couldn't have done this. He adores you."

"We got our stolen goods back, and I'll tell you all about it. That's another story, but first I wanted to get you up to speed on Greg and me. To the point, our marriage isn't the greatest. Actually, it's in shambles. Greg is not the man you think he is. I'm sure you painted a nice picture of him for the detective, but you didn't know the truth. That's my fault." Cici explained their difficulties and Greg's behavior that had been going on for some time. She told him about Pat's report.

"I wish you'd confided in me sooner, Cici."

"I didn't want to worry you, mom. Good grief, you're getting two knee replacements. You've been in pain for a long time. I'm glad you're finally getting this done."

"I go for my pre-op next week. My operation is in three weeks. Then the orthopedic surgeon is waiting for two weeks after this first operation, and I'll have the next knee done. I'm falling apart, Cici, but can't wait until this whole thing is over. Don't get old, Cici. Be happy. I'm sad to hear you and Greg have been having problems."

"Don't be. Mom, I'm getting a divorce. I'll be glad to get rid of him. I haven't told him yet. He'll be surprised when he finds out I hired a private detective," said Cici. "I can't imagine he'll be too upset that I want a divorce, now that he has a mistress."

"He does? When are you going to tell him you want a divorce?"

"After I see my lawyer," Cici said. "I don't think I want to be alone when I break the news to him."

"Good idea," said her mom. "When you met Greg, it was like he was your Prince Charming. I guess you looked to Greg for the security you didn't have with your father gone. And he seemed to offer you that. He's no Prince Charming anymore, is he?"

"No, not at all. Mom, you thought you did the best you could raising me after dad died. And you are right. Greg was a wonderful husband in the beginning. But not anymore," said Cici. "Life is so unpredictable."

"Good Lord, Cici," her mother said. "You've been through so much. It's mind-boggling. All I want for you is to be happy," said her mom. "I'm glad you got your stolen goods back. Who did it?"

"A man that Greg was friends with, Merv Grady."

"Why did he rob you?"

"Greg thinks he needed the money."

"He's evil, trying to kill you too. So glad they caught him. Keep me in the loop, honey."

"I will. I'm going to make reservations to fly out there when you are recuperating from your knee operation. I'll let you know all the details as soon as I can." Cici didn't want her to know that Greg was in jail facing an involuntary manslaughter charge. Not while she was facing major surgery. Not on the phone. She'd wait until she was with her in San Diego to have a real long discussion—about everything, even pouring out her soul to her. Face to face.

Crabbe took the plastic bag out of his patrol car and brought it inside the station. He removed his gloves and dialed the chief. "Where are you? I thought you were here," Crabbe asked Hulk.

"Left a little early," he said. "Queasy stomach," said Hulk.

Crabbe told him about the events at Merv's trailer and that Greg King was meeting him at the station to give his statement. "Going back to the scene tomorrow. Meet me there at his trailer. I'm going to notify Mrs. Grady after I get King's account of what happened again."

Mrs. Grady was home, writing up lesson plans for the next day. She got up from the sofa to answer the doorbell. She let Crabbe in. He saw her eyes widen. "Something's wrong. I can feel it. What did Merv do this time? Is he okay?"

He detested this part of his job. Crabbe sat down next to her on the sofa and told her Merv had been killed. "It looked like it could have been self-defense." He told her the story Greg had relayed to him.

He hated to see a woman cry. He was not successful in consoling her. Tears ran down her face, and Mrs. Grady's small stature made her look even more pathetic. Her short, auburn hair was pulled into two small ponytails. Her eyeglasses at the tip of her nose looked moist. She was dressed in her pajamas.

"I can't go to work tomorrow. I have to get a sub. At least my lesson plans are done." She wiped away her tears. "This is so shocking. I can't believe he's gone. I'll never see him again. How do you know for sure that Merv pulled a gun on Greg?"

"I only know what Mr. King said. He called 911 after it happened."

"Doesn't sound like Merv at all." She blew her nose and dabbed her cheeks with a tissue. "He couldn't have robbed and done that to Cici, Mrs. King, I mean. He really liked her. And he was Greg's friend. They did so much together. They had a lot in common. He helped Greg renovate his house. It can't be true," she said, shaking her head. "He was going to join AA. He said he wanted to come back to me after he could remain sober for six months. And I told him if he could kick his addiction, I'd take him back. I will never believe he tried to hurt Cici. Never. It's not in his character." She started crying again. "He's never hurt me."

"I'm so sorry, Mrs. Grady. There will be a thorough investigation." He stayed to talk with her a little longer.

"What do I do now?" she asked. "What about his stuff? His trailer? His truck? His tools?" She sniffed and wiped a tear away.

"Mrs. Grady, I think a lawyer could help you," said Crabbe.

"I'll call my pastor first," she said. Crabbe gave her his card and his condolences before leaving.

The next day Crabbe and Hulk examined the crime scene at Merv's trailer. "Geez, I feel like a sardine in here," said Hulk.

"Understandably," said Crabbe, joking.

"You think you're funny, don't you?" said Hulk.

After a thorough inspection of the premises, Hulk said, "It's hard to dispute that it wasn't self-defense. The lab completed the results of the fingerprints on the bag and ring. Grady's were on the plastic bag and the wedding band," said Hulk. "Also King's."

"I know we don't have anything pointing to a planned murder, but I can't help but feel that King came here just to kill him," said Crabbe.

"You just don't like the guy. He's a scumbag from what you've told me. I'll grant you that, but you're going to have to put your personal feelings aside," Hulk said.

"It's not my personal feeling. It's my gut feeling," said Crabbe.

"Aw, get over it, Joe. Get a beer at the Purple Moose and chill."

-ᴈ̣-

Cici kept her appointment in Salisbury with her lawyer around 4:00 p.m. She took a sharp right onto Main Street, where her lawyer's office was located. She was kept waiting for 10 minutes. Mr. Vaughn opened the door of his office, smiled, and asked, "Mrs. King?"

She was surprised to see how short he was. His shiny, bald head defined his protruding ears. The left one was pierced. Perched on his nose were round-rimmed eyeglasses, making his eyes look larger than usual. His office was small, neat, and organized. Behind his desk, mahogany shelves loaded with books stood like statues against the wall. Cici glanced at an 8 ½" by 11" silver-framed photo of a woman and two teenagers mounted on one of the shelves. She noticed the huge pile of thick folders on his desk. Heaps of work to tackle.

Pointing to them, Cici said, "Are those all divorces?"

He laughed and answered, "Most of them, but I'm behind in my filing."

"I'm glad you could see me. You seem to be deluged with work."

"Oh, but I enjoy what I do. It sometimes gets a little distressing mediating. So tell me what's going on with you. May I call you Cici?"

"Of course," she said. He seemed quite pleasant. She liked him instantly.

Cici told him everything. Discussing her marriage in the

beginning to the drastic changes in Greg's behavior rolled off her tongue. She told him about Greg's self-defense story and that he had been arrested.

"I definitely want a divorce. I'm ready to move on." Cici brought a copy of the surveillance report and the DVD that Pat had given her. "Here is a copy of the P.I.'s report," Cici said.

"I see you brought a DVD. I don't think I'll need that, Cici, but if you don't mind, leave it here just in case," Vaughn said.

"No problem. Mr. Vaughn, I don't want to go through marriage counseling or mediation of any sort. So what are my next steps in this process?" asked Cici.

"Have you told your husband about hiring a P.I.?"

"Not yet," said Cici.

"Well, I recommend you do that. Tell him you have an attorney. Give him my name, and tell him to hire a lawyer. Let him know you're filing for a divorce, and ask him to leave. You may want a friend or family member around when you do this. After he leaves, change the locks. In light of what happened to you recently, I would do that anyway. Let me know the name of his attorney when he hires one. Much communication will be handled through your husband's lawyer and me." Vaughn explained his fees to Cici and Maryland's law regarding property division and allocation of property and assets.

"I don't want the house. I don't want to live in it. I can't believe I'm saying this, but it's not important to me anymore. Too many bad memories." Cici said. "All I want is alimony each month. I can get a job. I don't want any of his inheritance he keeps in the safe at home, and I can live off our joint account, until everything is settled. There's a good amount in there." Cici told Vaughn the value of all of their assets. "I'm definitely not staying in the house after I tell him I want a divorce. I'll live somewhere else."

"Are you sure that's all you want? He hasn't treated you very well," said Vaughn.

"I don't care."

"Well, I'd like to focus on your future, you know. You have to. I can fight for you to live comfortably. You ought to rethink this. And, of course, there are lawyer's fees."

"Hmmm, you're right about that. I just want no hassling. I want this to be a smooth process. He did say he didn't want a divorce after reading a letter I wrote to him."

"Did you ever think about why he said that? He has a lot to lose if there's a divorce," Vaughn said. "Why should you be on the loser end? Let's sock it to him, Mrs. King."

"You could be right, but I don't want it to take a long time. I wish I could be a divorcee tomorrow."

"Well, I can't work that fast, Mrs. King," Vaughn laughed. "I'll do my best for you and keep your intentions in mind. But I'm going to settle for more than you want. Maryland law is on your side. Don't worry." They shook hands, and Cici left his office.

While driving back to Ocean Pines, Cici decided to call Amie. She pulled over to the side of the road and took her iPhone out of her purse. She told her all about Greg and Merv.

"That's crazy. It's so hard to fathom," said Amie. I just can't believe it."

"I know. I just left the lawyer's office. I really liked him. Pat's recommendation was great. I have a favor to ask you."

"What?" asked Amie.

"Could I stay at your house until I get settled? I don't feel comfortable sleeping in my own home anymore," said Cici.

"No problem, Cici. Be glad to help. Come over tonight," said Amie.

"Okay, thank you. I'll pick up a few things at my house. I probably will be spending some time at my house the next several days. I want to pack a lot of things, like my clothes, and some personal items."

"Oh, I have another favor to ask. Could you and Pat be with me when I tell Greg I want a divorce?"

Amie agreed. "Let me know when."

When Cici pulled into her garage, she saw a red car parked in front of her house. She knew immediately knew who it was. The license plate said EYES4U.

⚏

Della didn't like that Cici manipulated Greg. She wanted to help him. And she had an idea. She'd act on it after finishing her last sales call on Thursday with an ophthalmologist in Fenwick Island, Delaware, just 13 miles from Greg's house. Greg told her he was in Norfolk until Saturday. She wanted to see his wife alone. She knew Greg was the sole breadwinner and his wife didn't work. If she wasn't at home when she arrived, Della didn't care how long she'd have to wait for Cici to return to her house.

Della left the eye doctor's office and pulled up in front of Greg's home on Teal Circle. She looked into her rearview mirror and applied lipstick to her lips. She pinched her cheeks, looked into the mirror again, and rubbed a smear of lipstick off her front tooth. Twenty minutes later, she saw Cici's garage door go up and watched her drive her car inside. Perfect timing.

The garage door closed, and Della got out of her car. She rang the doorbell. Della's eyes scanned the front of Greg's home. Nice house. Cici opened the front door after hearing the chimes.

"Hello, my name is Della Summer. I would—"

"I know who you are," said Cici.

"You do? May I come in? I think what I have to say will interest you."

Not by the hair of my chinny-chin-chin. "I'm not interested in anything you have to say," said Cici.

Gee, she really is bitchy. "It's about your husband. It's in your and his best interests that you hear me out," said Della. "I won't take too much of your time. I promise," she said as nicely as possible.

Cici let her come into the great room. Glad that she had softened, Della smiled and sat down on the couch, crossing her legs. She didn't mince words and said, "Mrs. King, I'm in love with your husband. He told me he asked you for a divorce. He said you don't want a divorce."

"What are you talking about?"

"Hear me out," said Della. "I know that you want to hang onto this marriage. But Greg's so unhappy, and in the long run, hanging on to the marriage will make you just as miserable as he is. We're all adults here. I'm asking you to please let him go. Why are you being so unreasonable and mean to him? He loves me, not you."

Cici said, "Are you deranged? I have no intention of discussing my marriage with you." Cici stood up. She pointed at the front door. "Get out of my house."

"Not until you tell me you'll grant him a divorce. How come you knew who I was? Did Greg tell you about me?" asked Della.

Della rose from the couch. Cici took a step closer. "I asked you to leave. I'm calling the police if you don't get out of my house." She pointed to the front door. "Now."

As Cici leaned over to pick up her cell phone, Della grabbed her elbow and pulled her towards her.

"Get off me. Who do you think you are?" said Cici as she jerked her elbow loose.

Della put both hands on her shoulders and shook her. "Give him a divorce, you bitch. No wonder Greg hates you."

"You're the bitch, not me," said Cici. Della slapped her across the face. Cici slapped her back, and Della grabbed a chunk of Cici's hair and pulled the strands of hair as hard as she could. Cici kicked her in the shin, and Della let go of Cici's hair and whacked her hard on her cheek. With her fingers in a claw-like position she scratched Cici's face with her sharp nails, producing thin lines of blood.

Cici snatched a hardback book off the coffee table and threw it at Della's head, causing her to yell out, cover her one eye with her left hand, and lose her balance. She fell on the couch. Cici grasped her cell phone, ran into her bedroom, slammed the door, locked it, and dialed 911.

⚷

Greg sat in the holding area in Ocean Pines. His cell phone rang.

"Greg, it's me, Della." Sniffling, she said, "I've been charged with second-degree assault. I struck Cici."

He grabbed his head. The phone fell on the floor. Quickly picking it up, he asked, "What? You did what? Why on earth would you do such a thing?" asked Greg.

"She wouldn't talk to me when I went to your house." Della wiped her nose. "She pressed charges. She attacked me too. A doctor is going to look at me soon. I asked her to please give you a divorce, and one thing led to another. I thought I was helping you by putting pressure on her. Believe me, I didn't mean to hurt her. I'm so sorry. I want to get out of here. Can you believe this is costing me $14 a minute for long-distance calls? You have to call the facility to learn the hours you are permitted to make calls to me."

"Where are you?" asked Greg. *Don't want her to know about me and where I am.*

"The Berlin Police Jail. I contacted my lawyer, who is a friend of the family. He's going to call my brother to get me out on bail. They are so strict here." She blew her nose. Della started crying. "I hope my . . . boss doesn't find out. I guess you're heading to Norfolk, but can you persuade your wife . . . to drop the charges?" She blew into her handkerchief. "Please?"

"I'll see what I can do. This is incredible. Don't cry. Stay calm. I'll help you out of this. I'll be in touch. I love you." *I'll let her think I'm heading to Norfolk. Don't want to worry her more. What a wildcat!*

Greg's boss, Kevin Case, posted bail for Greg. It took an hour to do the paperwork and retrieve his personal items before driving back home.

Greg pulled into his garage that evening and saw Cici's car parked inside. He charged into the house and found Cici packing some of her things in the bedroom.

Cici looked up and dropped her makeup case when he stormed into the bedroom. She backed away from him. "What are you doing here? How did you get out of jail?"

Ignoring her questions, he asked, "Cici, what were you thinking? How could you do this to Della? Please drop the charges. Please try to understand. Della knew I was unhappy. In her state of mind, she lost it. She was only trying to help me. She wasn't even planning to hurt you. She just wanted to talk. She said you refused to even discuss things with her."

Cici took a deep breath and said, "Your paramour," she snorted, "deliberately hurt and scared me out of my wits. That woman is demented," Cici said.

"I'm sorry she hurt you. She told me she didn't mean to do what she did."

"Did you send her here?" asked Cici.

"No. I had no idea she planned to come to the house."

"She said you told her I didn't want a divorce. Am I missing something here?" asked Cici.

"We met by chance and fell in love. We discussed getting married someday. I told her you probably wouldn't want a divorce. I was thinking because of that note you wrote to me, you really wanted to save our marriage."

"Well, guess what? I do want a divorce. We never talked more after those letters. Because of the way you were acting, I hired a P.I., and he told me all about your little clandestine meeting at the hotel with her. The sooner the divorce, the better."

"What, you did what?" asked Greg.

"You heard me."

Greg clenched his jaw. He paused. "I'll only agree to a divorce if you drop the charges on Della. And I want the house, my 410k, and my inheritance . . . all my stuff."

"You can have all of your possessions. I don't want any of them. I hate living here now. You can get a lawyer and contact mine. I'm going to stay with Amie until I find a place. And I'm going to get a job."

"A job? That's a joke. What kind of job?"

Cici didn't answer him. "I know you're unhappy, but so am I. But I'm not dropping the charges," said Cici.

"You have to! I love this woman." He stormed around the bedroom. "She means the world to me. For God's sake, you can't do this. It'll destroy my life," yelled Greg, running his fingers through his hair, and pacing back and forth. "You've ruined Della's reputation. She'll probably lose her job," said Greg. He hit the wall with his fist, tipping over the lamp on the nightstand.

Cici jumped back and placed her hand on her chest, feeling her heart pounding way too fast. She said, "Your girlfriend attacked me. Your buddy, Merv, attacked me. When's it going to stop? How much do you think I can take? Della's not the victim here. I am."

Greg threw Cici's bag on the floor. Cici recoiled. Greg's face reddened. His eyes were like narrow slits, piercing and penetrating hers. Cici's eyes widened. Greg lurched towards her and raised his voice, "Drop the charges. Don't you get it? I can't marry her if she's in jail. You're so naïve. You think Merv gave you a concussion?" He punched her in the jaw. Cici fell and landed unconscious on the ceramic tile floor.

Shit! What have I done? Why did I lose control and hit her? She'll press charges against me now. They'll throw me back in jail. What's wrong with me? She was willing to leave and give me everything.

Swirling mind racing, Greg's eyes looked cold and calculating. He glanced around the room. Finding Cici's purse, he took out her wallet and keys. He picked up her cell phone from the nightstand. He raced outside to the pier and dropped Cici's phone, keys, and wallet into the river. Greg ran back into the house. He dragged Cici by her arms to the garage and stuffed her into her car's trunk. He grabbed his hammer from his tool chest, duct-taped her wrists and feet, slammed her trunk door, and headed towards the abandoned South Pines Golf Club.

Cici woke up inside her trunk. The air smelled of gasoline and oil. She felt the bindings around her ankles and wrists. Her heart wouldn't stop hammering in her chest. She felt the car reversing. *What the hell's going on?* And then she remembered she and Greg were fighting, and he hit her in the face. *Why is he doing this?* She banged on the trunk's door with her taped hands. She screamed, "Let me out of here!"

"Shut up," she heard Greg yell.

Then she remembered. *What did he mean by, "You think Merv gave you a concussion?" Did he mean he was the one who gave it to me?* Shivers coursed through her body. She was too terrified to make a sound. With her teeth, she bit and gnawed at the tape around her wrists. She worked and tugged on it—it seemed for years. She managed to make a small tear in the binding. She pulled hard and ripped the tape apart. She then tried her level best to loosen the tape around her ankles. It wasn't easy, but she was determined to make the utmost endeavor to get her ankles free. With her fingers, she tore at the tape. She tugged and tugged. It finally started to give. She stretched the tape by pushing her ankles outwards. Continuing to work at it with her thumbnail and forefinger, she poked and tore again at the tape around her ankles. Sweating and breathing heavily and taxing all her energy, she finally freed her feet.

Cici heard Greg's cell phone ring. He was talking to someone. She couldn't make out what he was saying. The muffled chatting stopped. *Where is he taking me? He's going to kill me.* Cici was shaking uncontrollably.

It was so dark inside the trunk. She didn't hear any cars whiz by. Cici felt the car turning. It was bumpy. Moving on a graveled road? The tires went over something. Maybe a rope? A chain? A branch? The car moved further on the bumpy road.

Cici felt the car stop. She tried to be still. She heard the trunk pop open. Cici felt his closeness. She kicked hard towards him with every ounce of her strength, and he stumbled backwards. She jumped out of the trunk and raced along a circular path. Terror paralyzed her. Her heart thumped faster. Greg got up from the dirt path and started to run after her. He shouted after her. "You can't get far. I'll catch you bitch."

Cici's adrenaline surged, and she looked ahead into the darkness as she ran. She ran half way around the circular path until it led straight to a debris-covered, narrow road. She kept running as fast as she could over stones and twigs. She wouldn't stop. "Damn!" Greg said. She heard what she thought was Greg dropping to the ground. Maybe he tripped on something behind her. She plunged forward, amazed at her speed. Greg got up and cocked his head to the left, listening for sounds. Cici heard a car's loud muffler in the distance and ran toward the sound. Her heart leaped into her throat. With a racing heart, she ran. Her clothes were drenched in sweat. Cici's eyes made out a huge, thick bush a few yards off the road, and she ran behind it. She crouched down and caught her breath. She heard Greg sprint past her. That was close. She went much deeper into the brush and hid again.

⚐

Greg doubled back. *Where the hell did she go? Did she find a hiding place? This is no game of hide and seek.* Greg was perspiring more than usual. If he couldn't find her, he was doomed. "Cici, where are you?" *Fat chance she'll answer.* He retraced his steps back to her car. Greg started the engine, turned on the high beams, and wound down the windows. He accelerated slowly along the path, looking out both side windows.

"Cici, there are animals out there. I know you're hiding somewhere. Come out." Cici couldn't get away. He had to find her. Greg headed toward the entrance to the golf course. He drove back over the chain on the ground. She could have made it out to the main highway. He turned left. He saw no sign of her. He pressed his foot on the gas pedal and picked up speed, heading back to his house. Greg parked her car on a quiet side street near Teal Circle. He jogged back to his house and headed back into the bedroom.

It was one o'clock in the morning. In his backpack, he packed some clothes, notions, and shoes. He emptied the safe of a lot of his inheritance money and crammed as many bills as he could squeeze into his backpack. Greg got into his SUV, stopped at an ATM for some extra cash, and headed south on Route 13 towards Norfolk. He was determined to make it to Florida. He turned off his iPhone. Gaining ground, he drove 80 miles an hour on I-95. *Be careful. Don't get a speeding ticket.*

He was screwed. *Shouldn't have made that comment to her about Merv. When she returns from the golf course, she'll probably get hold of Crabbe first thing.*

Cici felt it was okay to come out of her hiding place. She remembered Greg yelling out from the car that animals were out there. What kind? Foxes, wildcats, raccoons, werewolves? Cici decided to walk back to the main path leading to the clubhouse. The night was quiet. The outside, black darkness surrounded her. She gambled on finding the clubhouse. Her gamble paid off. She saw it as she circled the path.

The entrance to the clubhouse was unlocked. She stepped inside and put her arms out straight in front of her, for fear of bumping into something. Something stopped her steps. A wall? She put her hands out in front of her again and felt what must have been a tabletop or countertop. She brushed her hands across the countertop, getting dust on her palms. It was pitch black inside. Cici continued to feel her way in the darkness. She discovered an opening behind what appeared to be a U-shaped counter and stepped around it. Too tired to think, and feeling protected there, inside the U, she laid down on the floor and fell asleep.

The next morning, Cici woke up with a start. The brightness of the sun illuminated the deserted clubhouse. Her eyes snapped alert. Reflexively, her hand felt her sore jaw. In an instant, she was panic-stricken. The adrenaline surged. The floor felt cold on her body. *Gotta get up.* She looked around in horror. She squinted at the morning sun's light peeking through the broken glass windows. Is he out there somewhere? Would this monster of a husband come back? *Need to get out of here fast.*

Cici walked around the counter. She saw a couple of chairs turned over beside a table. At the end of the room, she noticed a bar and a small eating area. On the floor, she spotted several tees and smudged writing on a sign. She could just make it out. "Women's Golf Shoes on Sale." She made her way to the front door, nearly tripping over a large shard of glass. So far, no sign of Greg. The car was gone.

It was a chilly day. Glad that it was fall and not January, Cici walked away from the clubhouse. In the daylight, she saw more clearly how the circular pathway led straight to a debris-covered narrow road. This was easier. So many twigs and weeds covered the road, but she didn't care. She moved forward, making her way through the obstacle course of felled branches, browned leaves, and ragged pieces of bark. She often looked to her right and left, scared she might see Greg. She continued carefully over the stones and had difficulty avoiding the maze of branches, spiky burrs, and pinecones. Managing to get out of this mess last night was a miracle. She walked past the spot where she'd hid the night before. *And this used to be a golf course?* Her eyes locked on the road overgrown with weeds and twigs, watching her every step.

She lifted her head and could make out a clearing at the end of the road. *Thank goodness.* But then she heard someone's car honking in the distance. Next came the sound of a vehicle's engine coming closer. Its sound grew louder as she continued walking toward the clearing. Her heart pounded. *Is that the monster returning?* But the car drove by on the main road, passing the entrance to the golf course. *I'm almost there.* Getting a little closer to the exit lifted her spirits. She continued her trek, her eyes fixed on the road.

Cici spotted a chain on the ground across the golf course entry road. She stepped over it and onto the road's edge. She looked both ways and began jumping up and down. She yelled for help as drivers drove by. She frantically began waving her hands above her head. She waved like a fool.

Finally a lady in her early 30s, driving a van, pulled over to the side of the road opposite the entrance to the South Pines Golf Course, and her driver's seat window slid down. "Are you okay?" she yelled to her.

Exhausted, Cici said, "Oh, please help me. Can you drive me to the police station?" Pointing and turning her head towards the entrance to the old golf course, Cici quickly said, "I escaped from my abductor," and again pointing to the entrance, she said, "I hid in an abandoned clubhouse way back in there."

"Hurry, get into the car," the woman said.

Cici staggered across the street and climbed into the lady's van. Relief filled her.

"Thank you so much. I don't think many people would have stopped. I must look a bloody mess. You're such a Good Samaritan. Brrr, I'm so cold. Can you please turn up the heat up a little? What is your name?"

"Jean," she said. "Jean Tyler." She told Jean all about her night of terror.

Totally absorbed in a *Shrek* movie on the flat screen perched above his head, Mrs. Tyler's toddler in the back seat silently watched. As the van sped off, Cici asked, "May I please use your cell phone?"

Cici dialed Detective Crabbe. *Hurry, please pick up.*

CHAPTER 9

At the police station, Crabbe's phone rang. Crabbe quickly swallowed the last bite of his Egg McMuffin, gulped down the remaining orange juice in his cup, and picked up the receiver.

"Detective Crabbe, this is Amie Weiss. Cici King was supposed to spend the night at my house last night. She hasn't shown up yet. She's not at her house. Patrick McCombe and I went over there around 11:00 p.m. and knocked on the door. There was no answer. I had a key to the front door, and we went inside. No one was there. Mrs. King's car was not in the garage, but Mr. King's was. I saw her purse in the bedroom and rummaged through it. There was no sign of her keys, wallet, or cell phone, but her eyeglasses were on top of her bureau."

"I'm sure there's an explanation where she must have gone, Ms. Weiss," said Crabbe.

"I last talked to her late yesterday afternoon. She would have called me Detective Crabbe."

"Yesterday Della Summer was arrested at Mrs. King's house after an altercation. Mrs. King was a little shaky after that, but otherwise fine." He briefly told her what happened with Della Summer. "That was maybe around 7:00 p.m. and Mrs. King told me to she was going to pack and move out of her house. Mr. King hadn't left the police station yet. I wonder if Mrs. King had a change of plans after her encounter with Della Summer. If she doesn't return soon, or if you don't hear from her by 6:00 p.m. tonight, call me," said Crabbe. They talked a few more minutes and then hung up.

His cell phone buzzed, interrupting his thoughts about Cici. "Say again? You were what? He did what?" he asked. He shook his head in disbelief after listening to Cici on the phone. He sat down and tapped his pencil on his desk. Crabbe anxiously waited for Cici to arrive at the station.

Twenty minutes later Cici was escorted into his office. She entered, hair mussed, clothes wrinkled, and eyes red from crying. "Detective Crabbe, boy am I glad to see you," Cici said. "I know I must look a sight, but I've just been to hell and back."

"Sit down," said Crabbe, pulling out a chair. "You had Ms. Weiss really worried. What happened? Your face is badly bruised. You were rambling on the phone."

Cici told Crabbe about what transpired at the house with Greg and how she ended up at the golf course. When Cici mentioned Greg's remark about Merv, Crabbe agreed with her that Greg must have meant he gave her the concussion. Another might not agree. Crabbe never really believed that Merv was the perpetrator.

"Mrs. King, can we go to your house?" She nodded. Crabbe grabbed his jacket, and he and Cici got into his patrol car. When they got to Cici's house, they saw no cars in the garage. Crabbe tried to locate Greg without success. He put out an APB for Greg's SUV and also an APB for Cici's Buick. Before he left, he said to Cici, "Please call Ms. Weiss, and more importantly, get a doctor to look at you."

It wasn't long before Cici's car was located. After hearing the report on his dispatch in his car that Cici's sedan was found, Crabbe headed for Teal Circle again and turned right onto a street near Cici's house. Crabbe opened Cici's trunk and found the duct tape Greg had wrapped around her wrists and ankles and the hammer under the front seat. He bagged the hammer and the tape, hoping to find Greg's prints.

Before this, he had spent almost an hour talking to Cici about the events. He felt relieved she was now safe from Greg and admired her courage and strength. Crabbe wouldn't have minded talking to her longer. What an amazing woman.

⚕

After having her facial bruises photographed and being checked out by Dr. Chu at the hospital, Cici drove to Amie's house. Her facial injury only needed an ice pack. Cici sipped a martini at Amie's and was glad to be staying there until she got her own place. She still had to go back to her house to do more packing.

"I wish this whole thing would be over and they would catch Greg," said Cici. "Lord knows where he's hiding out. He's a smart guy, but so is Detective Crabbe. I hope the only reason he comes back here is to be thrown in jail." *Please find him soon.* She sighed and finished her drink. "In the meantime, I've got to search for a job. I checked the safe. Greg practically cleaned it out."

Amie said, "He's on the run. I'm sure the cops will catch up to him. You have to be traumatized. Glad you're okay. That was a very close call."

"Yeah, I've had two of them," said Cici.

"You know, I just remembered. Pat was advertising for a part-time receptionist," said Amie.

"Really? I'm interested," Cici said. "I'll give him a call. I'm going to look for condo rentals today too. I'm filing for a divorce, but now that Greg is a fugitive, I'm curious to see how to proceed. My lawyer got me to thinking. I think he was right. I guess I will split all of the assets."

"Glad you changed your mind," Amie said.

"This morning I found out that my mom's operation has been moved back. I'm going to have to fly out to San Diego. I'll make reservations today to fly out there," said Cici. "And I have to meet with my therapist first and call my mother," she said to Amie. "So much to do."

Cici had told her mom the latest shocking news. "You told me to keep you in the loop, mom. No, I'm not a basket case. Yes, I'm calm. The monster can't get to me right now. At least, I don't think he can."

"Maybe you should come out here as soon as possible, if you're so worried about Greg coming back," said her mom.

"I'll come out after I get a few things settled here," she said. "I can stay a week or so."

"Well, that Detective Crabbe was right to consider Greg a person of interest. You should have told me sooner about Greg. You may not be in this mess right now if you had told me. I could have advised you what to do."

"Mom, I have to go. Have lots to do. Talk to you soon." She rolled her eyes and shook her head.

Cici's internist, Dr. Sullivan, recommended Cici see a therapist, Eileen Frost, to help her through this difficult time—facing a divorce and nearly being murdered by her husband. How many wives experience that?

Two days later Cici met Ms. Frost. She was tall and slender. Her white pearl earrings contrasted well against her short, cropped, black hair. Tiny freckles dotted her face, and she wore bright red lipstick. Cici liked the way she decorated her office.

Chic, but simple. Cici accepted a bottled water and sat down opposite her.

"Tell me about yourself," she said.

Cici said, "I guess I'll begin when I was three."

"Begin wherever you want," she said.

"I don't remember this happening, but my father was killed in an automobile accident. My mom worked the afternoon/night shift at the hospital, and my grandmother watched me."

"What was that like?" Ms. Frost asked.

"I dreaded coming home from school. She was mean to me—yelling and complaining so much. I cried when she was nasty to me. Actually, I cried a lot. She called me 'Spongeface.' I hated when she did that. If I got on her nerves, she'd chase me around the house with Limburger cheese, and when she cornered me, she pressed the smelly cheese into my nose. Then there was the dreaded lunchtime. I hated the taste of tomato soup. She forced me to eat it once a week. She wouldn't let me leave the kitchen table until I finished every drop of it. One time I remember throwing up after I ate it, and she punished me, making me sit on a chair in the corner of the dining room for an hour."

Ms. Frost said, "Sounds horrible. How did you do in school?"

"I loved school and my teachers. My grades were pretty good. I wanted my mom to be proud of me."

"Didn't you tell your mother about the way your grandmother treated you?" asked Ms. Frost.

"No, I was afraid if she got mad at my grandmother, no one else could watch me, and my mom would put me in a foster home. I was also afraid my grandmother would beat me if I told on her."

"How sad for you," said Ms. Frost. "How long did your grandmother babysit you?"

"She stopped watching me when I was in third grade. I remember my mom telling me that my grandmother was sick. At the time, I didn't know what dementia was. My mom came home early one evening and found my grandmother heating a slice of pizza on top of the electric stove's burner for me to eat. After that, I remember my grandmother didn't come to watch me anymore. My mom was able to switch her hours to the daytime, and I was thrilled. And I was happy that my grandmother got caught cooking my dinner on top of an electric burner."

"How was your relationship with your mother after that?"

"It was fine. I love my mom," said Cici.

"Even though you believed she'd put you in a foster home if your grandmother couldn't watch you?"

"I was so young, so naive then. One of my school friends was a foster child and was taken away from her mother, who couldn't take care of her. My mom's sister lived in another state, and that's all the family we had. So who would babysit me? I thought social services would assign me a new family if my mother couldn't take care of me while she worked. Just like what happened to my friend."

"How is your relationship with your mother now?" asked Ms. Frost.

"Okay, except I don't see her much. I'm planning to fly out very soon to visit."

"It might be a good idea to confront your mother about your feelings growing up as a child," said Ms. Frost.

They talked more about Cici's relationships in high school and her endometriosis. Cici told her about Greg—how wonderful he had once been to her, their age difference, and how he had changed.

"Why didn't you leave him way before you did, after the way he treated you?" asked Ms. Frost.

"I felt that I was so lucky to have him. He was the total package. Intelligent. Handsome. I felt I disappointed him and embarrassed him. I had gained weight since we first got married, and I was guilty I couldn't have children. I felt I deserved his anger at first, but he got worse and worse. And then I discovered he was cheating. End of marriage."

"It's not your fault your husband acted the way he did," Ms. Frost said. "So many abused wives blame themselves."

"I agree," said Cici. "I'm ashamed that I was so weak. And I was blind not to see what was really happening." Cici respected her therapist and liked sharing her feelings with her. It was a new experience for her, confiding to a stranger she liked.

"I think that it will be good for you to get away. Does Dr. Sullivan know all about what you've been going through?" Cici told her he knew most of it. "You've had a difficult time to say the least. Let's make an appointment to see me when you return from your trip."

Cici drove to Amie's house, showered, and changed her clothes. She sat down at the dinner table with Amie and Pat. She was happy to hear that Pat and Amie were dating. They made a cute couple.

"Cici, sample some of this Cajun crab dip," Amie said.

"Sounds tempting," answered Cici.

"How did your session go?" Amie asked.

"Very well. Still processing it all. It's so hard to believe how my life has changed in one year's time," she answered.

She was excited Pat hired her. Cici asked, "Pat, may I start the job after next week? My mom needs me right now after major surgery on her knee. Will that be a problem?"

"Not at all. The current receptionist will be with me for three more weeks and she'll have time to show you the ropes."

"Amie, please keep an eye on my house. You still have my key, don't you?" Amie nodded.

"No problem. I made you an appointment to see that condo you wanted to see, over by Marina Cove. You have time to see it, don't you?" Amie asked.

Cici clapped her hands, threw her head back, laughing, and said, "Can't wait to see it."

A week later, Cici drove her car to BWI Airport and parked it in *FASTPARK's* lot. She then took a shuttle to Southwest Airlines.

She nabbed a window seat and gazed out at the clouds. *While I'm out there, not only do I need to help my mom, but I really need to talk to her about a lot that's been bothering me.* It was a long five-and-a-half-hour direct flight to San Diego's airport. Cici went to the baggage claim area, grabbed her suitcase off the rotating belt, and wheeled it outside. The sight of palm trees and the warm breeze on her cheeks felt welcoming. She spotted her stepfather's Equinox outside the baggage area and waved when he pulled up to the curb. They drove to Ocean Beach, about half an hour from the airport. Cici was looking forward to seeing her mother.

"How's she doing, Sam?" asked Cici.

"The operation went well, but boy is she in pain. The physical therapist is with her now. She's going to come three times a week. I'm glad you're here. I have to push her to do the required exercises between the PT's visits. I need your help with that," said Sam.

They pulled into their garage on Sunset Cliffs Boulevard. Cici hugged her mom when she saw her. Despite the operation, she looked fit, tan, and healthy. No evidence of gray showed in her bleached, blonde hair.

Cici loved their two-bedroom, stucco rancher that was a block from the Pacific Ocean. Its red-tiled roof accentuated the pale, yellow house. Orange hibiscus flowers in huge pots decorated the front patio. Sam showed her the guest bedroom, and he let Cici unpack.

"When you finish putting everything in the bureau, come out here. I made margaritas."

"Can't turn that down," Cici said. When she filled the bureau's drawers, she grabbed a drink.

"Your mom can't have one because of the painkillers," Sam said.

Cici's mom said, "Physical therapy is awful. Glad she just left. I hope it does the trick. So happy you're here, Cici. I need someone for company while Sam's at work."

"Isn't Sam able to take some time off now under the circumstances?" asked Cici.

"Yes, his job is only part-time, and he loves being a marshal at the golf course," she said. Sam walked into the bedroom.

"You just don't want me around making you do your exercises," said Sam.

"Cici can help me," she said.

"Have to let her have some fun while she's here," said Sam. "I'll let you two talk." Sam left the room.

"It's so great getting away," said Cici.

"You had a rough time this past year. Are you okay after your ordeal? Greg was despicable. Why did you let him treat you so badly?"

Cici didn't answer her questions right away. "Mom, I've thought a lot about my childhood after dad died. My grandmother treated me badly. Didn't you have any idea what she was like?"

"She was old-school. Very strict with your father. I had no idea she did what she did to you."

"I was stuck with her for five years of hell. I was so young then. I didn't know what to do. I was afraid to tell you before you switched your hours." She explained why she had been afraid.

Her mother said, "It was four years, not five. I'm sorry, Cici. I didn't realize how bad it was, and I should have tried harder to change my hours or work at another hospital."

"I think it really messed me up. My childhood days sucked," said Cici.

"Cici, I lost my husband. I worked like crazy to pay the bills and the mortgage. It was hard."

"I just wish it had been different. I wanted to please you so much because I could never please my grandmother. I studied all the time in high school and hardly went out. I wanted you to think of me as the daughter you always wanted. I still think that way. I never thought I could live up to that. When I met Greg, he made me feel wonderful about myself."

"Do you really think I was a bad mother?"

"Mom, I love you. I'm here for you. My grandmother was cruel. I just wished you could have discovered that sooner, and I wish I had been raised to be a tougher and a more positive person. I think this whole experience with Greg toughened me up. Not that I'm giving him any credit."

Her mother said, "I was so happy you married him. I felt you'd be fine with him even though I was 3,000 miles away. Too bad your good marriage turned for the worst. You kept your marriage troubles from me."

"What could you do? You were out here with Sam. And you were struggling to walk. You had your own problems," said Cici, getting testy.

"A little snippy today, aren't we? Cici, I was so looking forward to seeing you. This conversation is so negative. You're making me feel so guilty."

"Sometimes things need to be said. Getting it out in the open is a good thing," said Cici. "Now, show me those instructions for the exercises your PT wants you to do every day."

The following morning Sam brought Cici and her mother an oatmeal bar from the Java Café for breakfast. "After you help me with my exercises, why don't you drive over to Coronado

Beach and browse the shops in the hotel or tour Balboa Park?" her mother asked.

"Not this trip. Maybe next time," Cici said.

Cici worked diligently, forcing her mother to do her exercises. Her mother complained a little less about her therapy hurting her knees. "I'm glad we had our little chat, Cici. I am proud of you. You look like you've trimmed down a bit. I want you to know that you've always been the daughter I've always wanted. I'm sorry I failed you in not being more observant with your grandmother. It was wonderful having you here helping me. I'm going to miss you so much," said her mother.

The next day Cici walked to the edge of the Sunset Cliffs before she was to catch her flight home. She strolled along the cliffs and marveled at the pink and golden sunsets. *Goodbye San Diego.* She hated goodbyes, but the visit had been good for her.

Cici wore her brown skirt for the trip home and noticed it was too loose as she buttoned it at the waist. She chose a bulky sweater to cover the waistband. It would have to suffice.

It only took four hours to fly back to BWI Airport because of a cooperative tail wind. When Cici entered Amie's house that night, Amie said, "The trip must have done you some good. You've got color in your cheeks, and I don't see any of those muddy, dark circles under your eyes that you used to have."

"You're right, I'm glad I went, but it's great to be home," said Cici. "Looking forward to moving to my new condo on the cove."

Cici's cell phone buzzed. "Hello, Mrs. King. Detective Crabbe here. Good news. They've located your husband's Escalade abandoned in a parking lot off I-95 in North Carolina."

CHAPTER 10

Greg finished his McDonald's barbequed bacon burger, licked his lips, and threw his wrapper out of the car's window. *Gotta abandon the Escalade.* He drove further down a road off I-95 and saw what he was looking for—a car parked in a remote area. He removed its license plates and drove back to where he'd previously noticed a *For Sale* sign on a used Toyota Camry on someone's front yard in Rocky Mount, North Carolina. He left his Escalade in a convenience store parking lot and walked a quarter of a mile back to the Camry. The owner of the Camry was glad to be rid of it, and Greg purchased it for a reasonable price. He drove back to where his Escalade was parked, retrieved the stolen plates from the back seat, fastened the plates to the back of the Toyota Camry, and headed towards I-95. Greg peered into his rearview mirror. He wiped beads of perspiration off his forehead with his handkerchief. He stopped outside Fayetteville and bought a hair coloring kit, a Carolina Panthers T-shirt, a pair of jeans, a pair of low-magnifier readers, and a golf cap. Greg pulled into a rest stop on I-95 and changed into his new digs in a bathroom stall. He drove further south and found a cheesy-looking motel off the main highway in Latta, South Carolina. He checked in and prepaid for a night's stay. Standing in front of the sink in his bathroom, he changed his hair color from black to blonde. "Cool," he said, looking into the mirror. Greg glanced out the motel room window. *Looks quiet out there.* He put on his golf cap and new glasses, grabbed his bag, and drove towards US Route 301, not wanting to stay on I-95.

He stopped in Beaufort, South Carolina, and found a cozy sports bar, where he asked for a scotch. Greg watched their numerous flat screens and saw no news about him being a wanted fugitive. He downed his scotch and headed back to his car. He was concerned the license plates would be reported missing, so he ditched the car when he arrived in Savannah. There, Greg purchased a bus ticket to Jacksonville, Florida. He found a phone booth at Mini Mart in Savannah and dialed Della's cell phone.

"Thank God you answered," Greg said. "How are you?" he asked. "I didn't have the jail's number, so I took a chance and called your cell phone."

Della said, "I never thought I'd hear from you. My brother is planning to post bond for me. I wish your wife would have a change of heart. I want her to drop the charges," Della said, feeling her heart thumping.

"Not a chance," said Greg. "That's what provoked me. She adamantly refused to drop the charges."

"I want to apologize to her. Where are you? What in the world happened? On the news I heard you kidnapped and assaulted your wife. Greg, tell me it's not true."

"It's true." He explained the huge mess he'd created. "I was livid, and wanted you freed from jail."

"I can't believe it's come to this," she said. "If you're caught, you're facing a long time in prison."

"Della, I'm going to start a new life in hopes of never being caught. I know this is a lot to ask, but if I'm not caught, and have a decent lifestyle one day under a new name, would you consider joining me?"

"Uh, I don't know, Greg. I guess it could depend on how long it takes. I'm sick of how everything is going down. I feel so bad you did what you did because of me."

"Think about it. Please come and be with me. You can't call me. I don't have a phone. Right now, anyway, you can't. When I get settled safely somewhere, I'll contact you."

"Seriously, Greg, doesn't this whole thing seems hopeless for us?" she asked.

"Let's just see what happens. Trust me."

"Okay. I'll trust you, but I hope it doesn't take too long for you to get safely settled," she said.

Disappointed, he then hung up. *I was hoping she'd be a little more positive.*

Greg got on the bus headed for Jacksonville, Florida. He didn't want Della to know where he was. Not just yet. He'd wait until later to let her know.

⚔

The morning skies were clear when Cici woke up. In the guest bedroom, Amie had gently roused Cici. "Made coffee in the kitchen for you."

Groggy, yawning, and stretching out her arms, Cici said, "Amie, thanks for letting me stay here. I'll have a cup of coffee. That sounds good, and I better get dressed. Pat and his partner will be here soon."

Cici engaged the help from Pat, his partner, and Amie to help her move.

Cici said, "I hope we get it all done before the storm comes."

From the U-Haul truck, they unloaded a contemporary, white couch Cici had bought from a consignment shop. It had been greatly reduced after being there for two months. She took several lamps, the bedroom set in the guest bedroom, and some other items from her other house to decorate her condo. Her one-bedroom, rented condo looked out onto the Assawoman Bay, and she could see the Route 90 Bridge from her third-floor sliders. She loved the high ceilings and her view of the cove and marina. A mini place like the house she had. She spent the remainder of the day arranging furniture, hanging pictures, and unpacking boxes. The 30-mile per hour winds and heavy rains the weatherman had predicted never came, just some light showers.

Her cell phone vibrated. It was her neighbor, Mr. Cole, whose house they'd kept an eye on while they were away for six months. "Cici, I'm calling because I heard there was a terrible storm heading towards Ocean City, and I was worried about flooding in Ocean Pines, like we had once before. Is everything okay?" Mr. Cole asked.

"Yes, it kind of skirted us. It rained only a little. The storm quickly went out to the sea. Sorry, I guess I should have called you. Your house is fine."

"No, that's okay. I'm sure you would have called if there was a problem. Glad we dodged it," said her neighbor.

"Things around here haven't been normal to say the least. I have some shocking news to tell you. Guess you hadn't heard. First of all, I've moved to a condo near the Yacht Club. Second, and here's the shocker, the police are looking for Greg. He's a fugitive. He tried to kill me."

"What? Kill you? Horrific. That's incredulous. Cici, are you okay? I can't believe what I'm hearing."

"I told you it was shocking. Not sure I can talk about it. There probably will be a trial, and I'll have to testify. Rest assured, I'll look after your house, now that he's not around to do that." She hung up shortly after their brief conversation. *Not in the mood to talk about all of it with my neighbor.*

When Cici was just about to dial her lawyer's number, her phone rang and beat her to doing it.

"Hello. Mrs. King? This is Bradley Simms. I'm Della Summer's lawyer."

"What do you want from me?" asked Cici.

"I am calling on behalf of my client. She would like to speak with you, and she'd like to see you in person. She wants to apologize for what she's done to you. Would you consider seeing her?"

"I . . . I don't know. That's unusual, isn't it? Last time I gave in, and let her in my house, she tried to beat me up."

"She's very distraught over her behavior. She really wants to talk to you. It would be safe. We could conduct your conversation here at the Berlin Police Jail. She would be with me, and you would be in the inmate's visiting area, which is monitored closely by guards. If you're not too busy, she could see you today. I spoke to the warden, and he approved the visit, if you are agreeable. They have strict rules here for visitation."

"I want to bring someone with me," Cici said. Her conscience would bother her if she didn't go.

Two hours later, Cici put makeup over her scratches on her cheeks. She was satisfied they were concealed. She slipped on a pair of slacks that seemed a bit loose on her since the last time she'd worn them. She tightened her belt.

Pat McCombe and she entered the brick facility in Berlin.

"It's peculiar to have a police jail right here in this charming, historic little town of Berlin," said Pat.

Cici was escorted into the visiting room. Pat sat in the corner near the guard. Cinder block walls surrounded four long utility tables and chairs. Mr. Simms greeted her and led her to a table. Cici pulled out her chair, which scraped the painted gray cement floors. She looked up at the small, rectangular windows around the room. Della walked into the room handcuffed. Cici looked at her swollen, black eye where the coffee table book had hit her. Della lowered her head, sat down, and said, "Thank you for coming, Mrs. King. I am truly sorry for the pain I caused you. My intention was only to—"

"I know what your intention was," said Cici.

"I hope you will forgive me. I only recently learned what Greg did to you. I can't believe he would do that. It's terrible. And to think I wanted to marry him. I don't want anything to do with him. I hope he doesn't try to see me."

"I doubt that. He's may be somewhere down south. The police are looking for him," Cici said.

"I know, and I hope he's caught. This whole thing wouldn't have happened to you if I hadn't come to see you that day. It's amazing what love will make you do. My life has turned upside-down. My boss fired me. I certainly get it. But, I'm glad you came to see me. I thought you wouldn't come. It means a lot to me," said Della. "I take back all the mean things I said to you. Again, thank you for coming."

"You're welcome," said Cici and grabbed her purse.

Della went back inside to her cell, waiting for her brother to post her bail. She hoped to leave the jail in an hour.

"Mrs. King, wait," said Della's lawyer. "She appreciated that you came. She didn't mention it, but the injury to her eye is pretty serious." He went on to explain.

"Sorry to hear that," Cici said.

"Ms. Summer told me that Mr. King called her. She was nervous and tried to keep him on the line in case he mentioned where he was. Detective Crabbe thought that your husband might try to contact Ms. Summer, so he allowed her to keep her cell phone. Mr. King did say he would be contacting her again, but he withheld information about where he was," said Simms.

"Why couldn't the police trace his phone call?" Cici asked.

"Well, they did. It took longer than they thought. He called from a phone booth in Georgia. But what I was trying to say is, if and when he contacts Ms. Summer again, she's going to tell the police where he's hiding out. Hopefully he'll tell her this time where he is. He told her he wants her to join him when he gets settled somewhere. I'm hoping he'll call her soon."

"Do the police know this?" Cici asked.

Bradley Simms nodded. "Thanks again for seeing her," he said. "I know it wasn't easy for you. I wish you well."

Cici then walked out of the room with Pat.

"She asked you to recant your statement, I bet," said Pat.

"No, she didn't. Did you see that black eye I gave her? I actually felt sorry for her."

"Don't get too carried away," said Pat.

"No, I'm not. I'm thinking I might drop the charges," said Cici.

"You're kidding," said Pat.

"Pat, she was fired from her job."

"It's not your fault," said Pat.

"What do I have to do to drop the charges?" asked Cici.

"Well, you have to write your reasons down in an official Drop Charges Affidavit and take it to the police station. Then you have to contact the county district attorney to discuss your wishes to drop the charges. The state will make a determination. The prosecution has a great deal of discretion concerning the proceedings. It may be up to the prosecutor in the long run, but if you're not on his side, he usually can't win. And you can refuse to testify for the prosecution."

"I want to do this, but I have another matter to take care of first, after you drop me off," said Cici.

Cici called Frank Vaughn. She really wanted to move on with her life and find out what her options were, now that Greg was a fugitive. "Can we move this process along, even though we don't know where my husband is?" she asked.

"Yes, and now you really have grounds for a fault-based divorce. He committed a very serious crime. When he's caught, he'll be put in prison and be tried. I'm sure he'll be found guilty and will serve a long term in jail. In other words, it shouldn't be difficult to prove it's his fault the marriage crumbled and is beyond hope."

"What about my getting financial support? I may be waiting a long time, depending on when he's caught," said Cici.

"You have plenty in the bank right now. You are entitled to use your joint funds. No worries," said Vaughn. "I'm sure he'll be caught soon, Cici. If you and your spouse are in agreement about all the aspects of the divorce with regard to debts, the division of assets, and spousal support, we can file the petition for divorce and then arrange to serve him. There is another form to complete while he serves his sentence in jail, and that will be filed with the court."

"It sounds complicated," said Cici.

"It's really not, Mrs. King. Not in this case I feel. After your husband signs the petition, I'll draw up the settlement agreement, which he will have to sign. That will be filed with the court, and you may have to appear in court to answer questions. At the end of the hearing, your divorce will be granted."

"What kind of questions?"

"Questions about your marriage and the divorce agreement."

"What if he refuses to sign?" asked Cici.

"I'm dwarfish in height, Mrs. King, but you have an aggressive advocate here, working for your best interests. Be patient, and I assure you, your goals will be reached. He committed a crime against you. This will be easy. It may go faster than you think."

"Can you help me fill out a Drop Charges Affidavit?" Cici asked.

CHAPTER 11

Greg got off the bus in Jacksonville. He rented a room for the night in Atlantic Beach. He found a laundromat and washed his underwear and shirts. Greg stocked up on some more clothes at Target. *Hope to outsmart the police.* There was no mention of him on TV, but he wasn't that naive. He knew the cops would be looking for him. Especially Crabbe.

Greg dialed Della's number and then quickly hung up before punching in the last digit, bending his head down. His coins dropped back down the slot. He would wait until he felt more secure. Maybe she'd be more positive about joining him. He would travel further south, settle in, and look for a job. He needed to get some fake IDs. Greg felt his disguise was a good one, now that he was growing a beard.

The next day Greg took a bus to St. Augustine, where he contemplated whether he should purchase a car. He decided he needed to get a fake license and social security card before buying a car, and he located a public library. Yellow, blue and green shuttle buses were easy to hop in this town, coming every 20 minutes on A1A. He researched on the internet and discovered he could get a very good counterfeit driver's license produced in China. Instead of using the library's computer, Greg decided he would purchase an iPad, a printer, and a cell phone. He still had plenty of cash, enough to rent a place for a long time. But he had to get a job because he knew his money would eventually run out some day in the future.

Greg hitchhiked 38 miles farther south to Flager Beach and liked the small beach town. He paid cash for a bike and rode around the outskirts, backpack strapped around his shoulders. Many homes were for rent. He spotted a *For Rent* sign in the window of a small, 1970's white-clapboard rancher located near US-1. Greg liked its location. There were no houses on the right or left and only one home was down further on the opposite side. He didn't have to worry about neighbors close by.

He paid the landlord two months rent in advance and scribbled an illegible signature on the lease. His newly, rented home smelled musty and was minimally furnished. But it did have a washer and dryer. Greg set up his iPad on the dining room table and set to work. He filled out and downloaded a fake social security form and followed the necessary steps to create a card. He was able to have a driver's license as well as a birth certificate shipped to his address from China, after giving them the necessary information on the internet. He was no longer Greg King but Blake Thompson. He liked the sound of his new name. It had been easy to create a fake ID online, but he knew it may not be of high quality. And the police could probably tell the difference. But that was if he were caught.

Greg decided to buy a motorcycle. He chose a Honda Grom with a 125cc single cylinder. He parked his cycle near The Pelican, an ocean-front restaurant in Flager Beach. He sat outside at a table on the deck facing the ocean and ordered a fish taco. The Basa fish was tasty. He asked to see the manager.

"By any chance are you hiring?" he asked.

"My chef is looking for an assistant. What's your background?" he said. The manager was impressed that Greg knew a lot about fish and how to filet them. Even though Basa had no bones, they served all kinds of fish to filet. Greg was introduced to the chef.

"The way you prepared the fish taco was delicious," Greg said. The two of them chatted and Greg couldn't believe his luck. He was hired on the spot. The money wasn't great, but he could get by. Greg would work mostly in the kitchen and occasionally wait tables.

Greg's new life for approximately a month was moving along nicely. In fact, it seemed perfectly normal. He kept to himself when he wasn't working. He maintained a low-key profile and lifestyle. His co-workers at The Pelican were friendly enough and they all got along well. When he wasn't working, he rode his bike along A1A and on the many provided bike paths to keep in shape. And riding his motorcycle on US-1 was a rare treat. Almost as fun as playing golf. But golf would have to come later. He knew time spent in Flager Beach was temporary. Sitting at the dining room table, he scanned a map of the east coast and chose the best way to travel to the Keys. *My last stop. Della will love it there. I'd like to have a boat again.*

He was assigned to wait on tables at lunchtime the following week. Jimmy Buffet was appearing at the convention center in Daytona Beach, and the surrounding beach towns were expecting overflow crowds because of it. Inside The Pelican's dining area were dark-paneled walls and polished wooden tables and chairs. It was very rustic, but beachy. Pictures of pelicans were nailed to the walls. Greg walked out of the kitchen and inhaled the fresh, ocean air. The smell of burgers being grilled back in the kitchen made his mouth water. Greg wore his Pelican T-shirt and pale yellow Bermuda shorts when he approached a table of four elderly people. He stood behind a couple, each sporting white hair and facing the other two.

"Hi, I'm your waiter. My name is Blake. Can I get you a Happy Hour cocktail or something else to drink?"

The man whose back was to him whipped around and looked up at him. "Greg?"

Greg's eyes widened. "I'm sorry, sir. You are mistaken. My name is Blake."

"What, is this a joke? Come on, Greg. You know me. Fred Cole, your neighbor. I'd recognize your voice anywhere. I can tell it's you even with your blonde hair and beard."

Greg squinted and recognized his next-door neighbor, who was staying in St. Augustine for six months. Greg said, "I'll be right back."

"Did you see that?" the neighbor said to his wife.

Nodding she said, "Yes, I agree. It was him."

"What's going on? Who was that?" the other couple asked, unable to hide their curiosity.

"He's a fugitive from the law." The 69-year-old neighbor rose from the table and limped into the kitchen, where Greg had disappeared. Raising his voice and pointing, he said to the chef, "That man who is our waiter is on the run. The cops are looking for him. He's not really Blake somebody," said Mr. Cole.

The chef threw a towel over his shoulder and said, "I wondered why he left in a flash without a word. He just raced out of here and sped off on his motorcycle."

The neighbor hobbled to the kitchen's exit and looked outside. He scanned the parking lot, moving his head to the right, then to the left. He spotted Greg speeding away on his cycle on A1A, smoke trailing behind him. He dialed 911.

Greg headed home and leaned his cycle against the back wall of his house. He hurried inside, gathered his things, and tossed them into his backpack. He hopped onto his motorcycle and sped down US-1.

"God, please make this cycle go fast," Greg said. He revved the engine. *What are the chances of my bumping into my neighbor? Should I get off US-1? Where do I go now? Daytona's the next stop. Will I make it?*

The fake ID was worthless now. *In Daytona I'll get a bus ticket and head west to the gulf side, maybe Tampa. Hate to get rid of the cycle.*

It wouldn't be long until he'd reach Daytona. On US-1, behind him, he heard sirens. He glanced over his left shoulder and saw flashing lights. The police cars were coming closer.

He pulled off to the side at a gas station. Greg motored around to the back. Jumping off his cycle and grabbing his backpack, he ran towards the woods. Three police cars swerved into the gas station. Three cops got out of their vehicles and ran around to the back of the station. They spotted the overturned motorcycle and drew their weapons. One police officer scouted the area all around the gas station. The other two hastened into the woods.

Greg's brow was covered in perspiration. He dashed around trees and shrubs. Looking behind him, he didn't see anyone chasing him. He kept running. He couldn't take the chance to catch his breath. The woods were endless. He hoped to find a way out because it would be getting dusk soon, and he wouldn't be able to see where he was going much longer.

The three policemen split up. One went to the right, one ran straight ahead, and the other veered left. Greg saw an opening. Beyond the woods, he spotted a large development of Spanish-style, stucco homes. They were all cookie-cutters with red rooftops and one-car garages. One section was built around a lake. Greg headed towards those houses. He stopped behind a shed of one of the homes, resting his arms on his bent knees to catch his breath. His lungs burned.

Greg approached the rear of a house surrounded by numerous palms and evergreens. It was without a lanai, and a bluestone patio and screened door to the inside of the house took its place in the back yard. Greg opened the unlocked screen door. Beyond the kitchen, he saw a small hallway. He crept softly towards the front of the house. There in the living room was an elderly lady with gray hair, sitting in a wheelchair, petting her tan, Persian cat. He startled her when she looked up. "Don't hurt me. My money is in the bedroom." She held her cat tightly in her arms.

Greg asked, "Is anyone else here in your house?"

"No, just me," she said.

"The police are looking for me. They probably will search all the homes in this neighborhood. I need a place to hide in your house where they won't find me." She stared at him wide-eyed.

Greg grabbed the cat from her. "Don't hurt my cat, please," she said. Her arms shook as she held them out to Greg. She said, "Give her to me."

"Lady, I won't hurt you, but if the cops come here and you tell them I'm hiding in here, I swear I'll kill your cat," Greg said.

"No, please no. I'll do as you say. I promise. Don't hurt my baby," she said with tears in her eyes.

"Now, show me where I can hide."

She rolled the wheels of her wheelchair over the hardwood floor into the hallway. Greg followed her. Above her in the ceiling was a square-like shaped entry into the attic. She pointed above to the spot. "That's the way into the attic. It's a remote controlled electric automatic attic stair. The remote for it is in the kitchen drawer under the sink." Wasting no time, Greg made his way into the kitchen and found the remote to the attic stair. He also nabbed a sharp knife from the drawer. The old lady gasped when he returned, seeing the shiny knife in his hand.

The old lady cried out, "Please don't stab her."

Using the remote, Greg opened the electric attic door and the stairs automatically came down. He put the remote into his pocket. With the cat under his arm, he climbed up the ladder. He placed the cat inside the attic along with his backpack. Before closing the door with the remote, he said to the elderly woman below, "If the police come here, tell them no one has come to your house. Tell them you saw a man running in the direction of the lake. When they are out of sight and they're gone, let me know. I'll leave when I know there's no sign of them anywhere, and you can have your cat back. Remember what I said. Don't say a word that I'm here, or it's goodbye to your cat." He waved the knife in the air, then closed the door with the remote.

Once inside the attic, he looked around for the cat but couldn't find her right away. He tucked himself under the eave next to a mattress that partially hid him. He waited. *Ah, there she is.* Greg felt the cat rub herself against his leg and purr. He held the cat in his lap and petted her.

Greg heard the doorbell and knocking on the door downstairs from his position in the attic. He listened to male voices but couldn't quite make out what everyone was saying. *Had to be the cops.* He heard heavy footsteps on the wood floor below. Wheelchair lady told them he wasn't hiding in her house. Would she remember to mention that she saw a man running toward the lake? If she really loved her cat and believed her pet would be killed, she should do a convincing job. Greg heard a door slam. He remained still.

He heard her voice calling up to him. Staying well away from the electric stair up in the attic, and sitting in her wheelchair, she yelled, "You can come down now. They're gone."

Greg punched the remote button and the stair descended. Greg climbed down. "Give me my cat," she said.

"Not until I'm certain the coast is clear." Holding the cat, Greg peered out the bedroom and living room windows. A car was in the driveway. All was quiet. She rolled her wheelchair into the living room. "Is that your car?" asked Greg.

She told him it was her car. "I was so worried when they discovered that my back door was not locked. I thought they wouldn't believe me and think that I was hiding you in the house. They searched under the beds, in the closets, in my outside shed, in the car, and in the garage."

Greg went into the kitchen and opened the refrigerator door. He grabbed some grapes and pasta salad to eat with his one free hand. He nabbed a Diet Coke. Greg searched for more food and found pretzels and cookies to munch on. He cut the telephone wire on her wall phone. Walking back into the living room he asked, "Do you have a cell phone?"

"No."

He peeked out the window. Still holding the cat he said, "I need to have the keys to your car."

"The keys are in the sofa table drawer," she quickly said. "Give me my cat." Greg put the cat back into her lap. She held her to her heart and kissed the top of the cat's head. He grabbed his backpack and started the engine of her Toyota Avalon. Greg drove out of the neighborhood, not knowing where to go. He checked the gas gauge and saw he had half a tank. *Can't stop to get gas nearby. Cops may be sniffing around.*

Greg found his way to I-4 and headed from Daytona to Tampa. He passed a sign on the highway saying, "140 miles to Tampa." That would take him about two hours if he didn't stop anywhere. Greg stayed within the speed limit, but wished he could go faster. He stopped at a 24-hour Walmart and parked the car at the end of the last row that bordered a wooded area. He went inside and purchased some tools. Outside near his parked car, he crouched down and switched license plates from another car to his. After an hour on the road, his eyes drooped, and he nodded off for a second. He jerked awake and stopped at the next rest area. He bought a chocolate candy bar, hoping the caffeine would keep him alert.

When Greg arrived in Tampa a little after 1:00 a.m., he filled up the tank. He asked the cashier where the closest hotel was. He drove to a Hampton Inn and parked in its lot away from the entrance. He paid cash for a room with a double bed and fell asleep like a baby in its mother's arms.

In the morning, Greg woke up with a start. He rubbed his eyelids and squinted at the sun's morning light gleaming through the slats of the Venetian blinds. He left his room, grabbed an apple and bottled water from the continental breakfast table, and headed for Marco Island. It was about 181 miles if he drove on I-75. It took him two hours and 35 minutes. He pulled into the parking lot of the Flamingo Motel and checked into room number 8. The motel was small, only offering 11 rooms and only stretching half a block in length.

Greg was dying to go to the beach. He bought a solid green Guy Harvey bathing suit in a shop near the beach and was dressed in it when he came out of the dressing room. He paid 70 dollars for the suit in cash and stuffed his clothes into his backpack. He walked to the beach after he locked the back-pack inside the trunk of the old lady's car.

The stretch along the gulf was beautiful. Greg's feet weren't used to the sand composed of tiny, crushed shells. He spread SPF 50 lotion on his skin and jumped into the water, enjoying its warmth. He walked back to a spot on the crunchy sand and sat down. He observed the people on the beach. One skinny girl in a thong bathing suit was sitting alone on her towel, sunbathing and talking on her cell phone. She put her phone in her beach bag, got up, and walked down to the water's edge. She stuck her toe in the water and stepped further in. Greg walked over to her towel, picked up her beach bag, and removed her cell phone from the bag. He left the beach and headed for his car. He dialed Della's number after parallel parking the Avalon on the side of the road, next to the curb instead of in the motel's parking lot.

"Hi, gorgeous. It's me. How are you?" asked Greg.

"It's you! I'm fine. So glad to hear from you finally. Are you okay?" Della asked.

"You sound nervous. Are you out of jail and home yet?"

"Yes, I'm great now that you called. I'm not nervous. I just dropped a tumbler and was picking up some broken glass off the kitchen floor," said Della.

"Oh, well, don't cut yourself. I miss you, babe. I need you with me. I want to see you."

"I miss you too. Where are you? Are you safe?" she asked.

"Yes, I'm safe," said Greg.

"I want to be with you too. I've been waiting for your call. I was so worried about you," she said. "I wasn't sure you'd call me again."

"Of course I would call you again. When's the earliest you can meet me?" asked Greg.

"I can come after I pack some things," Della said. "I want to do this if you say it's safe."

"It is. You'll have to make a plane reservation to get here."

"Where do you want me to fly to?" Della asked.

"Marco Island," he said. "You will love it here."

Hulk called Crabbe. "Guess what? We heard from Della Summer. She said that Greg King told her where he was. She told him she would fly down and meet him at the Flamingo Motel, where he's staying," said Hulk.

"That's the best news I've heard in a long time," said Crabbe. He packed his bag and left to hop a plane to Florida. He flew into the Fort Myers airport and took Uber to Marco Island. He notified the police there of Greg's whereabouts.

Forty-five minutes later, Crabbe arrived at the sheriff's office near the Marco Island Jail, where they were waiting for him. The sheriff, his deputy, and Crabbe headed to the motel. They parked their unmarked police vehicle on the street. The deputy got out of the car and walked into the motel's office. He went back to the patrol car. "He's in room 8 now."

The three of them walked to the motel, careful not to be seen. Crabbe stood on one side of the door to Greg's room, gun in his hand. The sheriff stood on the other side, and the deputy went around the back of the motel. Not hearing a sound inside, they both kicked the door in.

Once inside, Crabbe heard the shower running. He banged on the bathroom door. "Come on out, Greg. We've got you," said Crabbe. The bathroom door slowly opened. Crabbe had his gun pointed at the door. Greg stepped out of the bathroom, the bottom half of his body covered with a towel. Color drained from Greg's face. He was speechless, but his eyes said it all.

"Get dressed," said Crabbe. The sheriff also held his gun on him. The deputy entered the room.

"Where's the car you stole?" asked Crabbe. Greg remained silent. "The elderly woman's daughter-in-law told us what you did. You really are a mean bastard. Threatening a poor, old woman that you would kill her cat. It will be a pleasure snapping the cuffs on you and bringing you back to throw you in the can. You couldn't hide forever, you know," said Crabbe.

"How did you find me?" asked Greg.

"Your lovely ex-girlfriend called us and told us where you were." Greg lowered his head. "Can't say I like the blonde hair." Greg raised his head and glared at Crabbe. "Come on, get moving. We're going for a little plane ride back home," said Crabbe.

Greg did as he was told, no longer the Alpha male. Crabbe enjoyed hearing the snap of the handcuffs around Greg's wrists. "Let's go," he said. "Deputy, check to see if that silver Toyota Avalon is outside near the motel."

On the jet back to Ocean Pines, sitting next to Greg, Crabbe ordered a beer. *Not supposed to drink on the job, but need to calm the nerves. And this calls for a celebration.* He turned to Greg, "We looked for you everywhere. All over North Carolina, South Carolina, Georgia, and finally Florida. You really cost the taxpayers. Have to give it to you. You kept us busy," said Crabbe. "You traveled 1,143 miles almost all the way to the southern tip of Florida."

Greg grinned. "I never knew how easy it could be to get a new name and start a new life. I liked it in Flager Beach, until my neighbor recognized me. No stress at all before that happened."

"Well, I guarantee you, you're heading for a lot of stress with a trial coming up and spending time in jail," said Crabbe.

Greg wiped the smile off his face. He shifted uncomfortably in his seat. His hands felt clammy in the handcuffs. The stewardess stared at his wrists.

"Don't like the attention you're getting? People staring at you in handcuffs?" Crabbe snickered.

"I'll get a good lawyer," said Greg. "Not the one you recommended."

"Good luck," said Crabbe.

Crabbe notified Cici when he landed. "Don't worry, Mrs. King. He can't bother you anymore. We're locking him up."

"Wonderful news," said Cici. "Now I can really move forward with the divorce proceedings and more importantly, my life. So much to do, but no more monster."

"No more monster," said Crabbe.

CHAPTER 12

Bail was denied because of the seriousness of the charges against Greg. It was argued that he could be a flight risk. The judge couldn't trust him if he was released. Greg was held in the Snow Hill County Jail, awaiting trial.

Greg called an attorney when given a phone privilege. He had hired a prominent defense attorney named Mike Stern from Baltimore to represent him. Greg assured him he had the funds from his farm inheritance to pay his fee.

Greg looked at the clock a few times, waiting in a small room outside his cell to meet with his lawyer. Stern finally walked in, introduced himself, and said to Greg, "They really have tight security here." He looked around before sitting down. "This room is a bit cramped." The small room's gray walls were dingy, and a fluorescent light shone down on Greg at the only table in the room. Two chairs were placed under the table facing each other. An officer stood in the corner. He stared ahead with his arms and hands clasped together in a V-shape under his belly.

Stern surpassed Greg in height. His single breasted jacket was classically stylish and made him look trim. His fitted black pants hugged his legs like Bradley Cooper's at an Academy Awards ceremony. Stern was in his late 40s. He was balding a bit at the crown, but otherwise wore his coal black hair a little long on the sides. His handshake was strong.

"Glad to meet you in person," Greg said. "Thanks for representing me and driving down here from Baltimore."

When the subject of the fees came up again, Greg said he spoke to the warden about the money he had in his backpack. The warden said he had the money locked in a safe. Greg said, "He will verify that I have the funds to pay you." Stern nodded, but was still going to meet with the warden about the funds.

"I've thoroughly familiarized myself with your case. I've read your statements and the police reports," said Stern.

Greg watched him press the *Play* button on his tape recorder. *Nothing like getting started right away.* Greg cleared his throat and was ready for his questioning.

Stern did the preliminaries—the date, time, location and name of his client. "Okay, in summary, you're here because you're facing charges of involuntary manslaughter, assault, attempted murder, and kidnap—"

Greg interrupted him, waving his hand. "I'm aware of all the charges. Let me explain what happened." Greg told him his self-defense story and what he thought Merv's motive was for robbing and trying to murder Cici. "He initiated my actions that led to his death. He's the guilty one, not me. I was fighting for my life. It was him or me. I'm not a murderer."

"Tell me about what happened to your wife after that."

"We had a very heated argument." He told Stern about his wanting Cici to drop the charges on his girlfriend and her refusal to do so. "Things got intense. I may have shoved her in my anger—I don't recall—and she tripped, hitting her head on the ceramic tile floor."

"Mrs. King said you struck her. She woke up in the trunk of her car. Did you put your wife there and bind her arms and legs?" asked Stern.

"I didn't put her in the trunk. I didn't bind her arms and legs. When she told me she wouldn't drop the assault charges on my girlfriend, I saw red. My girlfriend was facing a jail sentence, she'd lost her job, but she had remorse for what she did," said Greg. "I wanted to marry her."

"This isn't about her; it's about you."

"Wait, let me finish," said Greg. He chewed on his bottom lip. "I couldn't control my emotions and actions. I don't know what came over me. The minute I saw Cici lying unconscious on the floor from her fall, realization hit me. I thought she might press charges and blame me for it. I panicked. My mind was spinning and completely muddled. I put her in the car seat next to me, and I started to drive her to the ER, especially since she recently had that injury to her head. But then I wasn't sure if that was that right thing to do. I got scared. I didn't want to go back to jail if she lied and said I had assaulted her. She was furious I had been seeing Ms. Summer. To get even with me, she just made up that story that I kidnapped her and tried to kill her."

Stern said, "You drove her to an abandoned golf course, Mrs. King reported."

"No, no."

"The cops found a hammer under the front seat of her car. That doesn't look good," said Stern.

"Believe me I didn't have any intention of killing her. That hammer has always been there. She told me she felt safer having some kind of weapon hidden in her car. She said you never know what can happen to you when you're out driving alone. I drove towards the deserted golf course. I wasn't planning to take her there. She became conscious while sitting next to me. She was mad at me because we'd had that ugly argument about Ms. Summer. She jumped out of the car. She ran into the woods. I stopped the car to look for her. I lost her. I couldn't find her. It's the truth," said Greg.

"According to her, she somehow got free from the tape around her wrists when she was inside the trunk, and then when you opened the trunk, she ran like hell," said Stern. "You tried to find her and ran after her." Stern's serene, cool demeanor was to his credit.

"No, when she jumped out of the car, I yelled to her to wait and not go out there in the darkness. You never know what kind of animals are out there in the night. I yelled to her that I was sorry, and I would take her home," said Greg. "I searched and searched for her, but to no avail. So I went home and waited."

"You were on the run after that. There was an APB out for you," Stern calmly said.

"I panicked again when she didn't show up. I thought she had gone to the police," said Greg.

"You told Amie Weiss that you were with a guy from work when she called you that night to see if you knew where Mrs. King was. Who was that guy?"

"That wasn't the truth. I told her I didn't know where Cici was. I didn't want her to know that she was in the car with me, and I didn't want her to know we had a huge argument."

"This kidnapping charge is going to be a tough one to prove you're not guilty. I need to create reasonable doubt," said Stern.

"I know it doesn't sound good." He chewed on his lip again. "If you think it really looks bad, as a last resort, are you going to ask for a plea bargain?"

"I think you're jumping the gun here," said Stern.

Greg looked at Stern, who remained silent. Greg said, "I had mixed emotions. I didn't know what came over me. It's like I was temporarily out of my mind. I should have taken her to the hospital right away and not debated about what to do if she lied and said I hit her."

"You are facing stiff penalties if you're found guilty on these charges," said Stern. "Now this charge of involuntary manslaughter of Merv Grady... that's the killing of another unintentionally while doing an unlawful act, or a negligent act. If it's gross negligence, you would have been conscious of the risk to human life that your behavior created, and you acted with disregard to human life. The burden falls on the prosecution to prove that you somehow caused Mr. Grady's death. I will cast doubt on you not acting recklessly and not acting dangerously. You were protecting yourself from imminent death or serious harm. Now, this kidnapping charge. It's also a serious matter. You could spend up to 30 years in prison if proven guilty," said Stern. "I can create reasonable doubt on the involuntary manslaughter charge and prove it was justifiable self-defense," said Stern. "But kidnapping, assault, and attempted murder on your wife? That's a problem." Greg raised his hand to his mouth and his fingers squeezed his bottom lip together. "You weren't just taking Mrs. King out for a Sunday drive, and there's a photo showing her face black and blue," said Stern. "Did you have remorse for what happened to your wife?"

"Of course," said Greg.

"Have you spoken to your wife at all and told her you were sorry?" asked Stern.

"No, haven't spoken to her."

"That's too bad. I also want you to know about the prosecuting attorney. His name is Ted Berry. He's a first-rate lawyer.

Berry is tough, but so am I. The lawyers down here call him 'Bear,' but the inmates call him 'Teddy Bear,' just to badger him. He doesn't look like a bear; he's just good at winning cases. He's pretty proud of his record. He played a small role as a D.A. in a movie starring Al Pacino and Robert DeNiro when it was filmed in Baltimore. His office is lined with pictures from the movie."

"Oh brother, a movie star for a prosecutor. That's just great. He and Detective Crabbe are out to get me. Crabbe breathed down my neck a lot." Greg scratched his head. "When's the trial?" asked Greg.

"The trial will take place the end of December," said Stern. Stern started to rise from his seat.

Greg asked, "Do you have time to stay and chat a bit?"

"Why?"

"Well, the guy in my cell isn't exactly someone you want to hold a conversation with," said Greg. "It gets pretty lonely, being in here. You live in Baltimore?" asked Greg.

Stern looked at this watch. "Yes." He sat back down. "Used to live in Bowleys Quarters, but lost our home during Hurricane Isabelle. I live in the heart of the city, near the Inner Harbor. I usually jog three miles two times a week on the path they built circling the restaurants and businesses all the way to Fells Point."

"You look like you're in good shape. You should see my cellmate. He looks like a wrestler. What school did you graduate from?"

"I graduated from University of Maryland Law School and was the kicker for the Terps football team."

"Really? I played quarterback for the Salisbury Sea Gulls. Do you have kids?" asked Greg.

"I have a 13-year-old daughter we adopted from Peru." Stern looked at his watch again and eased out of his chair.

Greg grabbed Stern's arm. The guard stepped forward. "No touching."

"Sorry, wait, just a second, please," Greg said to Stern. "I'm not worried about the involuntary manslaughter charge. I hate to have the other charges end in a plea bargain. I hope you can prove reasonable doubt on those charges. But I trust you will advise me the best thing to do in this case, even if it has to be a plea bargain and you can't prove reasonable doubt." Stern sat back down.

Stern said, "Well, we have to have both sides come to an agreement. It is practical. You can avoid the time and cost of defending yourself at the trial and avoid the risk of a harsher punishment. And you wouldn't have all the publicity. The court system is saved the burden of conducting a trial on every crime charged. Let's just wait and see."

He turned off the tape recorder, gave Greg his business card, and put the recorder back in its case. "My advice to you is to say nothing to anyone at all about your case. I don't recommend you testify. They'll butcher you."

Greg slumped in his chair. *Maybe I should apologize to Cici.* He didn't want to spend 30 or more years in jail for kidnapping. Certainly not life. He didn't want to pay the penalty for the other charges. If proven guilty, he wanted mercy. He had no prior record. Not even a speeding ticket. He hoped his lawyer could work some magic. He was terror-stricken at the thought of being in jail a long time. He felt a glisten of cold sweat on his brow. *Am I on the road to ruin? Maybe Stern thinks it's hopeless. Maybe it is.*

CHAPTER 13

"Amie, I'm apprehensive about the trial and having to testify in front of a million people," said Cici as she took a bite out of her buffalo chicken wrap.

"A million?" said Amie.

"You know what I mean. Can you imagine if Greg was out on bail? I'd be looking over my shoulder all the time," Cici said. "The monster returns to get me. Stalking and chasing me like my grandmother."

"Oh Cici, get a grip. He's locked up tight. Stop worrying."

"You're right, but you have to admit, he was relentless and determined to kill me. I don't think he knows where I am. He might think I live at home, or I'm still with you," said Cici.

"You really don't feel safe, do you?" asked Amie. "Are you still seeing the therapist?"

"Yes. But what if he escapes?" said Cici.

"Not a chance," said Amie.

Cici nodded. "You could be right. I'm acting foolishly."

"Has the prosecutor contacted you?" asked Amie.

"Yes, and we had an initial discussion. He's middle-aged. He's easy to talk to. I found out he was divorced. He has a son. He feels bad about his custody situation. He wishes he could have his son more often. He only sees him 30 percent of the time because his job is so time-consuming. I heard a rumor that he's dating Nancy Kelly on WBOV-TV in the Delmarva area. She's drop-dead gorgeous."

"What's he think about Greg?" asked Amie.

"He thinks Greg is guilty as sin. I have to meet with him again next week."

"He is guilty as sin," said Amie.

"Did I tell you I'm meeting with the district attorney in the local jurisdiction to discuss my wishes to drop the charges against Della Summer?"

"Why do you want to do that? She could have poked your eyes out."

"Not if you keep a heavy book on your coffee table," said Cici. "I got to her first."

"I'm being serious, Cici. I don't understand you sometimes, Cici."

"I'm being serious too. When Della walked back to her cell that day after I visited her, her lawyer told me she has traumatic iritis from the book I threw at her. It resulted in her having permanent decreased vision in her one eye. I feel sorry for her."

"I don't," said Amie.

"My conscience would bother me if she spent time in jail," said Cici.

"That's not a convincing reason to drop the charges, Cici," Amie said.

Cici quickly changed the subject and later that night the two of them watched a scary movie on Showtime.

The next morning Cici met with the district attorney, Jane Fields, in her office. Her office was huge, and windows behind her desk faced a funeral home and Victorian houses lining the street. It was also located near the Berlin Police Jail.

Cici introduced herself and noticed her curvy figure. Her hair was coiled in a top-knot and her lips looked like they were collagen-inflated. Her thickly applied, black mascara enhanced her long eyelashes. She had a large bust, broad hips, and a small waist. Smartly dressed in her blue suit and high heels, she walked over to her desk and asked Cici to take a seat. She was probably the most attractive brunette and best dressed woman in Berlin.

"I've read your affidavit, but I want to discuss this a little more with you. You pressed charges against Ms. Summer. Assault and battery is a serious charge. Ms. Summer acted in a threatening manner and put you in fear of immediate harm. Didn't you feel you were in imminent danger?"

"Yes."

"Let's see here . . ." she read on. "Ms. Summer put her hands on you, shook you, slapped you, pulled your hair, and scratched your face. This is considered second-degree assault. She could face up to 10 years imprisonment, a fine not to exceed $2,500, and a misdemeanor reflected on her permanent record."

"I've read the police report. It does not say that I attacked her back. It does not say I gave her a severe eye injury. It does not say she was fired from her job. It does not say she had remorse. I submitted an amendment of the report in writing."

"I have it here on my desk," Ms. Fields said.

"I am not interested in sending the case to trial," said Cici. Cici lowered her head, "I feel she has suffered enough. Please consider dropping the charges, Ms. Fields."

"Mrs. King, making changes to a police report doesn't guarantee that I will consider dropping the charges. I will contact you with my decision, Mrs. King."

⌑

Greg hovered begrudgingly over his frank-and-beans dinner. He was moved to another cell and shared it with another inmate. In the room was a bunk bed, commode, and desk. Greg thought a flat screen would have been nice. Not much light brightened the room from a small, barred window.

Greg didn't care for the looks of his 31-year-old cellmate, Buzz Lynch, who was also awaiting trial. He was toned and fit. Not an ounce of flab on him. *Did he do push-ups in here?* With his stocky frame, he stood a little shorter than Greg. His prominent facial scars showed he'd had a bout with acne. He had a tattooed teardrop under his right eye. What was that about? His brownish hair was styled in a spiky Mohawk. *Is there a barber around here? His crooked nose must have been broken a few times. How do you make conversation with a Neanderthal? Crap. Just my luck to be stuck in here with him.*

Neanderthal man began to speak. "What did they get you for?"

Greg swallowed the last of his hot dog. "My lawyer has to prove I was justified in shooting a man. It was in self-defense," said Greg. *No way am I telling him the other charges.*

"Hah, I've heard that one before," he said. "So it was murder, right?"

"No," said Greg. "It wasn't." It was all Greg could say.

"Hope you have a good lawyer."

"Why are you here?" asked Greg.

"I'm being charged with second-degree assault after attacking my roommate. We were in a parking lot at the Tangers

Outlet on Route 50 and began arguing. I tackled him to the ground and left. My roommate accused me of slamming him against a truck and choking him. The cops arrested me, and here I am," he said.

"Any witnesses?" asked Greg.

"Yeah, one. My former girlfriend," said Buzz.

"That sucks," said Greg. "You like your lawyer?" asked Greg.

"Yeah, I guess. The trial is soon," he said.

Better watch my back with this guy.

Greg met with Mike Stern the following week. They skimmed over the events again, and Greg told him all about his background.

"How do you feel towards your wife?" Stern asked.

"Well, you know I'm in love with someone else. My wife is filing for divorce. When her lawyer gives me the settlement papers, I'll probably sign them."

Of course I'll sign them, he thought. *Cici doesn't want any of the assets.*

Greg asked, "Do you have anything positive to say about my current court case coming up?"

"I put some feelers out. I don't think the prosecutor is agreeable to negotiating a plea," said Stern.

Greg pounded the table with his fists. "Shit, are you serious? Must be because of my wife's insistence," said Greg. "She can be a witch when she wants to be."

"No, Bear isn't budging right now," Stern said. "You really messed up big time. Even if a plea deal was made, the judge has to approve it in the end. Look, Mr. King, you have to realize these are very serious charges. The prosecutor feels the same way and right now he wants you to have the maximum penalty. I'm sorry."

"Great. That's just great," clenching his fists. "So now what do I do? I could spend a long time in jail."

"I'll do my best," said Stern.

Greg went back to his cell, where he saw Buzz sitting on the bottom bunk, hunched over, with his head down and his eyes staring at the cement floor. A little leery of approaching him, Greg finally asked, "What's the matter with you?"

Sitting on the edge of the bed, Buzz ran his fingers through his hair, messing up his Mohawk. He said, "My lawyer called and said they had another witness who supports what my ex-girlfriend said she saw. Just my luck."

"Humph." Greg was silent a second. "Did you do what they said?"

He blurted out, "Hell, yes! But I thought my lawyer could get me off. I'm so pissed off."

"Sorry, man. That sucks," Greg said.

"It's a losing game now," Buzz said. "I used to be engaged to my roommate's girlfriend. When she met my roommate, she gradually lost interest in me. He stole her away from me. I've held a grudge against him ever since she left me. That's what the argument was about. I hated him for what he did. I hate her now too. She even kept the engagement ring I gave her. In that parking lot, in the heat of the moment, I wanted to strangle him to death."

"Don't blame you one bit," Greg said. "Lawyers." Thinking about his meeting with Stern, he said, "What good are they?"

CHAPTER 14

Jane Fields contacted Cici. "Mrs. King, I'm calling to tell you about my decision concerning Ms. Summer."

"Are you going to drop the charges?" asked Cici.

"Not exactly, but I agreed to her serving her entire sentence on probation, without any jail time. But there will be no option for the charges to be dismissed. She will have a conviction on her record."

"How long is the probation period?" asked Cici.

"Two years."

"At least she doesn't have to stay in jail," Cici said. "I'm sorry to hear the charges weren't dropped."

"Mrs. King, in my opinion, she was a breath away from being charged with a more serious crime. You are a very lucky woman you weren't hurt worse than you were."

Cici thought about what Amie said. *Yeah, she could have poked my eyes out.*

Later that day, Cici met with the prosecutor, Mr. Berry. Ted Berry had dull gray hair which matched his double breasted jacket. His hazel eyes sparkled when he spoke. "Need to prep you for the trial December 27," said Mr. Berry.

"I'm a little nervous about testifying," Cici said.

"I understand. This is a big deal, and you've been through so much," said Mr. Berry.

They discussed Cici's traumatic time again. "Just tell the jury exactly what happened. No need to fall for the opposing explanations. Your husband's lawyer may make it out to be not as bad as it sounds. How do you feel towards your husband?"

"I don't love him anymore. I'd be crazy if I did. He's evil. I don't feel sorry for him at all."

"Good. Glad to hear it. The trial will deal with four charges. Merv Grady's and your three. First of all, the defense lawyer is going to try to prove that self-defense is justified on Greg's part. Now, in your case, you will have to explain what happened from the time of your argument to when you left the deserted golf course. Let the jury hear how that all played out. You'll also be asked questions about your marriage and his behavior."

"Okay," said Cici. "Will you go over what I should and shouldn't say or what the best answers should be to proposed questions by the Defense?"

"Yes, of course. So, let's get started," Bear said.

⚵

It was a cold day in December for Greg's trial. One would have thought most of the residents in Ocean Pines were in Snow Hill. There were cars everywhere. Snow Hill, the county seat of Worcester County, and location of government offices, was about a 25-minute ride south of Ocean Pines.

Amie, Pat, and Cici proceeded to the double doors of the courthouse and walked through the security checkpoint once inside. They took the elevator up to the second floor. They sat in the front row. It wasn't long before the pews became packed with people.

Greg sat 11 feet away, in front of Cici and to her right. His beard and blonde hair were gone. He was wearing a tan suit and looked a little thinner, but he still made a good impression in his outfit. Greg's palms were sweaty. He frowned when he saw Cici sitting in the first row behind him. He noticed her classic-looking V-neck black dress and that she was wearing pearls. *All gussied up. Why couldn't she sit way in the back? Wish I didn't feel so edgy.* He had to look composed and not jittery. Greg wiped his hands on his pants. He glanced at the spectators and 12 jurors while waiting for the judge to enter the courtroom.

The jury consisted of seven women and five men. He watched the jurors periodically glance at him. One was exceptionally attractive. He thought he caught her eye and could have sworn she smiled back at him.

Mike Stern, dressed in a gray, herringbone suit and solid black tie, walked down the aisle, nodded to Bear the prosecutor, and sat down next to Greg. "Sorry, I had to take a leak," he said.

Greg looked at the spectators while waiting for the judge to enter the courtroom. He saw his golf buddies a few rows back. He nodded to them. Greg turned to Stern and said, "Look at that male juror with the long ponytail. He looks like he could be an inmate." Stern nodded. "What's the background of the jurors?' asked Greg.

Stern said, "The jury is comprised of two teachers, a waitress, three business owners, a motel manager, a golf pro, one salesman, two business managers, and one retiree. Seven of them are married. One is divorced. They also have selected two alternates in case a juror became ill." Greg observed Stern frown and cross his arms.

"Well, ponytail man doesn't look like a teacher," said Greg. Stern remained silent. "Something bothering you?" Greg asked.

"Judge is late," said Stern. He turned around and recognized several people in the courtroom.

"And you're satisfied with the jurors selected?" Greg asked.

Stern leaned closer to him and said, "Yes. The judge questioned the jurors to determine if they were qualified to act fairly and impartially and had no interest in the result of the case. It's all good."

People looked like they were getting antsy. There was a lot of chatter heard in the room. Finally, the judge walked into the courtroom, his brow furrowed. He stood a little over six feet in his black robe. His tanned face was in sharp contrast to his thick, premature white hair. Even though his hair was snowy white, he looked younger than 60. The bailiff said, "All rise. The Honorable Judge Donald Bell presiding."

He got right to the point. "Good morning, everyone. Sorry, I'm a little late. Please be seated." Everybody sat down. Judge Bell said, "The case today is the State verses Mr. Gregory King. The charges against him are involuntary manslaughter, assault, kidnapping, and attempted murder. Do the jurors swear that they will try the matter in dispute and give a true verdict in accordance with the evidence?"

The jurors all agreed to do so. "Before the opening statements begin," the judge asked, "Mr. Stern, how does the defendant plead?'"

"Not guilty, Your Honor."

Greg nodded and snuck a look at the pretty juror.

Depositions had already taken place in advance of the trial. Nine witnesses had given their testimonies under oath before the trial began, and the transcripts had been given to the judge.

The prosecutor, Bear, told Cici he didn't like Greg and thought he was too narcissistic. Bear wanted him to spend the rest of his life in jail.

Preparing for the case took a lot of time. Time away from his son. After this case, he was going to court to see if he could change his original custody agreement. He wanted 50 percent custody of his son. His ex-wife would be hard to persuade. She was bitter and unreasonable, even though he saw their son less than she did. He fell hard for another woman, and his wife was acrimonious. Bear adored his eight-year-old son, and he wanted the custody of him to be equally shared. He would fight for it and believed he could win. After all, he was the "Bear." He knew his reputation was vital to his career. How he was perceived was fundamentally important to him.

"Mr. Berry, are you ready to begin with your opening statements? . . . Mr. Berry?" asked the judge. Bear looked up from his pile of papers and cleared his throat.

"Sorry, yes, I'm ready, Your Honor," said Bear. He rose from his seat, dressed like the heavy hitters. He stood six feet tall, give or take an inch or two. He dressed professionally in his fitted, dark black suit and red tie. His wide forehead and prominent Greek nose gave him a refined-looking appearance. Bear walked in front of the juror's pews. Turning to the judge and then back to the jury, he said, "Your Honor, ladies and gentlemen of the jury, and opposing counsel, my name is Theodore Berry. It is the burden of the state to prove Gregory King is guilty beyond a reasonable doubt. That's exactly what I intend to do." He took a step closer to the jury box. All the jurors' eyes were on him. "Greg King killed Merv Grady. It wasn't self-defense. He had motive. And in this trial, I will prove that Greg King, the defendant, took substantial steps towards committing the murder of his wife. I will prove he knocked

Mrs. King unconscious and drove her to an abandoned golf course to kill her. You will hear how the defendant, Mr. King, couldn't stand his wife. He physically abused her. He had a mistress he desperately wanted to marry. Oh, he wanted to kill Mrs. King, alright. He had the motive." He took the time to look into each one of the jurors' faces. A plump lady juror averted his gaze and stared down at her notepad in her lap. "Ladies and gentlemen, take good notes. You will find him guilty of all the charges you hear in this trial without any doubt." Cici crossed her fingers.

Bear took his seat. He scribbled on his pad, then erased something and wrote again. He glanced over at the Defense table and caught Greg looking at him. Bear looked away. *Gonna put you away, buddy.*

⌁

"Mr. Stern, are you ready to begin your opening remarks?" asked the judge.

"I am, Your Honor."

Stern loved his job. He always looked up a judge's website before appearing in court to see if the judge had any unique rules. For his current case, he had asked other lawyers from Worcester County if Judge Bell had any pet peeves or unique practices. Stern researched Judge Bell's prior rulings. Representing a client was, for him, always empowering and thrilling. Stern was dressed in conservative business attire with a maroon handkerchief peeking out of his jacket's top pocket.

"My name is Michael Stern, and I'm representing the defendant, Gregory King. Ladies and gentlemen, Mr. Berry is dead wrong. I'll prove that Merv Grady's death was an accident. Mr. King did not pull the trigger. It was self-defense. The defendant, Mr. King, had a gun pointed at him. He had no choice but to protect his own life. I will also prove that Greg King is not guilty of attempting to murder his wife. You will hear that he did not assault her. He did not kidnap her. Witnesses will attest to his fine character. This man provided well for his wife. Greg King is definitely not guilty of any of these charges."

Stern went back to his seat. Greg patted his shoulder. "Good job," he said.

"Well, we have a long ways to go yet," said Stern. Greg saw someone approach the Prosecutor's table and whisper something to Bear.

"Your Honor, I ask the court to allow me to have a short recess. I have just been given information that another witness for the prosecution has stepped forward," said Bear. "I will need to question him before proceeding," said Bear.

"Your Honor, this is ridiculous. What kind of show is Mr. Berry putting on here? I know nothing about the introduction of a new witness."

Greg turned to Stern. "What do you think is going on?"

"I don't know, but I'm going to find out," said Stern.

"Mr. Berry and Mr. Stern, meet me in my chambers, now," said Judge Bell.

Greg was escorted back into a cell-like room in the court-house. He paced back and forth in the tiny room. An hour went by.

Stern entered the holding cell where Greg was waiting. Greg was biting his fingernails. "Don't do that in court," said Stern.

"What's going on?" asked Greg.

"Apparently your cellmate, Buzz Lynch, said you told him you killed Merv Grady and lied to the police that it was in self-defense. Did you talk to your cellmate about your case?"

"No. I only told him what I was in for. I knew this guy was shady. And you believed him?"

"No, but it doesn't matter what I believe. Lynch said you

told him you wanted Grady dead and shot him in cold blood. Did you make Lynch mad?"

"No, I stayed clear of him. He's somebody you don't want to be around, believe me. He's a bloody liar. I never told him anything at all. He's making it up."

"I don't put much credence into what he said," Stern said. "Bear appeased him, I think—making him believe he could get a plea deal. It's a far stretch. My paralegals are checking into Lynch's background. I'll do everything to assassinate his character. I think you're right. He's one shady guy."

"I don't want to be in the same cell with him," said Greg.

"That's already been taken care of," said Stern.

Court finally resumed after two hours. "Call your next witness, Mr. Berry," said the judge.

Buzz Lynch was led into the courtroom. He wore an orange prisoner's uniform and was in handcuffs. He stood by the judge and took an oath to tell the truth, placing both hand-cuffed hands on the Bible. He sat down after stating his name. Stern saw one of the female jurors wince at Lynch.

Bear adjusted his tie as he walked over to Buzz Lynch. "Why you are here today, Mr. Lynch?" asked Bear.

"I shared a cell with Greg. I mean, Mr. King. He confided to me about what he did."

"You're not his cellmate now?"

"No, I was transferred to a different cell."

"What did you think of Mr. King?"

"He acted like he was better than anyone, you know, kind of conceited."

"What exactly did he tell you?"

"He said he didn't kill Merv Grady in self-defense."

"Did he tell you why?" asked Bear.

"Um, he said he didn't like the guy," said Lynch.

"That's it?" asked Bear.

"Well, he said that Grady was going to report him to the police," said Lynch.

"Why was that?'

"He didn't say," said Lynch.

"He's full of shit," said Greg.

"Shhh," said Stern.

"Why did you come forward, Mr. Lynch?" asked Bear.

"Well, if he killed this Grady guy, what's to keep him from killing me one night in my cell? So, I thought I'd better contact you."

"He's a fucking liar," said Greg.

"Shut up," said Stern. Cici's eyebrows rose, watching Greg's face.

"Thank you. No more questions, Your Honor," said Bear.

"Do you wish to cross-examine?" the judge asked Stern.

"Yes."

Stern fumbled with his notes on the Defense table. He got up and walked over to the podium. "Mr. Lynch, have you ever been arrested before this?" asked Stern.

"Yes," he said.

"For what?"

"When I was eighteen, I got a DUI." Lynch leaned forward in his chair.

"Did you go to jail?"

"No."

"Did you go to prison when the cops found an unregistered gun and marijuana in your glove compartment?"

"Yes," Lynch said.

"How long was your sentence?"

"Five years."

"Must have been a lot of marijuana," said Stern. Spectators could be heard laughing in the room.

"Objection," said Bear.

"Sustained."

"Were you ever fired from your job, Mr. Lynch?"

"Yes," said Lynch.

"Why was that?" asked Stern.

Lynch leaned back in his chair and took a deep breath. "I embezzled money from my former boss."

A juror raised her hand to her mouth and shook her head.

"How much did you embezzle?" asked Stern.

"Almost three thousand dollars," said Lynch.

"Did you go to jail for that?"

"No, my boss didn't press charges."

"That's a lot of money you stole. Why didn't he press charges?" asked Stern.

"He was my uncle. I'm on a pay-back schedule each month."

"What's the balance? Two thousand, nine hundred dollars?" People were heard snickering in their seats.

"Objection," said Bear.

"Sustained. Mr. Stern, you're out of line," said the judge. "Quiet in the court," he said as he banged his gavel.

"Sorry, Your Honor. Mr. Lynch, how do we know you're telling the truth about Mr. King if you've been dishonest in the past?"

"I am telling the truth," Lynch said.

"Why are you in jail now?"

"I was charged with second-degree assault."

"Was that for allegedly attacking and choking your friend?" Stern asked.

"Yes."

"You don't want to go to jail for that, do you?" asked Stern.

"No, of course not. Who wants to go to jail?" he asked. Ponytail man in the jury box shook his head.

"Wouldn't you do just about anything to keep from going to jail?" asked Stern.

"Objection!"

"Sustained."

"For testifying today against your cellmate, Greg King, are you getting a plea deal from the prosecutor?"

"Maybe, but . . ."

"But what, Mr. Lynch?"

"Not exactly. He said he couldn't promise."

"Are you fabricating this story about Mr. King in hopes of getting a lesser sentence?"

"No."

"Did you know the penalty for your alleged crime could be up to 10 years in prison as well as a $2,500 fine?"

"Yeah, I knew that."

"How about the penalty for perjury, Mr. Lynch? No need to answer. That will be all, Mr. Lynch. No more questions, Your Honor," said Stern.

Stern sat down and glanced at Greg. "Don't look so forlorn. Wipe that look off your face. Keep the faith. You're not helping yourself by looking like a puppy who lost its owner," said Stern. "I bet Bear is sorry he called him as a witness."

"You're right," Greg said, half smiling. "Bet the jury will discount what he says because he was looking for a plea bargain."

⚎

Bear called his next witness and began his direct examination.

Greg said to Stern, "Oh boy, this'll be good."

Bear brushed something off this sleeve, walking near the podium. Amie took the stand, solemnly affirmed the truth, identified herself, and sat down.

"Hope you're doing well today, Ms. Weiss. You're a neighbor of Cici King. Correct?"

"Yes," said Amie.

"How long have you worked as a realtor at Cathell Realty?"

"I've worked there for 11 years."

Bear asked, "How long have you known Cici King?"

"About 12 years." A juror dropped her notepad and pen. Another bent down to pick it up for her.

Bear waited a moment. "You consider yourselves good friends?" he questioned.

"Yes."

"Very close?"

"Yes," she answered.

"Where did you first meet?"

"We met at a restaurant where we both worked, about 12 years ago. We've been friends ever since."

"Did Mrs. King tell you she was having problems with Greg King, her husband, the defendant?"

"Yes," Amie answered.

"Is her husband in the courtroom?" he asked.

"Yes." Amie pointed to Greg.

"Let the court know she pointed to Mr. King, the defendant. Did you suggest that Cici King hire a private investigator?"

"Yes, Patrick McCombe," Amie said.

"Why did you suggest she do that?" Bear asked.

"Mrs. King thought Mr. King could be having an affair. His behavior had changed, and he was not spending much time at home."

"How long were they married?"

"About 10 years," Amie said.

"Do they have a good marriage?"

"Objection! Calls for speculation, Your Honor," shouted Stern.

"Sustained. Rephrase your question Mr. Berry," said the judge.

"What was Mr. King's behavior like in their marriage?"

"After they were married, they seemed happy. Now, he berates her a lot and does it in front of others."

"Are you afraid of Mr. King?"

"I never felt comfortable around him. I really don't like him that much," Amie answered.

"Objection. Irrelevant, Your Honor," said Stern.

"Sustained. The jury will disregard her last statement," said the judge.

"Did he ridicule his wife in front of you?" Bear asked.

"Yes."

"What kinds of things did he say?"

"He often said he was looking for a second wife, because he would no doubt outlive Mrs. King," Amie said.

"Outlive his wife?" Bear asked.

"Yes. He said he was fit and healthy, and she was out of shape, fat, and unhealthy. He said she'd probably die earlier than he would."

Bear turned to Cici. "Mrs. King doesn't look fat to me." Pretty lady juror smiled at Bear.

"Objection."

"Sustained."

"Did Mrs. King discuss her husband's recent behavior with you?"

"Yes."

"What did she tell you?"

"Objection. Hearsay, Your Honor," said Stern.

"Overruled."

Amie mentioned Greg's distasteful and cruel behaviors. Greg shook his head.

"Ms. Weiss, tell us what you experienced the night of Mrs. King's alleged kidnapping."

"The night Mrs. King was kidnapped, she was supposed to spend the night at my house. She said she had to pack some things and would be over. At eleven o'clock at night, I really got worried because she didn't show up. I called her cell phone, but couldn't get through to her."

"What did you decide to do?" asked Bear. Amie told him what happened when she and Pat went inside her house.

"Did you think it strange that Mr. King's car was there and he wasn't?" She jumped when the judge swatted a fly on his podium.

Bear paused a moment.

"Yes, but I called him to ask him if he knew where Mrs. King was. He said he didn't know where she was and that a business associate had picked him up, and he was spending the evening with him."

"Did he seem worried that his wife was not home?" asked Bear.

"No," said Amie.

"Did Mrs. King show up and if not, what did you decide to do?" asked Bear.

"No, she didn't show up. In the morning I called Detective Crabbe and explained the situation to him. I told him it was unusual for Mrs. King not to call me. He told me she couldn't be a missing person until 24 hours or so. He said she may have had other plans since she probably had her cell phone, wallet, and keys with her," said Amie.

"Did Detective Crabbe think this was highly unusual, given what you told him about Mrs. King?"

"No, he didn't seem upset, but Detective Crabbe did ask me to get in touch with him by a certain time, if I hadn't heard from her."

"No more questions, Your Honor. Thank you, Ms. Weiss." Amie stayed in her seat.

⚖

"Does the Defense wish to cross-examine the witness?" asked the judge. Stern answered yes. The judge reminded Amie she had solemnly affirmed the truth. Stern rose and walked towards Amie.

"Good morning. Ms. Weiss. You mentioned you were neighbors and close to Mrs. King. Did Mr. King take pride in his home where he and Cici lived?"

"Yes."

"How do you know this to be true?" asked Stern.

"Mr. King liked fixing up his house. He hired a contractor almost yearly. He was always updating and enhancing his home. He thought it was the best house on the block."

"Ms. Weiss, could you say that he provided well for his wife?"

"Yes."

"Did he mind Mrs. King shopping and buying things for her home or for herself?" asked Stern.

"Not that I'm aware of."

"What did Mrs. King originally conclude caused the change in her husband's behavior?"

"She said she thought the pressures of his job were getting to him," Amie said.

"Have you ever seen Mr. King hit or beat his wife?"

"No."

"What does he do for a living?"

"He's the top salesman for his company," she said.

"How do you know this?" he asked.

"Because he's earned huge bonuses and raises, and his name has appeared in the business section of the newspaper for his accomplishments," Amie said. "And Mrs. King told me." Greg inched up a little taller in his seat with a smile on his face.

"Quiet in the courtroom," said the judge after hearing some chatter.

"That sounds like an *A* personality, a hardworking guy, and a very devoted employee. That would make any man relax at a bar from time to time, leave the house at different hours to check on his accounts, and be driven to be the best at his job, wouldn't you agree?" Stern asked.

"Objection. Leading the witness," Stern said.

"Sustained."

"Your Honor, I have a note written by Mr. King that can explain his inattentiveness and not being home much. It's in reply to a note written by his wife asking him if he wanted their marriage to work."

"Proceed," said the judge.

"I would like to mark this note, written by Mr. King, for purposes of identification and enter it into evidence as Exhibit One," said Stern. The judge admitted the evidence.

He gave the note encased in plastic to Amie. "Have you seen and read this note before?" he asked her.

"Amie said, "Yes."

"Who wrote it?"

"Greg King."

"Please read the second sentence until the end out loud," said Stern.

Amie read aloud, "I've been under a lot of stress lately from work. I don't want to talk about it, but I'll see you in two more days. I have a conference in Dover. I'm staying at the Inn. Take care of yourself."

Stern took the note from Amie and held it in the air, waving it back and forth as he walked over to the jury and smiled.

"Ms. Weiss, did you suspect Mr. King was involved in Mrs. King's disappearance that night she was supposed to spend the night with you?"

"No."

"Why is that, Ms. Weiss?"

"Well, he told me he was out with an associate. He often goes out at night and comes home late." *Greg's a slick one. Maybe Stern already knows it.*

"No more questions, Your Honor," Stern said. Amie sat down and patted Cici's hand.

❧

"Mr. Bear, call your next witness."

"Your Honor, my next witness is delayed in traffic due to an accident on Route 50. May we please resume after lunch?" asked Bear.

The judge banged his gavel and announced court would resume at 1:45 p.m. Greg was escorted back to his holding cell and served lunch. After eating, he fell asleep on his cot. At 1:30 p.m., the bailiff woke him up and brought him back into the courtroom.

Pat hurriedly parked his car and sprinted towards the courthouse. He made it in time to testify. Bear called him to the stand and began to question him after he was sworn in.

"Good afternoon. Glad you made it back safely to court. Please state your name and occupation."

"My name is Patrick McCombe. I'm a private investigator for Discovery Investigations in Bishopville, Maryland."

"How long have you worked as a P.I.?"

"Nine years. Prior to that, I was a detective on the police force in Salisbury," Pat said.

"Were you hired by Cici King to observe Mr. King's activities?" he asked.

"Yes."

"Why did Mrs. King want you to observe her husband?"

"She was suspicious that he was having an affair."

"When was that?" Bear asked.

"In October of this year."

The sun drifted into the court's windows. Pat shielded his eyes from the glare that shone on his face with his right hand.

"Explain to the court what your investigation discovered," said Bear.

"I saw him with another woman. I observed them both enter his hotel room, where they remained until the next morning. I witnessed them on the balcony of Mr. King's room in various stages of undress. It was clear to me that it was a romantic meeting, not business."

"Maybe wife number two?" said Bear.

Stern noticed a juror smirked. "Objection," shouted Stern.

"Sustained. Mr. Berry, curb your remarks like that from now on," the judge said.

"Sorry, Your Honor," said Bear. "We'll now show the jury Exhibit Two, your surveillance report, on PowerPoint for the jury to read."

The courtroom was still as the jury read the report to themselves. Only an occasional cough was heard. Cici turned to Amie. "I hope Greg is having a stroke," she said.

Greg said to Stern, "Was it really necessary to put that up on PowerPoint?"

"Shh," said Stern.

When the jury was finished reading, Bear asked, "You gave the report to Cici King. What was Mrs. King going to do with the information?"

Pat answered, "Give the report to her lawyer and ask Mr. King for a divorce."

"Thank you. No more questions, Your Honor."

"Does the Defense wish to cross-examine?" asked the judge.

"Yes, Your Honor," said Stern.

Stern cordially greeted Pat. "Was this the only time you observed Mr. King spending the night with this so-called paramour?"

"Yes."

"Then your job was over when you discovered the two together?" he asked.

"Yes."

"Having a one-night stand with a woman when a man is out of town doesn't give him motive to murder his wife. Do you agree, Mr. McCombe?"

"I agree," said Pat.

"No more questions, Your Honor," said Stern.

Judge Bell spoke, "I will have to end today's session. We will delay hearing the testimony from the next witness." With the bang of his gavel he said, "Court will resume Monday morning, at 9:00 a.m."

CHAPTER 15

Cici wasn't wearing her fat clothes in her closet anymore. She now could select from outfits she had saved from back when she was slimmer. Her slightly tight, green plaid skirt looked becoming on her. As she sat in court, she said to Amie, "That Stern is doing a good job. I hope the jury sides with Bear, though."

Judge Bell rushed into the courtroom, his black robe trailing behind him. He called the court to order. After all were seated, he said, "Call your next witness, Mr. Berry."

"Will Mr. Frank Vaughn please come to the stand?"

Mr. Vaughn swore to tell the truth and stated his name and occupation. His head peeked out above the podium. His neck and the rest of his body were hidden behind the stand.

Cici whispered to Amie, "He needs a telephone book to sit on."

"Behave," Amie whispered back.

Bear asked, "You are Mrs. King's attorney, correct?"

"Yes."

"Did Mrs. King waive her client/privilege so you could testify today?" asked Bear.

"Yes, she did," said Vaughn.

"Why did she need your services?" asked Bear.

"She told me she wanted a divorce," said Vaughn.

"Did she explain why?"

"She said it was because of her husband's changes in his behavior and infidelity."

"Did she give you the field report from private investigator Patrick McCombe?" asked Bear.

"Yes."

"Did she say she knew how Mr. King would react to her getting a private investigator?"

"No."

"Did her husband know she wanted a divorce?"

"Not when she first came to me. She told him their marriage could not continue the way it was if he didn't change. He told her he did not want a divorce."

"Did he later know she definitely wanted a divorce?"

"Yes. She told him before the alleged kidnapping that she hired a P.I. and wanted to divorce him."

"Did he agree to a divorce then?" asked Bear.

Vaughn said, "Yes, under his conditions. Mrs. King said that he told her he wanted all of the assets, to include the house, the pontoon, his 40lk, his inheritance, and then some."

"In other words, Mr. Vaughn, he simply said he wanted everything. Correct?" asked Bear.

"Yes," said Vaughn. He looked at Greg and saw him shift in his chair.

"How did Mrs. King feel about that?"

"Mrs. King said she didn't want any of his possessions. She said she wanted to be a divorcee as soon as possible," said Vaughn.

Vaughn glanced over at the jury. They seemed restless. One juror yawned. One was nodding off.

"Has Mr. King signed a division of assets agreement yet?"

"Not yet," said Vaughn.

"Thank you, Mr. Vaughn. No more questions, Your Honor." Stern did not redirect.

⚓

"The State calls Detective Joseph Crabbe."

In long strides and in his custom-made suit, Crabbe crossed the room towards the stand. His posture remained plumb-line straight as he raised his right hand and swore to tell the truth.

"Detective Crabbe, you are the lead detective in this case, correct?"

"Yes, I am."

"Are you a detective for the Ocean Pines Police Department?"

"I'm a WCBI Detective. My office is in the Ocean Pines Police Station."

"I see. That stands for Worcester County Bureau of Investigation. Correct?"

"Yes."

"How long have you been on the force?"

"Almost 30 years."

"You have a reputation for solving many crimes, correct?"

"I've solved a few."

"In fact, you've solved more than a few, and you've received commendations seven years in a row. Correct?" Bear asked.

"Yes."

"I'm glad you're a cop where I live," said Bear, turning to the crowd, nodding his head. Some spectators chuckled and nodded in agreement. Cici smiled at Amie.

"When did you get involved with this case?" asked Bear.

"Back in October, when Mrs. King was attacked in her bathroom and robbed, and Mr. King became a person of interest."

Two lady jurors looked at each other. One raised her eyebrows.

"Objection," said Stern.

"Overruled."

"Did they find out who did that?" asked Bear.

"There is evidence that points to Mr. Merv Grady," said Crabbe.

"Do you have evidence that shows Mr. King allegedly assaulted Mrs. King?" asked Bear.

"Mrs. King said that Mr. King punched her during an argument before allegedly putting her in the trunk of her car. I have a photo of Mrs. King's injury to her face," said Crabbe.

"I will submit this photo as Exhibit Three—the photo of Mrs. King's badly bruised cheek, the night of the alleged kidnapping," said Bear.

"Can you prove that Mr. King put her in the trunk of her car and allegedly kidnapped Mrs. King other than just her testimony?" asked Bear.

Crabbe said, "Her DNA, that is, her saliva, was found on the duct tape due to her gnawing on it to get it off her wrists when she was inside the trunk of the car. Also strands of her hair were found inside the car's trunk where the tape was. Mr. King's fingerprints were found on the hammer."

"Are you aware of how Mr. King has treated Mrs. King in their marriage recently?" asked Bear.

"Only from Mrs. King's and Ms. Weiss's previous statements to me in October. And also, as I said, when Mrs. King said Mr. King slugged her hard on the face before he drove her to an abandoned clubhouse," said Crabbe.

Stern's face was flushed as he pulled in his chair closer to the table.

"What statements did she make in October?" asked Bear.

"Objection, Your Honor," said Stern.

"Overruled."

Crabbe explained Cici's descriptions of Greg's disgusting behavior.

"What did Mr. King do after Mrs. King was allegedly kidnapped?"

"Mr. King took flight to Florida, changed his name, altered the color of his hair, grew a beard, and obtained a false ID."

"No more questions, Your Honor," said Bear.

Stern glared at Crabbe. He stood close to Crabbe. "Detective Crabbe, did you go to Mr. Grady's trailer the night of his death?" asked Stern.

"Yes, I did."

"Was Mr. King there, and if so, what did he tell you happened?" asked Stern.

"Yes, he was there. He told me he discovered the stolen items from his house hidden under Mr. Grady's futon. He said that when Mr. Grady accused him of being the perpetrator, Mr. Grady aimed his gun at Mr. King. Mr. King then said he tried to get the gun away from Mr. Grady, and the gun went off, killing Mr. Grady."

"Did the surroundings look like there was a scuffle?"

"Yes." Crabbe described the appearance of the room. The pretty juror smiled towards Greg.

"Detective Crabbe, was there any evidence at all that proved it was not self-defense?"

"Only that his cellmate said Mr. King admitted to killing Mr. Grady."

"Surely, you don't believe he's telling the truth?"

"Sorry, I don't have a crystal ball," said Crabbe.

"Were you aware, Detective Crabbe, Mr. King and Mrs. King had an argument before the night of the alleged kidnapping?"

"Yes."

"Were you aware that Mr. King said Mrs. King lost her balance and fell in their home and hit her head on the tiled floor before Mr. King and she were in her car?"

"No."

"Were you aware, Detective Crabbe, that Mr. King said that he did not put her in the trunk of her car, but in the passenger seat beside him?" asked Stern.

"Objection. Hearsay."

"I'll allow it," said the judge. Stern smiled as he looked over at the jury.

"No."

"Were you aware that Mr. King was taking Mrs. King to the hospital because she fell and hurt her head?"

"No."

"Were you aware that Mr. King said Mrs. King jumped out of the car from the passenger seat and ran into the woods?"

"No."

"Were you aware that Mr. King searched for her, couldn't find her, and waited for Mrs. King to return to their home to apologize for their argument?"

"No. I was aware that he skipped town," said Crabbe.

"Just answer yes or no, Mr. Crabbe," said Stern. "Were you aware that there have never been any submitted reports of domestic violence on Mr. King?" A juror with a dark tan scooted up in his seat and grabbed the railing of the partition.

"Yes," said Crabbe. There was a burn in his stomach.

"Were you aware that Mr. King panicked and was afraid Mrs. King would lie and say he struck her, so he decided the best course was to go to Florida for fear of going to jail?"

"No."

Bear was scribbling away on his pad.

"No more questions, Your Honor."

Greg said to Stern, "Beautiful job."

"May I redirect, Your Honor?" asked Bear.

"Proceed," said Judge Bell.

"Detective Crabbe, did you see Mrs. King right after she left the golf course?"

"Yes. She was immediately driven to the police station by a Mrs. Jean Tyler after she picked her up in front of the abandoned golf course."

"How did Mrs. King seem?"

"Tearful and frightful. Her hair was disheveled, and her clothes were a mess from hiding and spending the night in the deserted clubhouse. Dark bruises were on the left side of her face. Mrs. King explained to me what happened to her."

"No more questions, Your Honor."

Crabbe stepped down from his podium. The burn in his stomach was still there.

On the miserable, cold morning of Cici's testimony, she laid in bed stretching and yawning before she turned over on her front. She stared up at the ceiling fan. She was glad she'd hired a P.I. She was glad Greg was in jail. She was glad they were separated and getting a divorce. *But what if the jury believes Stern and he's found not guilty? Or what if he has a short prison sentence to serve?* If so, suppose he'd come back and harm her? What if she didn't get enough money to support herself? She felt a headache coming on. Cici got out of bed and got dressed for her day in court. Looking at her reflection in the mirror, she felt the outfit she wore passed the test for her day to testify. Dressed and ready, she left for court.

Cici looked around the courtroom and stared at the paneled walls and American flag behind the judge's black, leather chair. Looking through the glass windows, the gray skies made the courtroom inside look depressing. Her heart beat at tremendous speeds as she waited to take the stand. Cici walked to the podium, looking thinner and shapely in her newly purchased navy blue suit from Macy's. She tried to form a smile when

Bear approached her. She raised her right hand and swore to be truthful.

"Mrs. King, we know you've had a rough time these past months. How are you feeling?" asked Bear.

She sighed. "My whole life has fallen apart. I have a lot of anxiety about my future. I'm horror-stricken by what has happened. I'm ill at ease right now and apprehensive," said Cici, twisting her handkerchief in her lap.

"Apprehensive of what, Mrs. King?"

"Apprehensive of how the trial will turn out. I am frightened if my husband's found not guilty. I'm worried about not having enough money to pay the bills."

"Are you getting support during this difficult time?" asked Bear.

"Yes, I'm seeing a therapist." Bear walked toward the jury and nodded his head.

"Is it true your husband had been unkind to you, and you noticed a change in his behavior over a period of time?"

"Yes, this past year," answered Cici.

"Did you try to talk with him about it?"

"Yes, and I wrote him a note."

"I would like to enter Exhibit Four, a note written by Cici King to her husband." Bear gave the protected note to Cici. "Please read the note aloud, Mrs. King." Cici read the letter aloud, her hand trembling.

"Did he and you discuss the problems in your marriage after he read your note?" asked Bear.

"I tried to discuss it with him, but he said he was too tired to talk about it when I broached the subject. He just wrote me a note afterwards." She glanced at Greg and saw him shaking his head.

"Mrs. King, your husband has been charged with assault, kidnapping, and attempted murder of you. Please explain his actions and changes in his behavior before this alleged attempt on your life occurred," said Bear. Cici's eyes started to well up.

She began to explain his nasty behavior. Cici looked at the jurors and watched the expressions on their faces as she told the court how her 10-year marriage had deteriorated in the past year. One lady juror wiped the corner of her eye with a Kleenex.

"One night he came home very drunk. I had left my car parked in the driveway, and he went ballistic because I absent-mindedly blocked the space he uses to park his car inside the garage. He was so enraged at me for preventing him from entering the garage where he usually parks. He yelled the words, 'Leave. Get the hell out of my house.' He threw a lamp against the wall among other things, and his madness frightened me so much, I left and drove around for an hour or so. I should have left him then or gone to a shelter. I was such a fool."

Tears rolled down her cheeks. She dabbed her eyes with her hankie.

"Are you alright to proceed, Mrs. King?" asked Bear.

"I'm okay. I'll continue."

"Tell us what happened the night of the kidnapping," said Bear. Cici explained all the events of that night to the jury. One female juror gasped and put her hand over her mouth after she heard Cici explain how she hid behind a bush, fearing for her life.

"I was petrified. I knew he was going to kill me," she said with watery eyes.

"Objection!"

"Sustained," said the judge.

"Did your husband ever imply to you that Mr. Grady didn't give you a concussion?"

"Objection, Your Honor."

"Sustained. Move on Mr. Berry."

Bear looked at the jury and shook his head back and forth. "Mrs. King, have you spoken to your husband at all since he was apprehended?"

"No."

"So he never apologized to you for his behavior after that night of the argument?"

"No."

"Did you tell your husband you hired a private detective and wanted a divorce?"

"Yes."

"How did Mr. King react to hearing that?" asked Bear.

"He said he would grant me a divorce, if he could keep all of the assets."

"How thoughtful," said Bear.

"Objection."

"I've asked you to curb your comments, Mr. Berry. You're on thin ice," Judge Bell said.

"Sorry, Your Honor. It won't happen again."

"What is the value of your assets?"

"Objection."

"Overruled."

Cici said, "Almost two million dollars." Murmuring could be heard in the room.

"Thank you, Mrs. King. No more questions, Your Honor." Amie smiled at Cici and gave her an okay sign with her fingers, but Cici wasn't looking forward to the next line of questioning.

It was Stern's turn to cross-examine her.

"Mrs. King, what was your reaction when you found out Mr. King was having an affair?"

"I was furious. I hated him for what he did." She looked at Greg as he smirked.

"So furious that you would lie to have him thrown in jail?" asked Stern.

"Objection."

"Sustained."

"Mrs. King, have you been prescribed any medications?" Cici was wringing her hands in her lap.

"Yes."

"What are they?"

"I used to take Ambien as needed for sleep," said Cici. "I used to take Losartan for high blood pressure."

"How long were you on the blood pressure pill?" Stern asked.

"About two years, but I'm off the blood pressure med now, because I've lost weight. My blood pressure is fine."

"Are you taking any other prescriptions?"

"No."

"Did you ever take an anti-depressant?"

"Objection!"

"Sustained."

"Some of the side effects from Losartan are anxiety, confusion, depression, memory impairment, nervousness, and panic disorder. Side effects of Ambien can be forgetfulness, depressed mood, and hallucinations. Did you know that?"

"The doctor told me not to read the little pamphlet about it. He said patients get freaked out reading all of those side effects in the inserts, and he said not to worry about it. He said it was a safe drug." A couple of jurors nodded their heads, smiling.

"Were your medications being monitored closely by your doctor because of their side effects?" asked Stern.

"Yes, of course."

"Mrs. King, a short time ago, you were in the hospital for the treatment of a concussion after you were robbed in your home. Significant blunt force to the brain can rattle it. Since you were greatly traumatized recently, and you were taking very potent medications with severe side effects, Mrs. King, couldn't you have misjudged the way your husband treated you?"

Wiping her tears away, Cici said, "No, I don't thin—"

"Never mind," Stern said. "I withdraw the question. No more questions, Your Honor," said Stern.

"Mrs. King, you may step down," said the judge. Court was then dismissed for lunch.

Cici emerged from the courthouse. She wasn't smiling when she walked down the courthouse steps. She met up with Pat and Amie outside. "I feel like Stern made me look like a mental case," Cici said. "I hope the jury doesn't think I am."

"It's just a lawyer's tactic, Cici," said Pat. "Besides, I saw a couple of the women on the jury look like they were sympathizing with you when you were describing Greg's actions." Cici said she saw that too.

"Cici, the suit you're wearing really flatters your figure," said Amie. "You really looked good up there testifying."

"Thanks, I've lost 16 pounds. Don't ask me how I did it," said Cici.

The courtroom was still packed after lunch, and Cici saw Greg's boss seated back in the fourth row. She edged into the pew and sat down, facing the front of the courtroom. She watched Greg speaking to Stern. People were talking too loudly.

The judge entered the room. "The Honorable Judge Bell. All rise."

When all were seated, Bear produced a stack of papers from his briefcase and set them on top of the table.

"Are you ready to proceed, Mr. Berry?"

"Yes, Your Honor."

"Mr. Berry, please call your witness."

"Mrs. Jean Tyler, please come forward." After being sworn in, Bear asked, "Why are you here today Mrs. Tyler?"

"I can vouch for Mrs. King's whereabouts after the alleged kidnapping. Early in the morning, I saw Mrs. King at the side of the road, waving her arms back and forth, trying to get someone's attention in front of the abandoned South Pines

Golf Course. One half of her face was swollen and purplish. She told me what happened to her and that she needed a ride to the police station. I drove her immediately there."

"What did she tell you?"

"Objection."

"Overruled."

"She was very distraught. She said Mr. King had put her in the trunk of the car, and when he opened the trunk, she jumped out and ran to get away." She explained the rest of Cici's story.

"Did it ever cross your mind that she was lying?"

"No," said Mrs. Tyler.

"Did she say she jumped out of a moving car and ran into the woods to escape from being with her husband?"

"No."

"Thank you, Mrs. Tyler."

The judge said, "Any questions, Mr. Stern?"

"No, Your Honor."

"The next witness, please."

Mrs. Tyler waved to Cici as she left the courtroom.

⚖

"Will Ms. Della Summer please come to the stand?"

Della walked towards the front of the courtroom in her spiked heels and tight, mauve mini-skirt. As she paraded up the aisle, swaying her hips, with not a reddish hair out of place, Della caught many an eye, including Greg's. She wore dark, tinted eyeglasses and had a paisley, pinkish scarf around her neck. She stood, raised her right hand, and swore to tell the truth, and nothing but the whole truth, so help her God.

Greg tapped his fingers on the table. Stern placed his hands on top of Greg's. Greg stopped the finger-tapping.

Bear approached the witness stand. "Please state your name and occupation."

"Della Summer. I'm unemployed," she said. She snuck a peek at Cici.

"How do you know Mr. King?" Bear asked.

"We were lovers. I fell in love with him at first sight. He felt the same way," Della said. She wasn't looking at Greg when he smiled. He turned his head and glanced at Cici to see her expression on her face. Cici remained stone-faced. His eyebrows raised. He saw Lisa, the mojito girl, sitting behind Cici, staring hard at him.

"How long have you known Mr. King?" asked Bear.

"Almost two months. I met him in October."

"What information did Mr. King give you about his wife, Mrs. King?" asked Bear.

"Mr. King frequently called her a 'bitch'. At first he told me he was divorced. Then he later told me he lied. He told me he'd like to be rid of his wife. He said he wasn't keen on getting a divorce before he met me, because he wasn't willing to give up all of his belongings."

"Did he tell you why he lied at first?" asked Bear.

"Yes, he said he thought if I knew he was married, I wouldn't want to be with him," said Della.

"Did he try to contact you when he left town, and if so, what did he tell you?" asked Bear.

"After he made his getaway, he called me. He never mentioned where he was. I heard about what he'd done on the news. I asked him if it was true, you know, about kidnapping and assaulting his wife. He said it was true and explained how he took her to the golf course. He then said he wanted me to join him when he established a new life. I told the police," she said. Greg stared at Della and shook his head.

"How did you feel when he admitted he kidnapped and assaulted Mrs. King?" asked Bear.

"Seriously? Who would have thought it? I was astounded. I never thought he'd be capable of such a horrific thing," said Della. "I felt sick to my stomach. I had to keep him on my cell phone to see where he was hiding out. After his phone call, I was scared. I really didn't want to see him again. Not after what he did to Mrs. King. No way," said Della. "He could have done that to me." Greg covered his face in his hands, elbows resting on the table. The elderly juror shook his head and then jotted down some notes.

"Objection. Speculation, Your Honor," said Stern.

"The jury will disregard Ms. Summer's last sentence."

"Did he ever tell you he assaulted Mrs. King before this?"

"Objection."

"I'll allow it," said the judge. "Continue, Mr. Berry."

Greg looked up at her.

"No, he didn't," said Della.

"Did you tell him if he got caught, he'd probably go to prison for a long time?" asked Bear.

"Yes, I did."

"What did Mr. King say?"

"He said he could make a new life for himself," said Della.

"Did he contact you after that first phone call?" asked Bear.

"Yes, and thank goodness for that," said Della.

"Why is that?"

"Because I wanted the police to find him. He told me he wanted me to meet him in Marco Island at a motel. I informed the police of his whereabouts, and Detective Crabbe nabbed him at the motel," said Della.

"No more questions, Your Honor," said Bear.

"Do you wish to cross, Mr. Stern?" asked the judge.

"Yes, I certainly do," said Stern.

"Ms. Summer, did you assault Mrs. King?"

"Objection. Relevance?" asked Bear.

"It's pertinent, Your Honor," said Stern.

"Overruled."

"Yes, and I hate myself for that," said Della.

"Did the district attorney, Eileen Fields, lessen the charges because Mrs. King requested she drop the charges on you?" asked Stern.

"Yes, and I'm grateful to her for that."

"Because of that, you do not have to spend time in jail. Isn't that correct, Ms. Summer?"

"Yes, it's true," Della said.

A bird banged into the glass courtroom window. People jumped and looked up at the source of the noise. Judge Bell's head quickly turned to the left, and he looked at the window. The jurors stirred. Chatter was heard throughout the room.

Judge Bell banged his gavel. "Order in the court! It wasn't a flying missile. It wasn't a rock. Ladies and gentlemen, be calm, please. It was just a bird. Just a poor bird. Proceed, Mr. Stern."

Stern shook his head. "Are you so grateful to Mrs. King that you didn't have to go to jail, you thought you'd testify for the prosecution?"

She placed her arms crisscrossing her breasts, and took a deep breath. "In my heart, I'm so grateful to Mrs. King, but I am testifying because I want the court to know what kind of a person Mr. King is. I feel sorry for Mrs. King, being married to such a creep and all," she said.

"No more questions, Your Honor," said Stern, his face suddenly reddening. His neck was almost the color of his scarlet handkerchief.

"You may step down, Ms. Summer," said the judge. Della strutted past Greg and out of the corner of her eye, her good eye, she saw Greg cast a glance her way.

Della drove her red Kia over the speed limit on her way back to Wilmington. She had fallen hard for Greg and his good looks. *What a loser.* After hearing her testimony, would he find her and hurt her if he was found not guilty?

⊣⊐

"Mr. Berry, do you have a next witness?"

"Yes, Your Honor. The State calls Mr. Ronald Cole."

Mr. Cole limped with a bamboo cane to the stand and sat down after his introduction. His white hair was combed forward towards his brow, covering a prominent bald spot on the crown of his head. He had bushy eyebrows and a clear, smooth, rosy complexion. He wore a sleeveless, blue sweater over a white long-sleeved shirt and a blue-striped tie knotted under his shirt's frayed collar. He was sworn in.

"Mr. Cole, did Mr. and Mrs. King watch your house in Ocean Pines while you were living in Florida?" asked Bear.

"Ahem, yes." His eye twitched. "Mrs. King watches it now."

"Did you see Mr. King in Florida after Mrs. King was allegedly kidnapped?" asked Bear.

"Yes. I called Mrs. King about checking out my place after a storm hit Ocean City near my house. During our conversation, she told me Mr. King was a fugitive from the law, and he abducted her and tried to kill her. My wife and I saw him in a restaurant in Florida after my conversation with Mrs. King."

"Tell the court what happened when you saw Mr. King in Florida," said Bear.

"A little while after Mrs. King told me what Mr. King had done, I saw him. He was our waiter in a restaurant in Florida. I recognized him even though his hair was bleached blonde and he grew this stupid-looking beard." Cici and Amie started giggling.

"Order," said the judge.

"Did he say hi to you after you recognized him at your table?" asked Bear.

"No, he went into the kitchen and drove away on his motorcycle." Greg's reddish cheeks showed his embarrassment.

"So you are saying he didn't come back to the table and serve you, but high-tailed it out of the restaurant because you recognized him. Correct?" asked Bear.

"Yes," said Mr. Cole. "The chef saw him bolt out of there too."

"No more questions, Your Honor. The Prosecution rests," said Bear.

"Do you wish to cross-examine, Mr. Stern?"

"No, Your Honor."

"Court will resume tomorrow morning at 9:00 a.m. for the Defense. Have a good evening, everyone." He banged his gavel.

CHAPTER 16

New Year's Eve morning at 7:30 a.m., as Stern sipped his coffee and ate his cheesy omelet in the General's Kitchen, he glanced at his notes in preparation for the court's session. He wiped his mouth with his napkin, put his notes away, and paid his bill. He got into his Mercedes and drove to Snow Hill. His wife was joining him in Ocean City at Fager's restaurant for a big New Year's Eve bash that night, and he was looking forward to enjoying himself. And he was looking forward to having his first witness testify.

Judge Bell marched into his courtroom. Court reconvened on time.

All rose. "Be seated," said the judge. "Today the Defense will call its witnesses."

Stern turned to Greg and said, "Hulk is the next witness."

"Hulk?" said Greg.

"Yes, you'll see," said Stern. "Will Mr. Hank Phillips please come to the stand?"

The Chief of Police lumbered to the front of the courtroom.

His button-down, white shirt protruded over his enormous belly as he walked toward the front of the courtroom.

"I see what you mean," said Greg. "Hulk doesn't look like a chief to be messed with if you intend on breaking the law."

Stern turned to Greg and said, "He walked into a bar one day on the Boardwalk to arrest a couple of rowdy guys and came out with one under each arm." Greg nodded and smiled.

Hulk told his name, put his right hand up, and plopped his 6'4", 350-pound body down in his seat.

"Chief Phillips, are you familiar with the case involving a robbery at Mr. and Mrs. King's home?"

"Yes, I was present the day Mrs. King was assaulted and robbed in their home last October."

"Were you at the crime scene after Mr. Grady was shot?"

"Yes."

"Are you very familiar with the case involving Mr. King and Mr. Grady?"

"Yes."

"Do you believe Mr. King killed Mr. Grady in self-defense?" asked Stern.

"I do," said Hulk.

"Why is that?" asked Stern.

"At the scene of the crime, Mr. Grady's DNA was found on the plastic bag that contained the stolen items from Mrs. King's house. Mr. Grady's fingerprints were also found on Mr. King's wedding band."

"Do you believe Mr. King's story of the events that occurred in Mr. Grady's trailer to be true?" asked Stern.

"Yes, I believe Mr. King defended himself because his life was in danger. I believe they fought over the gun, and it discharged as described by Mr. King."

"Thank you, Chief. No more questions, Your Honor," said Stern.

"Do you wish to redirect, Mr. Berry?"

"No, Your Honor," said Bear.

"No more questions, Your Honor. You're free to go, Chief Phillips."

Hulk stepped down and looked at Greg. Greg and Stern were both giving him a big grin. Hulk didn't smile back.

Hulk squeezed through the courtroom door, avoiding a reporter. He walked down the steps to the first floor. Breathless, Hulk paused and heard, "Hulk, wait up!" Catching up to him, Crabbe said, "Hulk, I still believe King is guilty of Merv's death."

"Not a chance," said Hulk.

"Why not?" asked Crabbe.

"Joe, come on. You really don't know what they said and what went on in that trailer. You can have all the theories you want. There's no evidence to indicate King murdered him in cold blood. I had to go with what we had. You could be right, Joe, but you just have to stop letting it eat you up like this. Move on. With the kidnapping and assault, King's probably going to go to jail for a very long time anyway," said Hulk. "Let's drop it, Joe. I'm sick of talking about it. I'm disappointed Bear didn't question you though. I wish King would take the stand, but we know that's not going to happen," said Hulk.

Back in the courtroom, the next witness took the stand. After he was sworn in, he stated his name and occupation.

"My name is Kevin Case, and I'm the CEO of Delmarva Food Distributors, located in Dover, Delaware."

"What is your relationship to Mr. Greg King?" asked Stern.

"I'm his boss," he answered.

"How long have you known Mr. King?"

"Almost 20 years."

"Has he worked with your company that long?"

"Yes," said Mr. Case.

"Do you remember why you hired him?"

"Yes. Greg, I mean Mr. King, was a just a young, country boy when I interviewed him. I remember..." Mr. Case laughed, "He showed me his transcripts from high school and college, even though I didn't ask for them. He was captain of his high school football team and its star quarterback. His grades were pretty good. Mr. King was offered a college football scholarship and worked at night to help with some of his expenses. He had the spirit of independence and motivation to leave the farm where he grew up and enroll in Salisbury University. He graduated with a business degree. I admired his drive and ambition."

"What kind of an employee is Mr. King?" asked Stern.

"He's one of the best salesmen in the company," said Mr. Case. "He hasn't lost any of our major clients. He's a hard worker and works well with others."

Stern asked, "Has he ever been dishonest?" asked Stern.

"No, not that I'm aware of."

"Then, from what you're saying, he sounds like a model employee." A juror yawned, and another was writing down notes on his pad.

Mr. Case answered, "Yes, I think he is."

"No more questions, Your Honor."

"Do you wish to cross-examine, Mr. Berry?"

"No questions, Your Honor," said Bear.

The judge said, "Due to it being New Years' Eve, court is adjourned a little early today. "Court will resume Thursday morning, January 2. Happy New Year, everyone. Stay safe, and use your designated drivers tonight. I don't want to see anyone here in my court for any DUI." He banged his gavel.

Cici, Amie, and Pat spent a quiet evening watching the New Year come in on TV. Stern and his wife enjoyed a great evening dining and dancing. Crabbe spent his New Year's night alone with Old Bay. Bear and his girlfriend watched the fireworks on a midnight cruise in the Assawoman Bay.

New Year's Day came and went. January 2 it was back to business. Judge Bell stood in front of his large podium and said, "Happy 2014, everyone. The Defense will continue presenting their witnesses in the case State vs. Gregory King." Stern called his next witness to the stand.

Dr. Tim Chu sat down after the preliminary questions were done.

"You are one of the attending physicians at Atlantic General Hospital. Is that correct, Dr. Chu?" asked Stern.

"Yes, I am."

"How do you know Mrs. King?" asked Stern.

"I was on duty in the emergency room at Atlantic General Hospital on October 1, when Mrs. King arrived there by ambulance."

"Dr. Chu, why was Mrs. King brought to the hospital?" asked Stern.

"After examining her, I diagnosed her with a concussion," said Dr. Chu.

"Did Mrs. King know how she got the concussion?"

"No, she was very confused and couldn't remember anything," said the doctor.

"Did she complain of any symptoms?" asked Stern.

"She complained of a headache and nausea."

"Did you test her mental abilities while she was there?"

"Yes, I tested her ability to pay attention, remember things, and solve problems."

"Did she pass your test?" asked Stern.

"Pretty much," said Dr. Chu.

"Did she go home the same day?" asked Stern.

"No, she stayed overnight for observation," the doctor said.

"When she went home, did you follow up on her care?"

"Yes."

"And did she experience any problems after she was discharged from the hospital?"

"Yes, she experienced headaches, and her memory still was fuzzy about how she got the concussion," said Dr. Chu.

"Did you meet Mr. King at the hospital?"

"Yes."

"Can you describe how he reacted to his wife's trauma?" asked Stern.

"He seemed very upset and concerned," said Dr. Chu.

"Like a caring husband, doctor?" Stern asked.

"Yes, I guess you could say that," the doctor said.

"Thank you, Dr. Chu. No more questions, Your Honor," said Stern.

"You wish to cross, Mr. Berry?" asked the judge.

"Yes."

"Were you the only attending physician that day when Mrs. King was brought to the ER at Atlantic General Hospital?"

"Yes, I was."

"Are you still treating Mrs. King?"

"No, I was following her progress a month after her concussion, and I told her to call me if she was experiencing any problems."

"Is it normal to experience headaches and memory loss after a concussion, doctor?"

"Yes."

"How long would the average patient with a concussion experience headaches?" asked Bear.

"It all depends on the patient. A couple of weeks or longer."

"Did Mrs. King experience headaches after a couple of weeks?" asked Bear.

"No, her headaches disappeared," said Dr. Chu.

"What about her memory?" asked Bear.

"She has no recollection about how she got the concussion, but I'd say she made a full recovery."

"Dr. Chu, when you've prescribed a barbiturate, don't you always tell your patient to call you immediately if he or she experiences any side effects from taking the drug, or any other drug for that matter?"

"Yes, of course," said Dr. Chu.

"Were you also aware of the blood pressure medication Mrs. King was taking and its side effects?"

"Yes, I was."

"Has Mrs. King ever experienced any side effects, like memory problems, or hallucinations, or confusion?" asked Bear.

"No," said the doctor.

"Thank you, Dr. Chu. No more questions, Your Honor."

Dr. Chu nodded to Cici as he left.

"Call your next witness, Mr. Stern," said the judge.

One of Bear's paralegals hurried down the courtroom aisle and handed him a note, which he immediately read. Stern turned to look at the both of them.

"Uh . . . Excuse me, Your Honor and counsel. Your Honor, may I ask for a recess? I've just been handed a note from my associate that says a witness has come forward and wants to take the stand for the prosecution."

Stern, his eyes squinting, turned to look at both of them. He abruptly stood up and said, "Your Honor, I didn't know about this new witness. This is absurd, Your Honor. Here we go again. How dramatic. We are not filming a movie, here," he said. "Your Honor, he's probably trying to denigrate my client and sway the jury." Stern had wanted to call one of Greg's golf buddies to the stand so he could attest to Greg's fine character after Dr. Chu's testimony.

"Now, now, Mr. Stern," the judge said. "Proceed, Mr. Berry."

"I assure you, Your Honor and counsel, I was unaware of this witness coming forward," said Bear.

"Both of you in my chambers now," said the judge. Bear wanted his associate in the room also. Bear, his associate, and Stern marched into the judge's chambers. "Now what's going on, Mr. Berry?"

"My associate, Miss Norton, told me my office received a call this morning informing them a witness wanted to testify for the State as soon as possible. She just handed me the note when you asked Mr. Stern to present his next witness. This new witness who wants to testify for the State has come forward with justifiable information about the case."

Miss Norton said, "Your Honor, the witness just found evidence that can exonerate Mr. Merv Grady from committing attempted murder and robbery."

"Who is this witness?" asked Judge Bell.

"Mrs. Grady, Merv's wife," said Bear.

CHAPTER 17

After the judge agreed to a recess, court was adjourned and set to reconvene the next morning. Bear said to Miss Norton, his paralegal, "I'm anxious to meet Mrs. Grady. Has she left to come here?"

"Yes, she's on her way," said Miss Norton.

Bear and Miss Norton stepped into a small, private room in the rear of the courthouse building, where they would conduct the deposition. Bear removed his lightweight sport coat and hung it on a clothes tree in the room. Twenty minutes later, the court reporter and Mrs. Grady were walking down the hall. The court reporter opened the door to the private room.

Mrs. Grady just about burst into the room. Bear's eyebrows raised as he watched her sudden entrance into the room. "I couldn't wait to get here and show you what I found," said Mrs. Grady, a bit out of breath. She had her hair pulled back in a bun and wore a white turtle neck sweater with brown slacks.

"I'm curious to see what information you have for me," said Bear. "Please sit down." Bottled waters were brought into the room by the bailiff. They sat around a dark brown walnut table. Ample light filtered into the 10' by 12' room from four large windows.

"Mrs. Grady, my questions and your answers will be recorded by the court reporter and produced in the form of a transcript. Mr. Stern, the Defense Attorney, will meet with you after we talk."

"Mrs. Grady, this is Miss Norton, my associate. I believe you two have spoken on the phone already." Bear said, "All depositions are a serious matter. Okay, are you ready to begin?" She nodded and slipped on her round, steel-rimmed granny glasses. "Listen to the questions carefully, and answer them precisely. Remember you're under oath."

Bear said, "Rachel Grady has come forward today, January 2, 2014, as a witness for the prosecution." Mrs. Grady took a sip from her water bottle and began to answer Bear's questions. The four of them talked for a little over a half an hour. After completing Mrs. Grady's deposition, Bear discovered he would need to question one more witness.

Stern arrived in the room after Mrs. Grady's deposition was taken. His meeting with her only lasted 20 minutes.

Bear's office contacted the other witness, and Bear notified the court and Mr. Stern of the addition.

Friday morning, court convened at 9:00 a.m. sharp. Mrs. Grady maneuvered through the crowd and found a seat next to the aisle in the middle of the courtroom. She picked at her fingernail and took a deep breath. She blinked at the gray, January sky outside the court window and remembered the weatherman on the local channel said that Ocean City might get an inch or two of snow. *So unusual for the beach town.*

People were in the halls and seated inside the courtroom. Cici turned to Amie and said, "I'm so anxious to hear what

Merv's wife is going to say. Mr. Berry told me she could clear Merv's name."

"I'm wondering too. I'm going to keep my eyes on Greg's face and see his reaction to whatever she says," said Amie.

Judge Bell said, "Mr. Berry, representing the State, has two unexpected witnesses who have come forward today. We will hear new evidence from these witnesses. Mr. Berry, begin the proceedings."

"Two?" said Cici, as she looked at Amie. Amie shrugged her shoulders.

"I call Mrs. Rachel Grady to the stand."

Greg lowered his head and stared at the table.

After Mrs. Grady identified her relationship to Merv Grady and stated she was an elementary school teacher in Ocean Pines, the questioning began.

"Mrs. Grady, please tell the court why you have come forward today and not before this," said Bear.

"After my husband, Merv Grady, died, I inherited some of his belongings, one of which was his pick-up truck. Recently, I just got around to rummaging and sifting through its compartments. Inside the glove compartment, I found my husband's calendar booklet. He was a handyman and recorded his weekly jobs in the booklet. I flipped the pages and looked at the number of jobs he had completed each month. When I turned the calendar page to October, and saw that on October 1, he had written down, *Deck at Edwards*, I had to check if he started my neighbor's deck that day."

"I'd like to ask the court if I may enter this calendar into evidence as Exhibit Five," said Bear. The judge approved.

"Mrs. Grady, what is the significance of October 1?"

"That is the date of my father's birthday, and because of that, I'll always remember that Mrs. King was robbed and attacked on my dad's birthday. My husband couldn't have been at Mrs. King's house that morning to rob and attack Mrs. King. He was too busy building a deck for my neighbors, Mr. and Mrs. Edwards, two doors down from me."

"Were you home that day to see your husband, Mr. Grady, working on your neighbor's deck?" asked Bear.

"No, I was teaching that day, but I called my neighbor, Mr. Edwards, and asked him if he was home that day my husband was to start building their deck."

"Was Mr. Edwards, your neighbor, at his home October 1 when Mr. Grady was there?" Bear looked at the jury. Their eyes locked on him.

"Mr. Edwards was home and so was his wife. I never believed my husband tried to rob and kill Mrs. King. Not in a million years." Cici patted Amie on her hip after hearing Mrs. Grady's remarks.

"No more questions, Your Honor," said Bear.

"Mr. Stern, do you wish to question the witness?"

"Yes, Your Honor."

"Mrs. Grady, how do we know that it's not you who wrote *Deck at Edwards* in the calendar, and not your husband?"

Mrs. Grady's lips parted as she heard his question. She deeply inhaled and blinked rapidly. She exhaled and then leaned her body back in her seat. "If you don't believe me, you can have my handwriting analyzed. My husband's printing looks like chicken-scratch." Laughter was heard in the courtroom.

"Order in the court," said Judge Bell.

"It's very easy to tell the difference between his handwriting and mine," said Mrs. Grady.

"Mrs. Grady, because you were so doubtful that your husband couldn't possibly have tried to kill Mrs. King back in October, and you wanted your husband's reputation cleared, aren't you lying about the calendar?"

"No, absolutely not," she said.

"No more questions, Your Honor," said Stern.

"You may step down, Mrs. Grady." She leered at Greg as she passed him.

"Call your next witness, Mr. Berry," said Judge Bell.

"Will Mr. Edwards please take the stand?"

A very short, older man shuffled down the aisle. He wore khaki pants and a light pink shirt. He was bald and stooped over somewhat when he walked to the stand. The tremor in his right hand was very evident when he was sworn in.

"Thank you for coming today on such short notice. Please state your name and occupation."

"Christopher Edwards, and I'm retired."

"Your testimony is very crucial today. We need to confirm if Mr. Grady was working at your house on Tuesday, October 1. Was he there that day, and if so, what time did he arrive?"

"Yes, he was there the entire day. He arrived early in the morning, around 8:00 a.m. Yes, he worked on the deck all day long, except when my wife gave him a tuna fish sandwich and a bottle of Gatorade for lunch. He finished eating that and got back to work."

"Mr. Edwards, how can you be positive that he was there that particular day?"

"Both my wife and I are positive. My wife said we needed a deck built, and she wanted it started after we got back from staying at our beach house in Cape May the whole month of September. We had called Merv before we left and scheduled it for October 1. Easy to remember that date for an old guy like me." Laughter could be heard. "It took him four days to complete the deck, and it's just beautiful. Merv's a nice guy. He—"

"Thank you, Mr. Edwards. No more questions, Your Honor. The Prosecution rests," said Bear.

"Do you wish to redirect, Mr. Stern?"

"No, Your Honor. The Defense rests."

"You may step down, sir," said Judge Bell. "Closing arguments will begin Monday morning at 9:00 a.m. Court is adjourned until then. Have a good weekend."

Greg was hunched over as he was taken back to his cell. Stern walked back to Greg's cell after some of the people had cleared out of the courtroom.

"Greg, I need to tell you something. In light of the new evidence brought into court today by Mrs. Grady, you are suspect in the attack of your wife back in October. You no doubt will be charged with attempted murder on your wife, and there will be another trial. Obviously, Grady never had the bag in his possession. You did. Everything points to you."

"I found the bag in my neighbor's back yard. I just had a hunch it was Merv who robbed us," said Greg.

"Is that the best you can do?"

Greg looked at Stern and said, "Try real hard and get me a plea bargain this time. If you don't mind, I want to be left alone right now."

"I'll see what I can do," Stern said.

⚟

It was the day of the closing arguments. Amie looked at Cici as she was chipping off her pink nail polish in the courtroom. "Cici, you picked all the polish off your thumb. Are you nervous?"

"Yeah, I'm nervous and sick over this," she said. "Can't believe the trial is over and the closing arguments are going to begin. I can't tell which side the judge is on. He sure does frown a lot. Look at him. He's frowning now," said Cici. "Amie, I can't believe Greg attacked me and tried to kill me. He had the bag. Merv is innocent. Greg planned the whole thing." She shook her head.

Amie said, "He's a dirtbag."

"Yeah, but his boss made him out like a saint," said Cici.

"He's going to be convicted," said Amie.

Cici fanned herself with her hand. "It's warm in here," she said. "They need to turn on the air conditioner. I can't wait until this is over. Look, Mr. Berry is getting up now."

Bear rose from his seat and walked over to the jury box. He looked at the 12 of them, smiled, and began, "Ladies and gentlemen, in my opening statements, I said I would prove that Greg King abused his wife. You heard how he abused her verbally and physically. He insulted her, he didn't want sex with her, he frequently stayed out late, he was unfaithful, and he loved another woman." Bear pointed to Greg.

Cici whispered to Amie. "Greg's got his arms folded and is looking out the window. How pretentious."

"That man couldn't stand her. He was so angry at her because he thought she kept him from marrying his lover, Della Summer," said Bear.

Cici watched the jurors' faces. One was jotting down notes. Another looked disgusted.

"Ladies and gentlemen of the jury, I'm going to keep this short. You know why? Because it's a no-brainer."

Cici observed two jurors whispering to each other, and she poked Amie to look at them.

Bear said, "Witnesses supported Merv Grady had an alibi the day of the attack. Mr. King's self-defense story was a lie. Mr. Grady couldn't have had the bag of stolen goods." One juror sneezed twice, interrupting Bear.

"Gesundheit," said Bear. The stout female juror smiled.

"I ask you, ladies and gentlemen of the jury, do the right thing, and find Greg King guilty of involuntary manslaughter. That's also known as 'criminally negligent homicide' because it is an accidental killing caused by a person's criminally liable recklessness or criminal negligence. A fight took place in the trailer bedroom of Mr. Grady. Mr. King knew Mr. Grady didn't harm his wife. Mr. Grady was furious that Mr. King would blame him for the crime. Who grabbed the gun first? Mr. King or Mr. Grady? They fought over control of the gun and Mr. Grady ended up getting shot in the head. And ladies and gentlemen, you should find Mr. King guilty of assault, kidnapping, and attempted murder of his wife. You heard Ms. Summer, Mr. King's lover, say that Mr. King admitted to kidnapping and assaulting Mrs. King. Why do you think Mrs. King feared for her life when her wrists and feet were bound in the trunk of her car? Mr. King said he didn't put her in the trunk like she said. Why was her hair and saliva found in the trunk? Why did he try to escape after punching her and taking her to the golf course against her will? You know why." The elderly juror nodded his head. "Attempted murder charges consist of two elements. The offender takes some action toward killing another person, and the offender's act is intended to kill a person. An act that shows an intent to murder is luring, stalking, or taking someone to a specific location. The abandoned golf course in this case is where the murder was intended to take place." Pretty lady seemed totally absorbed in his speech. Bear stared into pretty lady's eyes. "And he had the weapon," nodding his head. "Didn't he?"

"Yes, the hammer," pretty lady blurted out. "Oh my God, sorry," she said, and placed her hand across her lips.

"The hammer," said Bear. "Yes. His fingerprints were on it. There's absolutely no doubt about it. Guilty as sin. Thank you."

"Amen," said Cici. "I almost screamed out 'Hammer!' myself." Cici scanned the courtroom. She turned around and saw two reporters scribbling on their pads in the back of the room, against the courtroom wall. Her elderly neighbors seated across the aisle caught her eye and waved to her.

Some of the jurors were reading their scribbled notes, and some kept their eyes glued straight ahead, looking at Greg. Greg slumped a little in his seat. "Sit up," said Stern.

The courtroom was still. Some people were smiling, and one person gave Bear a thumb's up. He pretended not to see him.

"Wonder what Stern will say," said Cici. Amie was twisting a handkerchief in her hands.

Sitting tall in his seat, Stern portrayed a picture of confidence. The judge asked, "Mr. Stern, is the Defense ready?"

"Yes, Your Honor." Stern wore a tailored brown suit and sported a bowtie as he walked towards the jury.

"Looks distinguished," said Cici.

Standing in front of the jurors, Stern said, "Ladies and gentlemen of the jury, Greg King is not guilty of the charges. Mr. Berry was right about one thing. There was a fight in Mr. Grady's trailer bedroom. They were fighting over the gun, and it discharged—right into Mr. Grady's skull. Mr. King had to protect his own life. It wasn't even his gun. It belonged to Merv Grady. It's justifiable self-defense." A blond-headed, male juror began coughing loudly. He popped a lozenge into his mouth. The other jurors looked at him with annoyance.

"There have never been any reports of physical abuse on Mrs. King. If it were so, why didn't she file charges? Yes, Greg King was unfaithful to his wife. He loved another woman, but that doesn't make him want to attempt to commit murder. He wanted to divorce her, not kill her. The night Mr. and Mrs. King had an argument over Mrs. King's refusal to drop the charges on Ms. Summer, Mrs. King accidentally fell and hit her jaw on the tiled floor. She accused her husband of striking her. He did not. No one witnessed Mr. King drive Mrs. King to the golf course. He put her in the car to drive her to the hospital. No one can prove he attempted to murder her. She ran out of the car, and God knows where she went. The meds she took can cause confusion and delusions. Mr. King couldn't find her and drove home. Mr. King was so upset about the situation Mrs. King created, he wanted to get out of town because he was afraid she would lie to the police that he kidnapped her and assaulted her. He was afraid of going to jail. Mrs. King lied about the abduction, because she wanted revenge and was furious he was seeing another woman."

Bear looked up from his papers on his table. He wrinkled his forehead after hearing Stern's last few statements. "I have provided you with reasonable doubt. I must repeat to you, ladies and gentlemen of the jury, Greg King is not guilty of these charges. Vote not guilty. Don't let me down."

Cici said, "Are you kidding me? Do you really think the jury will believe him?"

"I really doubt it," said Amie.

Judge Bell said, "Mr. Berry, will there be a rebuttal?"

"Yes, Your Honor, thank you. Ladies and gentlemen, thank you for your patience. The burden of proof. That's what I have to give you. Gregory King is guilty. He hated his wife. He didn't want to give Mrs. King any of their assets. He had a temper he couldn't control. His lover was in jail, and he blamed the wife he despised for his lover's imprisonment. So, enraged, he planned to kill Mrs. King that night. Mr. King is a monster. Put him away, ladies and gentlemen. Thank you."

※

Judge Bell said, "Ladies and gentlemen of the jury, you have a serious task ahead of you. Please give careful consideration to your decisions on whether the defendant is guilty or not of the charges. In order to return a verdict of guilty, in a criminal trial, the charges must be proven beyond a reasonable doubt. If you have any questions, the foreperson you select can summon the bailiff. I will help with any clarifications. While you deliberate, all of you will be under the supervision of a court officer. I would like the alternate jurors to remain in the courthouse while the 12 jurors deliberate and come to a final verdict. Good luck." He banged his gavel and said, "Court is adjourned." Cici saw that Judge Bell was no longer frowning.

Noise filled the air. People walked out of the courtroom chatting, and someone was laughing boisterously.

Cici thanked Bear for his handling of the case. "You did a wonderful job."

"Well," Bear said, "have to keep up my reputation as a tough prosecutor, or else they'll start calling me 'Teddy Bear,' which I would hate." Cici laughed and tried to leave the courtroom with Amie and Pat as quickly as possible. The room was packed so tightly, they could barely step through the crowd.

Greg was ushered back to his cell. He mumbled thanks to Stern. The 12 jurors left their seats to deliberate.

Outside, the threesome conversed. "I think Mr. Berry did a great job," said Cici. "Don't you think Greg will be found guilty on all counts?"

"It's hard to predict. I can't imagine he'll be found not guilty. *We* all know he's guilty," Pat said.

"The longer the jury deliberates, the better it is for the Defense," Amie said. "But I agree with Cici. Mr. Berry did a fantastic job. And he proved Greg had a motive. It should be a slam dunk."

CHAPTER 18

George, the oldest juror of the 12, wanted to be elected the foreman. He looked around the room where the group would deliberate. He noticed a huge, rectangular mahogany table in the center. A ceiling fan hummed above the table. No sunlight could enter the windowless room except for a skylight in the ceiling in the rear of the room. A sink and small refrigerator bordered the back wall, and on the table in the middle of the room was a container of sharpened pencils and markers. Small writing pads for the jurors were next to the pencils. Lined chart paper was clipped to an easel near the table, and a unisex bathroom was situated beside the entry to the room.

George wore small, round, black spectacles similar to Harry Potter's and was dressed in a white long-sleeve, button-down shirt, khaki pants, and brown loafers with no socks. George walked over to the fridge to check its contents and found ample bottled water for everyone. He carried some over to the table. *Time to take charge.*

"Here, let me help you," said Tracey, one of the jurors.

George, now a retiree from serving as a parole officer for 17 years, got the attention of the others and said to the group of 11, "I think it might be a good idea to get to know one another before getting started. Why don't we take a seat around the table?" He noticed a stack of labels next to the pads. He distributed the name tags to everyone. "After writing your name on a label, stick it on yourself, so everyone can know who they're talking to." George didn't want to sit at the head of the table because he knew they had to decide on a foreperson. *Don't want to appear too domineering.*

Liz, who seated herself next to George, said, "I hope this doesn't take too long. I think it's pretty easy to come to a verdict. I'm anxious to go home to my eight-month-old daughter."

George couldn't help but stare for a second at the rhinestone earring which pierced her nostril. He said, smiling, "I certainly understand, Liz, but we don't want to convict someone because you think he *probably* did it. We have to focus on the evidence and the law." He thought she looked to be in her late 20s and didn't care for her kinky perm. George encouraged everyone to tell a little bit about themselves.

A stocky man named Eric spoke up. His gray hair was pulled back in a ponytail. He had bright blue eyes and a scar on his forehead above his nose. His gold top incisor showed when he smiled. He rolled up his shirt sleeve, revealing not only his muscular arm, but also numerous, colorful tattooed snakes and skeletons. "I guess you all wouldn't be surprised that I own a tattoo parlor, since I'm covered in tattoos." When he rolled his sleeve down, the only tattoo left showing was an anchor on the left side of his thick neck.

"Were you in the Navy?" asked George. He could smell cigarettes on his breath.

"Yes, were you too?" asked Eric.

"No, but I'm a Vietnam vet, retired with a wife and two grown children," said George.

"I lost my brother in Iraq," said Eric.

"Sorry," said George.

A man with blondish hair parted in the middle and dressed in a light blue, collared polo shirt coughed and cleared his throat. "I'm Gary, and I sell mattresses. In a nutshell, I'm a bachelor and love being single. I had a rotten divorce, but that's all behind me now." He curled his blonde mustache with his thumb and forefinger.

"I sure could use a mattress right now," said Bill. George laughed. "I guess I'll go next. Bill's the name. I own Crabs Ahoy." He was as skinny as a young Jerry Seinfeld.

"I thought I knew you from somewhere. It was killing me. I couldn't think where," said Ann. "We buy your steamed crabs often."

"Great. Keep coming. Anyway," said Bill, "I'm 52, married with five kids and live on Manklin Creek. I love fishing. Every year I go out on a charter boat and participate with a great crew in the White Marlin Open in August. Almost won it one year," said Bill.

Ann, who wore tights, flats, a loose, long white and black striped blouse, and what looked like a mild case of rosacea on her face, said, "Love to watch those charter boats come in with their catch. I'm a hair salon manager, and my boyfriend plays in a band every other Saturday at the Cove."

There was a momentary silence, and George said, "Herb, Tracey, let's hear from you."

"Okay," a very pretty blonde dressed to the nines, said, "I'm Tracey, and I own a boutique with my mom on Route 50. I'm single and can't wait to get started discussing this case."

Fit and tan Herb said, "I'm an assistant golf pro at Eagles Landing. I'm married to a golf widow because I'm on the course six days a week."

"Lucky you," said Gary.

Brenda, a heavyset African-American, had a contagious, hearty laugh and said, "I teach the second grade." She had nicely coiffured hair and played with her large, hooped pierced earring. She said, "I love my job, but I've always wanted to serve on a jury."

"I'm a teacher too—at a private school in the town of Berlin," said Mary. "I've been married for eight years and have two sons. I teach kindergarten." Her hair drooped around her pale cheeks. "I'm really glad I was selected to be a juror."

"Who's left to introduce themselves?" asked George.

Karen, who looked to be six feet tall before she sat down, said, "I'm a motel manager in Ocean City." George noticed she had a facial tic when she spoke. Karen removed her tortoise shell bifocals and rubbed the lens with a Kleenex. She brushed her brownish bangs away from her eyes and said, "I'm glad to be here and away from overseeing the staff at the motel. It's not so busy now, but I still need a break."

A dark-skinned Hispanic woman with streaked, highlighted hair said with a slight accent, "I'm Helen. I manage a Dollar Store. I'm proud to say I have twin boys who are amazing, and I'm legal. I've been in this country all my life, in case you were wondering."

George cleared his throat and said, "Okay, well, nice to meet all of you. We all have varied backgrounds, and I know we are all anxious to get started."

"What about you, George?" asked Brenda, sipping from her bottle of water.

After telling Brenda and the others about his past, he said, "So now that we know a little about each other, our first order of business is to choose a foreperson."

The pretty boutique owner said, "George you're doing a good job already. I think it should be you."

Brenda said, "Yeah, George you seem like a good discussion leader and are really organized."

"I have no problems with you being the foreperson," said Herb.

George said, "Is anyone interested in the job besides me?" asked George. The room was still. The group unanimously chose him.

"Okay," said George. "Let's go around the table and talk about the case. Speak up anytime, though, when you have something to say. Don't be afraid to express your views. Brenda, would you please take notes? I'll write down key points on the chart so that everyone can see them."

"This will be an interesting task for us," said George. He explained that the case fascinated him. There was nothing like the thrill of participating in a criminal trial and watching clever lawyers do their job. *Bear was a bit of a smart-aleck at times. Judge Bell's a very no-nonsense guy.*

"Alright, everyone, let's discuss each charge, one at a time." George looked at his notes. "We'll begin with the charge of involuntary manslaughter."

Eric started and said, "I think this Greg guy is guilty of involuntary manslaughter. He must have planted the stolen stuff in Grady's house. It took the blame off him. That must have been his motive, and he probably wanted to get rid of Grady. I don't believe it was self-defense."

Herb said, "Are you saying that only because Merv Grady had an alibi the day Mrs. King was attacked and robbed?"

"Yes," said Eric.

"Well, it's a good theory, but I think we need to have more discussion," said Herb. "That means Grady couldn't have had the stolen goods from Mrs. King's house. Eric might be right about King planting the stuff or King bringing the bag in with him. He could have planned to kill him. If so, how was he going to kill him? The gun belonged to Grady. Did he have a weapon with him? There's no proof he did. Maybe Grady got so angry at King for accusing him and trying to set him up for the attack and robbery, he pulled his gun out on King. They could have fought for possession of the gun, and it went off, killing Grady. It could have been self-defense. And I don't believe his cellmate's story," said Herb. George scribbled on the chart.

Mary said, "They were close friends. Maybe King knew where Grady hid his gun. Maybe he got to it first. Maybe all along he planned to murder him. He had motive, like you said, Eric. Maybe he tried to kill his wife and gave her the concussion. King was a person of interest for that. He didn't want to be the one charged with attacking and robbing his wife."

"I don't want to rule out Mr. King's cellmate's story. But how did Mr. Grady's fingerprints get on the plastic bag and King's ring?" asked Gary.

"Somehow his prints got on the bag. He could have grabbed the bag to look at it more closely. I don't know how his prints got on the wedding band, though," said Bill.

George said, "Let's look at the evidence. Merv Grady had an alibi, so Grady wouldn't have had the bag." He looked at his notes. "Lynch, the cellmate said King told him he killed Grady. We are voting whether King murdered Grady unintentionally. Detective Crabbe told us Mr. King's story about what happened. Is King's story credible? Can it be dis-proven? Does anyone have anything to add?" Silence. "Okay, before we vote, let's define involuntary manslaughter."

"It's the crime of killing another person unlawfully but unintentionally," said Helen.

Karen said, "Wait. I agree with what some of you said. There was a scuffle. King grabbed Merv's gun, they each struggled to get it, and it discharged, killing Grady. It was unintentional. And reckless."

"But King's lawyer said Grady pulled a gun out on him. He wasn't being reckless in defending his own life," said Helen.

"How can you be sure what actually happened? Mr. Stern wasn't there." said Ann.

"King's story is all fabricated if he said he found the stolen stuff under Grady's bed. Grady couldn't have possibly committed the crime. King is a liar," said Bill.

"Does anyone have anything else to add? Are we ready to vote on this charge?" asked George. They all voted.

"Do we put our names on the paper?" asked the waitress, Liz.

"Not necessary," said George. Some of the jurors laughed. Liz blushed and said, "Well, I didn't know."

George collected all of the papers and looked them over. He finally said, "We have five holdouts who voted not guilty. Let's keep this discussion flowing."

Brenda said, "We don't know if both of them grappled with the gun, and it discharged, killing Grady. But the room was a mess after the shooting. Because of the mess in the room, Grady could have pulled out his gun, and they fought over it, but you can't be 100% sure."

"The Chief of Police thought it was self-defense," said Ann. "I think that speaks volumes. Boy, is he huge. He's the biggest man I've ever seen."

"Yeah, but that was before Mrs. Grady testified. It just seems fishy to me. Mr. King had that bag. Mr. King had some kind of a plan when he went to Mr. Grady's place," said Tracey.

More discussion followed. One by one, they gave their opinions. But they were still deadlocked.

"Let's come back to this later and discuss the kidnapping charge next. Who wants to go first?" asked George.

"I will," said Brenda. "Just let me say first, that I vote guilty on this one. I believe Greg King is guilty because they found the duct tape—"

"That duct tape could have been in the trunk for some other reason. No one saw King wrap it around her wrists and ankles," said Eric.

"Let Brenda finish," said George.

"Mrs. King described in detail the events of that night. I don't think she made it up. Do you really think she got to the golf course by walking there by herself?" asked Brenda. "Or jumping out of a moving car? Was he going 30, 40 or 50 miles per hour? Her body would have landed on the road, hitting it hard and would have been badly injured at that speed."

"Did the prosecutor prove that she was in the trunk? No one saw King put her in the trunk and drive her there." said Gary, the salesman.

"This guy is bad news. From all that I heard in court, he's a horrible husband. He's an unsympathetic, extremely cold, violent, amoral, and vicious man. I believe he was so full of rage and furious at his wife when he found out she refused to drop the charges on his girlfriend, Della Summer. The man is a sociopath. He's guilty in my mind of driving her to the golf course," said Brenda.

"Mrs. Tyler picked her up in front of the golf course. She saw her bruised face. Mrs. King testified that she was driven there by her husband. She even had her saliva on the duct tape in the trunk when she tried to bite it off her wrists. What other proof do you need?" said Tracey. Brenda jotted down notes.

George said to Tracey, "Her hair strands too. We think along the same lines, Tracey." She smiled and thanked him. "Is there any more discussion about the kidnapping charge?"

"I think it's bullshit that he said he was driving her to the hospital. His wife had a bruised, purple face and recently had a concussion, and he's driving the opposite way from where the hospital is?" said Eric. "That neighbor, Mr. Cole, said Mrs. King told him she was abducted. Come on, people."

"Yes," said Liz. "Mrs. King's husband abused her physically in the past. He was really nasty to her, as you heard. He didn't love her. He loved that Della woman. He had a motive for kidnapping her and driving her to the deserted course. Why do you think he went to the trouble of taking her there? He wanted to finish her off, in my opinion. He wanted Della. He kidnapped her, alright." Liz spit out her gum into her hand.

Bill said, "King wanted to keep all of his assets. I believe he really didn't want a divorce, especially after meeting Ms. Summer. He drove her to that golf course to kill her."

"Remember, we have to focus on the evidence, but all opinions are valid. And ask yourself, did the state prove its case? Should we vote? Any more comments?" asked George.

All voted guilty of kidnapping.

They moved on to the next charge—assault of Mrs. King.

"One of the exhibits was a photo of Mrs. King's swollen, bruised face. The photo was taken at the police station, dated the day after she was at the golf course, and had been presented in court by Detective Crabbe. Let's pass that around for everyone to see," said George.

Helen grabbed the photo and said, "Yikes. The photo is definitely graphic. Mr. King has slapped her around in the past. I do believe Mrs. King. I believe he knocked her out before driving her to the golf course. That would make it easy for him to put her in the trunk of the car. Mrs. King said she woke up inside the trunk. I don't believe that she fell on the floor."

"Come on people. Did you forget about his mistress, Ms. Summer? Remember King called her when he was on the run, and she asked him if he really kidnapped and assaulted his wife? He didn't deny it," said Eric.

Everyone looked at their notes. A balanced discussion followed along the same lines as Helen's and Eric's.

"Let's show a raise of hands on this one," said George. "Guilty or not guilty of assault?" Everyone's hand went up for guilty.

"Okay, let's move on to the next charge, attempted murder of Mrs. King. Has everyone had a chance to comment? I encourage everyone to speak his or her thoughts. We've had fair discussions so far." He swatted a gnat away from his face.

Motel manager Karen spoke up. "Well, I was thinking, if he really wanted to kill Mrs. King, why didn't he hunt for her a little harder than he did? You would have thought he'd hunt for his wife and find her, even if it took all hours of the night."

"What about Mr. King leaving immediately and heading for Florida?" asked Liz.

"What about it?" asked Karen.

"Well, if he wasn't guilty of trying to kill her, why would he want to skip town? Why would he want to change his name? Why would he want to leave his job? His money? His precious home? His girlfriend? For the hell of it? Doesn't make sense to me, except he was running from the law and he was guilty of the charge," said Liz.

"Right!" said Mary. "It's so logical." Mary's cell phone buzzed. "Aw, I miss you too, sweetie. Mommy can't talk right now. I'll call you when I can. Love you." She disconnected. "Sorry, guys."

"Let's all turn off our phones, so we don't get interrupted," said George.

"I still say there is no real proof he tried to kill her. Okay, granted, he drove her there. I'll concede to that, but I believe you have to vote not guilty on attempted murder, because there's no proof," said Eric. "The hammer under the driver's seat doesn't mean he was going to use it to kill her, even if his prints were on it. Of course they'd be on it. Tools are kept in cars all the time." His hands patted his chest pockets. "I need a cigarette."

"Have to wait," said George.

"I don't have tools in my car, let alone a hammer or duct tape," said Mary. Mary was very soft-spoken. "I think that Mr. King is—"

"Speak up. We can't hear you," said Karen.

"Ahem," said Mary. "I believe Mr. King is guilty of attempted murder of his wife. Mrs. King said she feared for her life. Do you think he just wanted to kidnap her without harming her and leaving her at the golf course? Doesn't it make sense that his intent was to kill her and abandon her somewhere off the beaten path?"

"Mrs. King never said that he tried to kill her with a hammer or any other way," said Ann.

"Alright" said George. "Bill, Herb, Tracey, what do you say?"

"I think the prosecutor knows his stuff. He was very convincing. I believe Mr. King had in mind to kill his wife using a hammer and leave her dead at that abandoned golf course. Have you ever been there? It's so isolated and desolate. This guy reeks evil. He picked a great place to hide a body. It's like putting puzzle pieces together once you are given all of the evidence. I definitely think it's a no-brainer," Herb said.

"I hear ya. Points well taken. I'm in agreement," said Bill. "Remember the law. A conviction for attempted murder requires a demonstration of an intent to murder, meaning that the perpetrator either tried to murder and failed or took steps towards committing a murder."

"Tracey?" asked George.

"Guilty," said Tracey.

Gary stood up. All eyes were focused on him. "Listen up, guys. You want to know what I think?" Not interested in hearing any replies, he said, "It seems plain to me as night follows day:

That man tried to kill his wife. He treated her like dirt. She's lucky to be alive."

George said, "Merely causing serious bodily harm to someone is not sufficient to prove attempted murder unless there is evidence of actual intent to kill the person. Taking someone to a specific location where the murder is intended to take place is an act that shows an intent to murder. Mr. King did have something in the car that could do the job."

"Okay, let's write our vote on paper. Then fold it," said George. When they were done, George counted the 12 votes. "Okay, looks like we have two voting not guilty. We will need more discussion. Please remember, don't convict someone because you think he *probably* did it."

"I need to use the bathroom," said Gary.

"Alright, let's hold up on the discussion," said George. "Hey, will someone ask the court officer to turn down the ceiling fan a little?" Bill said he would ask him.

"I'm starving," said Brenda. "If we don't come to a unanimous decision, maybe we can go out and get a pizza," she said.

"I vote steamed crabs from Crabs Ahoy," said Eric, laughing.

"Dream on," said Bill.

When Gary returned, George said, "Okay, we need to come to an agreement. The judge doesn't want to hear we are hopelessly deadlocked. Be open-minded."

Discussion resumed on the attempted murder charge of Cici. They finally handed in their votes.

"Now let's get back to Mr. King's charge of involuntary manslaughter." Pointing to the chart, George said, "I'll start. You know, I was thinking that Greg King planned to blame Merv Grady for the robbery and assault, and that of course probably means that King is the guilty one for that crime. Let's say he planted the stolen goods at Merv's trailer. Let's say King didn't want to kill Merv; he just wanted to cast suspicion on him. While he was at the trailer, maybe King's plan was to call the police after he pretended to discover the loot under the futon. The police would then arrive and arrest Merv, but his plan backfired when Merv got out his gun and aimed it at Greg."

More than half of the jurors nodded their heads, but the 12 of them convened for another 45 minutes.

CHAPTER 19

Cici couldn't stand to look at Greg. She couldn't fathom her marriage ever coming to this, and worst of all, she couldn't believe Greg was so hideously evil. Cici hoped he would be found guilty beyond a reasonable doubt on all counts. The whole court experience took a toll on her. What would the outcome be? Would she still get half of the estate if he went to jail? She was assured by Frank Vaughn he would do battle for her. Suppose he got off? Would she be safe? Would he go back to Della? Would he stay in Ocean Pines?

"Do you think the jurors will deliberate a long time?" Cici asked Amie.

"What do you think, Pat?" asked Amie.

Pat looked at his watch. "It's already been a little over 2 hours."

Cici finished the last of her cappuccino in the Snow Hill Coffee Shop. "That's not good, is it?"

"It's hard to tell," said Pat. "When you're selected to be a member of the jury, and your decision effects a person spending a long time in jail, you want to be absolutely sure you're making the right decision."

"Are you okay, Cici?" asked Amie.

"Yes, but it's so stressful waiting." Cici's cell phone buzzed.

"Mrs. King, this is Detective Crabbe. They've reached a verdict."

"Thank you. I'm on my way," she said. They immediately left the coffee shop. As they approached the courthouse, they saw people everywhere. They crowded outside and inside the courtroom. Cici and Amie ploughed through the crowd.

Cici said, "I bet this is the most excitement this little town has ever had. No wonder today it's so packed with people." Cici, Amie, and Pat were fortunate to get a seat close enough to the front of the room, because Detective Crabbe had saved space for them there. People crowded the halls and extra folding chairs were placed in the rear of the courtroom.

Cici glanced at Bear. He was flipping pages in his folder. She felt perspiration on the back of her neck and deeply inhaled, then let out her breath.

The noise in the courtroom suddenly halted when the judge entered the courtroom. "The Honorable Judge Donald Bell. Please rise."

All rose. Cici stared at the expressionless faces of the jurors, except for the older juror. "Amie, look at that elderly man on the jury. He's smiling and talking to that pretty lady next to him. He must be happy about the verdict."

"Or he has a crush on her," said Amie.

The only sounds in the room were the shuffling of papers on Stern's table and a sneezing juror. Cici felt that Amie could hear her heart pounding.

The judge spoke to the jurors, "The Court wants to thank the jurors for their patience and their commitment to serve. It has been an interesting case, and now it's time to hear your decision. Foreperson, has the jury reached a verdict?"

The appointed male foreperson stood and answered, "Yes, Your Honor."

The judge said, "The clerk will read and report the verdict." George handed her the paper.

Cici's heart was thudding louder in her chest.

The clerk read, "We, the jury, do find the defendant, Mr. Gregory King, on the charge of involuntary manslaughter, not guilty." Cici saw Greg smile and tap Stern's shoulder. She looked at Amie and said, "Are you kidding me?"

"And the second charge?"

She read, "We, the jury, do find the defendant, Mr. Gregory King, on the charge of kidnapping, guilty."

"On the charge of assault, we find the defendant, Mr. Gregory King, guilty," said the clerk. And lastly, "We do find the defendant, Mr. Gregory King, on the charge of attempted murder, guilty." Cici looked at her husband as he whispered in Stern's ear. Greg shook his head. He covered his face with his hands. Was he crying?

The judge announced, "Sentencing will take place in three months. Thank you, ladies and gentlemen of the jury. You're free to go." He banged his gavel. "Court is adjourned."

Greg looked up at Stern and said, "Wish Bear wasn't so tough and you could have gotten me a plea bargain."

"You know I tried," said Stern. Greg turned around and stared at Cici. She saw the corners of his mouth slide downwards, and she rose from her seat and immediately turned her back on him. Cici glanced in the rows behind her. She saw Joe Crabbe two rows back. Their eyes locked. She smiled at him, and he nodded and smiled back.

C HAPTER 20

Four Months Later

Amie had a stroke of luck. She couldn't wait to call Cici and share the news with her.

"Cici, you won't believe this, but guess what?"

"What? You're pregnant?"

"Hah! No. I won the OPVD (Ocean Pines Volunteer Fire Department) New House Raffle."

"You're kidding. No way."

"Yep, it's true. I get to claim my newly built home on the Assawoman Bay in two weeks. Wait till Pat hears. He'll be blown away. Can you believe I paid $100.00 for my raffle ticket out of only 63 tickets?"

"That's great news, Amie. Congratulations. It's what you've always wanted."

"Oh, and I need your advice. Could you come with me on Saturday to help me choose my bridal gown?"

"I'd love to," said Cici.

"Pat and I decided to have a small wedding on the beach at the Ocean Beach Club."

"Love that idea," said Cici. "You two were meant to be."

"Of course, I want you to be my bridesmaid. We can pick out your dress, too."

"I can show off my new body," said Cici.

"Absolutely. How much did you lose anyway?"

"Twenty-nine pounds of blubber," said Cici. "No doubt that I lost my appetite from the stress of the robbery, assault, abduction, trial, and finalizing all this divorce stuff. Look at these tights I'm wearing. My flat stomach's back."

"And Zumba lessons helped too, I bet," said Amie.

"Yes, and that too."

"Well, you have one big stress out of the way. Greg is gone forever from your life, spending time in the Worcester Correctional Institution—and without a water view," said Amie. "Plus, I'm sure you didn't forget, he's facing a second trial for attempted murder because of the introduction of new evidence at the end of the trial from Mrs. Grady."

"I don't want to go through another trial," said Cici. "What's the point? Why not forgo the trial and plead guilty for a plea bargain. What are they going to do, slap him with more time until he's 105 years old?"

"Makes sense to me," said Amie. "Hey, Cici, has the divorce been finalized?"

"My lawyer has filed the papers, and he served the documents to Greg while he was in prison. Greg can't stop the legal process of divorce. He can, however, delay matters by being uncooperative, just to be nasty. I'm still waiting for him to sign the papers. My lawyer said that criminal conviction and incarceration are automatic grounds for an at-fault divorce. Vaughn's really done a great job keeping the process on track for me. I'll walk away with a greater share of the marital goods.

I never wanted his inheritance money. That's his anyway. Greg was using some of it to pay Stern and his divorce lawyer. I'm still living off the money in our joint savings account right now. That will last for a while. I should be fine after all this is settled. There's a lot—too much to mention it all. Real estate, mutual funds, bonds, crystal, coin collections, CD's . . . "

"Wow. What if Greg is uncooperative?" asked Amie.

"After two months, that time is up this week, I can request to enter a default judgement."

"Sounds like a lot of work, but I'm glad you have a skilled lawyer," said Amie. "I wish I had known about him when Carl and I got our divorce. By the way, I have scheduled two showings of your house on Friday. So far I've had nothing but compliments on your home," said Amie.

"I hope it sells soon."

"It's only been on the market for two weeks, Cici."

"I know. I would never want to go back there and live. I'm perfectly happy in my condo," said Cici. "Didn't you show the house yesterday?" asked Cici.

"Yes, to a young couple. They loved it, but they thought it was overpriced," said Amie. "I think it's very competitive with some of the houses in Terns Landing. You won't have any trouble selling it. Remember, Greg always said it was the best house in the neighborhood."

"Oh please, Amie, don't remind me about him," said Cici.

Amie said, "I'm going to put my house up for sale next week, now that I've won the raffle. I'm worried I won't sell it quickly because it's not on the water and hasn't been updated much. I'll get someone to stage it for me, and that might help. I'll keep the price a little lower than some of the other comparable homes."

"You know your market. Oh, I forgot to tell you. I talked to my mom. She's walking in her neighborhood every day, and

Sam and she are thinking about riding their bikes on the trail once a week."

"Modern medicine. That's great, Cici," said Amie.

⊣⊢

Amie and Pat lucked out on their wedding day. The ocean was calm and the air was still. The temperature was mild. The sun peeked out among the fluffy, cumulus clouds that dotted the blue sky.

Cici walked down the sandy aisle with Amie following her, carrying a large bouquet of white tulips. Amie was dressed in a white, A-line bridal gown with a fitted bodice. It flowed out to the ground, with an unbroken line. She wore her blonde hair long with a rhinestone clip above her ear. Pat wore a dapper suit, pink shirt, and bow tie. A red carnation boutonniere was tucked in his buttonhole. They said their vows below a flowered archway among a small crowd of about 15 people.

"I now pronounce you man and wife. You may kiss the bride," said Judge Bell. Everyone cheered, and Crabbe clapped and winked at Cici.

C HAPTER 21

Detective Crabbe was feeling guilty. He was angry at himself for not doing a better job to prove that Greg was guilty of Merv's death. He never believed it was self-defense. If he could have proved otherwise, Cici wouldn't have been assaulted and kidnapped. Crabbe felt protective of Cici. He thought she really looked great, even after all she'd been through. When she came to the police station after she was kidnapped, he was struck by her bravery and found he was attracted to her. Her beautiful, sparkling, green eyes were captivating. He loved that she let her hair grow longer. He kept staring at her at the trial. She was intriguing. When she smiled at him, as he was leaving the courtroom, he felt his heart skip a beat. It was wonderful seeing her so happy at Amie and Pat's wedding.

He dialed her cell phone, asking if he could meet her somewhere. "I'd like to talk to you about something that's been bothering me," he said. "Could we meet somewhere?" he asked.

"When do you want to meet?" Cici asked.

"Are you busy now?" he asked.

"Not really. Have a pedicure appointment in two hours. Would you like to come here to talk?"

Cici gave him her new address.

Cici was wearing dark, black tights and a light green top that accentuated her eyes. Her mocha colored hair fell over her shoulders. Dressed in jeans and a black T-shirt, Crabbe walked into her condo and glanced around.

"I love this place. One bedroom or two?" He swerved around. "Wow! What a view! You can see all the way to Ocean City's skyline." Crabbe and Cici walked outside onto the deck. "The cool air feels good on your face," said Crabbe. He held onto the wrought-iron railing as Cici pointed upwards at the V-shaped formation of geese that flew by. "There are white caps on the bay." They remained silent for a minute as they watched the bobbing water in the cove. Crabbe turned to Cici. "How do you like it here?"

"I love it. Only one bedroom. I feel nice and safe here. My little cocoon. Come back inside. Please sit down. What is it you need to tell me, Detective Crabbe?" asked Cici.

"Don't you think we should be on a first-name basis?" he said.

"Of course," said Cici.

"Well, I hate to admit it, but I feel I didn't do my job. My gut tells me Greg murdered Merv. If I had been more thorough, I could have prevented him from hurting you. When I think how close you came to being killed out there on that golf course, I get sick inside."

"You want to know the truth? I just can't be killed," said Cici.

He laughed and said, "I think you're on to something there."

"Is that what you wanted to tell me?" said Cici.

"Yeah, I think I'm losing my touch. I never even checked if Grady had an alibi that day when you were robbed. I never even questioned him," said Crabbe.

"Don't be so hard on yourself," said Cici.

"No, you're wrong. I should be. I've decided to retire. I've been in it for too long. But I'm glad I worked on the Operation Identification (Operation ID) program in Ocean Pines. It discourages burglary and theft by marking properties with identifying numbers. The program has shown a dramatic result in burglary reduction."

"That's good to hear," Cici said.

"Anyway, I'm putting in my resignation tomorrow. Pat has been asking me to work with him now that his partner is leaving. So I accepted his offer. It'll be less stressful than my current job. It's time. And I have a position at night teaching criminology at Wor-Wic Community College."

"Well, you have to do what makes you happy. And you shouldn't be plagued with regrets. I worked part-time at Pat's agency a little while. Aside from his partner, it was just the four of us—a retired cop, Jim; his wife, Barbara; and a female detective, Emily Kirk, specializing in spousal abuse. Everyone there was so nice. I enjoyed it there, but needed more money. Now, I'm working full-time."

"Oh, really? Where Cici?" he asked.

"At a women's shelter in Salisbury. It's very rewarding. My therapist helped me get a job there."

"That's great. You would be exceptionally good at that."

"Can I get you something to drink?"

"No, thank you." He glanced at his watch. "Have to hit the road. I really should be going, because my dog, Old Bay, is overdue for a walk. He's getting older and has arthritis. Cici, Old Bay is 10 now. He really needs more room. I'm planning to put my condo on the market and move to a bigger place. I'd like to get a house with a yard. Maybe here in Ocean Pines."

"Gosh, everyone is selling their house—me, Amie, and now you. You should have Amie as your agent."

Cici looked at him as his gaze held hers. The mood suddenly changed. Cici was silent. Crabbe wanted to kiss her. He reluctantly had to break their trance.

"Thanks for seeing me. I can see myself out."

"Joe, I think you're an outstanding detective."

"Thanks," he said, smiling. Crabbe turned away and walked to the door. Cici stood there watching him, with his back to her. He paused, placing his hand on the doorknob. His shoulders raised, and he took a deep breath. He turned around. Her eyes were on him.

He grinned, nodded, and said, "Cici, you said I have to do what makes me happy." He asked, "By any chance are you busy tonight? I'd like to take you out to dinner at the Shark."

CHAPTER 22

Della couldn't get her job back, even though she wasn't serving a jail sentence. She still had the misdemeanor on her record. But she got lucky. She landed a job working out of her home for a cosmetic company, similar to Mary Kay. Della's income afforded her to keep her condo on the 21st floor with her view of the Delaware Memorial Bridge.

Della didn't wear tinted glasses anymore. No one could really tell her vision was disabled in her one eye. Even though her sight was limited, she was still grateful to Cici for her efforts in trying to persuade the district attorney to prevent her from serving a jail sentence and paying a hefty fine.

Della had thrown away letters that Greg wrote to her from the jail. She despised him. She had driven to Snow Hill to hear the sentencing for Greg's crimes. Traffic had been heavy, and Della had stopped on the way twice. The drive had taken more than the usual two and a half hours.

She pressed her remote key to lock the Kia and glanced at her new vanity license plate. It no longer read, "EYES4U."

She'd replaced it with the word, "MAKEUP." Della sat in the back of the courtroom, making sure Greg couldn't see her. She didn't mind if Cici noticed her and she would thank her again if she saw her. The same judge was presiding. She watched Cici take the podium and describe the hell she went through with Greg. She listened to Detective Crabbe give his opinion of Greg's detestable actions. The prosecuting attorney, Bear, was even there. A pretty, blonde neighbor of Cici's attested to Greg's miserable character.

Judge Bell said, "Federal criminal code makes kidnapping a serious felony offense." Judge Bell handed down a sentence of 25 years for kidnapping, 15 years for assault, and 30 years for attempted murder, served concurrently. Della felt relieved. Justice was served in her mind. She computed the math—Greg would be seventy-one when he got out, but then there would be another trial. *So he'll probably never get released.* She left the courtroom quickly and headed back to Wilmington.

The day's events brought back painful memories and stressed her out. She pulled into the parking lot of Spike's Tavern, which was near her condo. It was a small place. She headed towards the L-shaped bar, slid onto a stool, and ordered a cosmo. She never had been in there before and admired the décor. Pictures of the Delaware Memorial Bridge and ships in the port lined the silica sand textured, white walls. Casual beige sofas and a chic, glass-top, coffee table were arranged around a cozy fireplace.

Della took a sip from her drink. She needed that sip. She took another and couldn't help but notice the good-looking guy in a V-neck sweater at the bar sitting opposite her. He smiled at Della, and she nodded back. Della signaled the bartender. "See that guy over there in the black sweater?" The bartender turned around to look.

"Whatever he's drinking, send another one over to him, and put it on my tab, please," she said.

Greg signed the division of assets agreement for Cici. It irked him that she got so much. Stern told him in the first trial that Judge Bell wanted to avoid imposing 'triple punishment' for the same course of conduct and decided the multiple sentences would be served at the same time. Greg didn't have to worry about a second trial. A plea bargain had been granted by the prosecutor. Greg pleaded guilty to attempted murder of Cici back in October. His sentence for that was life imprisonment with the possibility of parole. He told Stern the bottom of the river was where he'd find Cici's wallet, cell phone, and keys.

Greg rode in an uncomfortable bus to his home prison where he would be spending the next decades. The bus made a few stops at other police departments and prisons, picking up and dropping off convicts. After his arrival, he was stripped, disinfected, and subjected to a very thorough inspection to make sure he wasn't smuggling anything into the prison.

His cell was approximately 8 feet by 8 feet. It had one window, two metal bed trays, a sink, and a toilet. An additional metal bunk was placed above the bed. He steered away from the "bad guys," even though all inmates were allowed to roam outside their cells and visit other prisoners to socialize. He realized after his experience with Lynch that there were no friends to be found in prison. But deep down, he hoped he'd find someone to hang out with.

He was petrified of his cellmate, Cutter, who adopted a skinhead look. His cellmate poked fun at him for trying to achieve points to earn privileges. He was worse than Lynch. He heard that Cutter had murdered a 73-year-old woman, whose body was discovered in a pond at an Ocean Pines park. Greg found out later that Cutter had killed his own mother. Greg knew of Cutter's infamous reputation: if Cutter felt another inmate wronged him, he'd badly cut him.

Greg asked if he could be moved to another cell and be assigned another roommate. He got his wish. They moved him to a cell where the other inmate lost part of his leg due to a blood clot from another time in prison. Greg felt much safer with him than Cutter.

He sorely missed his scotch, his pontoon, his job, and Della. In his mind, he had forgiven Della for her testimony in court. He had written her letters and hoped to receive one back, but he had received no mail. He knew it was a lost cause and eventually gave up writing to her.

Greg was receiving help with coping with the length of his incarceration and was accepting that prison was going to be his home for a long time. Greg was being taught how to live and survive in a prison environment weekly.

There were armed guards watching everyone from above while Greg ate in the cafeteria. He had no phone privileges. He became very depressed and suicidal. He agreed with his prison therapist in writing that he would not harm himself for designated periods of time. After several sessions with the therapist, eventually Greg's depression improved and his suicidal thoughts diminished. But he still continued his sessions with the therapist. If he ever was to be granted a parole hearing, he knew he'd better shape up and act the role of a model prisoner.

Greg's cell was unlocked every morning at 5:15 a.m. Roll-call occurred at 5:30 a.m. each morning in his cell. Greg participated in morning exercises and made his bed. He got breakfast and a lunch bag, usually with four pieces of white bread, two pieces of ham, and a packet of mayonnaise. Sometimes he got a peanut butter and jelly sandwich. Dinner was at 5:00 p.m. Greg needed to buy a lot of soups, cereals, crackers, and packaged tuna from the commissary, because he felt he never had enough to eat. His locker next to his bed was stuffed with so much food, other inmates were pretty friendly with him.

He could take walks by the prison wards but was watched by a guard. He took classes in anger management, but was escorted to them. They opened the yard after breakfast, and Greg could go outside, or he could participate in programs. After lunch, Greg had to remain in his locked cell so the staff could have their own lunch. Dinner was usually stews and filling foods like pasta and rice. He worked hard at being a model prisoner and achieved the necessary points allowing him access to a radio, TV, or the internet.

After meeting with his therapist, he was assigned a job in the kitchen as a dishwasher. They paid Greg 65 cents an hour. Greg thought the work was very mundane, but it was something to do, and it passed the time. Anything was better than this way of life. Even living back on the farm with his awful parents would have been better than this.

Instead of participating in a program, Greg decided to spend some time in the yard, even though he wasn't much of a socializer. He needed some fresh air. He sat on a wooden bench against the tall chain-linked fence. Greg closed his eyes and leaned his head against the fence, feeling the sun's warmth on his face. It felt so good. A shadow blocked the sun's rays. Greg opened his eyes. He looked up and saw Cutter standing before him.

"It wasn't very nice of you to leave my cell," Cutter said. Greg remained silent. "My new cellmate smells like a garbage truck. I don't think he knows what a bar of soap is. You fucked up. It's payback time."

"What?" asked Greg.

Cutter pulled out his makeshift knife and plunged it twice into the front of Greg's neck, severing his two carotid arteries. He keeled over as Cutter walked away and mingled in the crowd.

DANA PHIPPS was a former teacher of special and elementary education in Baltimore, Maryland. She served as Director and owner of a Sylvan Learning Center in Westminster, Maryland. At Sheppard Pratt Hospital in Baltimore, as an education specialist, she was a liaison between the schools and the hospital where she advocated for obtaining the appropriate educational placements and programs to meet the specific needs of emotionally handicapped adolescents.

She is the author of two children's books, *Emily and Hurricane Isabelle* and *Emily and Her Pouting Puffer Fish*. She spends her summers in Ocean Pines, Maryland with her family and enjoys playing golf. *Murder in Ocean Pines* is her first novel.

ACKNOWLEDGEMENTS

It goes without saying that *Murder in Ocean Pines* is a work of fiction. Names, characters, events, and incidents are used in a fictitious manner. Any resemblance to actual persons, living or dead, or actual events, is purely coincidental. Many people were instrumental in helping me write this book. I would like to thank them all.

Special thanks goes to editor, Tamra Tuller, who aided me in the development of this story and book design. I want to thank author and writing instructor, Kathryn Johnson, for her helpful comments to improve my manuscript. I am sincerely appreciative to Carole McShane, free-lance author and former columnist of the *Baltimore Sun*, for giving generously of her time, referrals, and support. I appreciate the editing suggestions from Charity Bustanante, literary agent.

Thank you, Jay Merker, Special Agent at the U.S. Department of Homeland Security, and former Captain Steve Tucker of the Northumberland County Rescue Squad in Reedville, Virginia. Many thanks goes to Reginald L. Pryzylski, President of Absolute Investigative, Services, Inc. and Victor Aulestia, Director of Investigations, for their expertise and sharing of knowledge in private investigation matters. Marge, Sandy, and Vicki, thank you for your input. Gil and Anne, thank you for your informative emails.

I mustn't forget how grateful I am to Rob for his support. And friend, Eileen, for her time and encouragement.

Personal thanks and love to my kids - daughter Holly, who proofread and spent hours helping me on the computer. Thank you, Casey, for improving the manuscript in countless ways. I value all of your feedback. And as always, my husband, for his patience and trying hard not to interrupt me while I pounded away on the keys. Thank you for proofreading, being my tower of strength, and for putting up with me.

9 781943 290567